ETA: DOA

Joey DeVecchio saw the game plan too late. And the moment he saw it, he went for the door handle with both hands. But the big man pulled him back by the shirt collar. He smashed Joey's face into the top of the wheel twice in fast succession. Then he twisted around in his seat, gun in his left hand, and shot Joey DeVecchio twice in the back of the head.

The big guy grunted, calmly turned the car's engine off, and walked back upstairs into the airport.

He had no problem at all finding a taxi that took him to the city.

Murder with a Twist

L.V. SLYKE

AVON BOOKS ◆ NEW YORK

MURDER WITH A TWIST is an original publication of Avon Books. This work has never before appeared in book form. This work is a novel. Any similarity to actual persons or events is purely coincidental.

AVON BOOKS
A division of
The Hearst Corporation
1350 Avenue of the Americas
New York, New York 10019

Copyright © 1994 by Henry Schlesinger
Published by arrangement with the author
Library of Congress Catalog Card Number: 93-91644
ISBN: 0-380-76797-X

First Avon Books Printing: January 1994

AVON TRADEMARK REG. U.S. PAT. OFF. AND IN OTHER COUNTRIES, MARCA REGISTRADA, HECHO EN U.S.A.

Printed in the U.S.A.

RA   10   9   8   7   6   5   4   3   2   1

DEDICATED TO

My parents—
who were generous with their love
and kept their fears to themselves
and to
Melissa Suzanne

Acknowledgments

Tom Colgan, who is truly one of the best; Peter Stern, last of the good-guy New York landlords. Neil Gordan, who read carefully, and Dan Goldin, who offered greasy chic. Both of them good guys. And to Luis Lima, who let me run outrageous tabs that fed the kids.

Murder
with a
Twist

Barmy's was nobody's kind of place, not anymore. Squeezed between a maternity shop and a bakery, the narrow blue front could have been anything, maybe even a bar, which it was. Years ago, when the place was popular, this was part of its charm. It was what the columnists and guide books called "anonymous mystique." But by the time the mystique wore off, it was just anonymous, and more than a little shabby.

What Barmy's had going for it was cheap rent and a cheap payroll. And for a bar in New York, that's enough. The streets of the city are littered by the remains of bars with cute names, distinctive interiors, and bone-crushing rents. Greedy owners and thieving staffs only speed up the inevitable.

Now, here's the history lesson. There'll be a quiz later.

In the sixties, when the East Side above Seventy-ninth was wide open, the place was a pimp bar called Players' Ground. There was table-stakes poker and two Indian Head slot machines in the back room. That lasted into the early seventies, until the house dealer got a little fast with the cards.

"Make it happen outside," the manager said to the first officers on the scene, holding out four hundred bucks in folded fifties and twenties. The two cops looked from the money to the dealer, then back again. There was a sucking chest wound and a widening puddle of blood from a leg wound forming on the floor near the jukebox. The dealer was as good as DOA and the Knapp Commission was still making headlines.

"Not this time," the cop said, shaking his head and showing the manager an upraised palm.

The manager walked back into the empty bar, poured himself a triple brandy, and watched as the cops applied first aid, which meant covering him with a blanket and asking if he saw the guy who shot him. An era was coming to an end.

Miles Barmy was working at a bar down the street that catered to what was then called the "swinging singles scene." Looking past a profusion of turtlenecks, he kept mixing the Beefeater martini, and watched the ambulances and police units roll up Third Avenue. A month later, at ten in the morning, Miles stood behind the landlord and the owner's lawyer as they ripped down the police crime-scene seal and put the key to the lock. Twenty minutes later he bought out the fifty-year lease, furnishings, and remaining stock.

The three of them celebrated the deal over glasses of Chivas. Miles poured, smiling broadly, and suppressed the urge to charge both of them four bucks apiece. He walked straight from the bar to the joint he was working and quit. The rest of the week he spent hustling up the cash to make good on the postdated rubber check he'd written. He knew only two things: that he had to own the bar and that he would own it without partners.

He sold his records, his stereo, and his car. With a day left, he was still two grand short. He sold his girlfriend's car. Then Miles began writing rubber checks to every bar that would take them. It was ten to three when he walked into a Chase Manhattan branch office, closed out his account, and left at a trot with a cashier's check, rushing to the final meeting.

First thing, Miles had Kee, the Chinese porter, ancient even then, bleach out the bloodstain with Clorox. A week later he hired two guys from Bayside to knock down the wall to the back room, doubling the square footage. When the building inspectors came around, the smaller one said, "You got permits?" And Miles said, "Yeah, I'll have my guys put them in the trunk." One of the inspectors tossed his car keys to Miles, and the three of them sat at the bar watching the plaster dust settle as the Bayside guys loaded two cases of Canadian Club in the city car. When the operator came around offering a juke, pool table, cigarette machine, and "any other fucking thing ya want," Miles beat down on the split from fifty-fifty to sixty-forty and got him to throw in a pair of external speakers by promising to supply his own records.

Miles was paranoid, greedy, charming, and street-smart. He was a cunt-hound, a rascal, a romantic, and a user. He was a New York City bar owner. It was his greatest and only talent. It was a true calling that could not be duplicated by all the slick corporations and hit squads of big-money consultants armed with traffic surveys, focus group videos, demographic models, and visions of mirrored glass, shining brass, and hanging plants.

Years later, a consultant posing as a customer asked Miles about it. And he answered, "You bring in the pussy, and the pussy draws the guys, the paying customers." The consultant, obviously a sensitive guy, grimaced slightly. "Two other things," Miles added, smiling. "The women have to feel good. Safe. And the guys don't have to actually get laid. They just have to believe there's a better chance of it happening out of your joint than the one down the street."

It took about four years for Barmy's to become the hottest place on the East Side. The kind of place where celebrities show up to drink for free. A card over the register listed the phone numbers of three freelance photographers who would trek out at three in the morning to shoot the celebs. By four the next afternoon, a publicist would have the photos and neatly typed captions messengered to columnists at the *New York Post*, the *Daily News*, and *Rolling Stone*.

Then came the eighties. Wall Street and real estate money flowed over the bar in torrents. Two full-time doormen screened the clientele, and a limo was on call to drive home the better customers. Twenty-four-year-olds were pulling down a hundred and sixty grand a year in junk bonds. At night they rented limos and put hundred-and-fifty-dollar bottles of Dom on their gold cards.

The party lasted for years. The money, the music, and the drugs were all numbing.

Then it stopped. Later, it would seem as if someone had shut off a spigot. But it had been slower than that—everyone was just having too good a time to notice. A great deal of ugliness and fear followed. And nearly everyone was left scrambling in the wreckage.

Incredibly, Barmy's was left standing, but just barely.

Even now, years after the boom, one of the old patrons would return for a single drink and say, "I remember when this place was *hot*. What happened anyway?"

And Max Bally, the bartender, would answer, "Not much."

ONE

Joey DeVecchio, all five foot eight and 132 pounds of him, stood waiting in a No Smoking section of Kennedy Airport, chain-smoking Merits. It was his wife that made him switch to Merits, because they were better for him. And instantly, he jumped from one pack a day to two, sometimes three and a half. But today, he'd set a new record. Not even midnight yet, and already halfway through his fourth pack.

This was his last chance to make it right with the boys. They knew he'd been skimming from the car services he ran for them, but they couldn't prove shit. And that probably got them more pissed off, that they couldn't prove nothing. The greedy fucks, a couple hundred a week was pocket change to those guys.

He'd left Brooklyn early because of the construction on the BQE and because the weather report said snow. But once he got there, there wasn't anything to do except smoke. He already had a couple of drinks at the bar, browsed the newsstands, and checked departure times for Vegas, Tahoe, and Reno out of bored curiosity. He was hungry, but the idea of eating airport food turned his stomach. So he smoked instead and thought of the menu of his favorite diner on Queens Boulevard.

Now he was waiting for a guy. He didn't even know the guy's name, except it was something foreign. The boys told him he wouldn't need a name.

"He's from the islands, ya know?"

"You ain't sending me to pick up no spook," Joey had said. "I don't chauffeur no *yom* 'round."

"He ain't black," came the grim answer. "He's from the other islands. South Sea. Ya know what they look like, them people?"

Joey ran a mental check of the Brando movie *Mutiny on the Bounty* through his mind. But all he could think about was the broads. Good-looking women wearing dresses that reminded him of his aunt Tina's slipcovers. "They're like Ricans, without the accent."

"He'll be big. Ya won't be able to miss him," came the answer. "Just give him the package and get him to a hotel. Don't fuck this thing up, Bonanza."

Joey winced involuntarily at the nickname. It was a neighborhood thing, from when there were two Joeys. First he was Little Joey. Then Little Joe. And finally Bonanza. It was one of those things that stuck with a guy, like from high school to when they put him in the ground. "I won't fuck nothing up," he answered. "I'm looking for a big spic. I got it."

"He ain't a P.R. He's Polynesian. Fuck this up Bonanza and you'll be making video poker collections up and down Westchester Avenue in the Bronx."

Joey stiffened, rising ever so slightly higher in his just-polished Ferragamos, his chest puffing out the dark blue of the double-breasted suit with the covered buttons. "I won't fuck nothing up."

"Better not."

And now he was waiting to babysit a big spic who wasn't a spic.

*   *   *

The first passengers came off the plane and down the long corridor past the metal detector. Four or five guys in suits, Connecticut and Westchester types carrying briefcases and tan raincoats. First-class passengers, Joey thought. Probably not even paying for first class. Upgrades and corporate charge accounts.

Then a couple of young chippies in tight jeans and down coats. Young enough to be college girls, maybe. Could be they were tourists.

And then Joey saw the guy. He was coming down the brightly lit hallway, just ahead of two more business types. Even though he was walking slow—strolling— the business types didn't pass. "Jesus Christ Almighty," Joey whispered to himself. The guy was a gorilla. A real fuckin' knuckle-scraper. Wait 'til he told the guys at the bar about this.

The guy was huge. Six two or six three and must have run three hundred and fifty pounds. He looked like a Rican linebacker. The guy had a big face, flatlike, slicked-back hair, and no neck. Shit, he was big. But big the way a lot of those biker types are—you just fucking knew there was muscle under all that fat. The guy was wearing a flower-print shirt stretched tight around his stomach and arms. Over his right arm was a shearling coat that looked brand-new. There was a brown plastic carry-on bag in his left hand.

The guy walked straight for him and the closer he got, the bigger he got, until finally, he was standing right next to Joey, who wasn't quite up to his armpit.

"You Bonanza?" the guy asked. The guy didn't have an accent, but it was hard to tell. The voice wasn't much more than a grunt.

Joey tilted his head slightly back to look up at the guy. He'd dealt with gorillas before; the best thing to do was not back down. Let them know respect is a two-way street. None of them were ever as tough as they wanted you to think. "Yeah," Joey said.

"Good," the guy answered and walked past Joey as if he knew where he was going.

Joey had to take two or three steps at a run to catch up. "Hey, you know where you're heading, pal?"

The guy stopped and turned. "New York City."

"Yeah, that's a start," Joey said. "You got any fuckin' clue how to get there?"

The guy turned slowly and looked down, like he was studying a roach that fell into a cup of day-old coffee. "That's what you're for."

It was something about the guy's eyes that spooked Joey. They were dark and flat—nothing in them at all. *Murder one* eyes, Joey thought. He didn't know who this guy was, what his business was, or why the boys called him in from wherever he was from, but the big bastard was mean. Stone cold. "Yeah, well then, follow me, huh?"

They walked the rest of the empty corridor in silence. Joey didn't talk again until they reached the terminal's main lobby. "You got any luggage?"

"No."

"Like to travel light, huh?" he tried, smiling.

"Yes." The guy didn't smile back.

It had been a long flight—nearly thirty hours in all. The Hawaiian Air flight to Honolulu was five hours, then an eight-hour layover. The next plane took him to St. Louis, where a tired-looking man in a brown raincoat and scuffed brown shoes met him at the airport cafeteria. The tired-looking man gave him an opened quarter wrap with the name Bonanza and a description written on the inside. Then he dug into a pocket and pulled out a battered envelope with ten thousand dollars in fifties in it. Written on another quarter wrap inside the envelope was a woman's name and two addresses. The big man barely had enough time to finish his ham sandwich before boarding the plane with a too narrow seat for New York.

Joey tried again on the escalator. "First time in New York, huh?"

"Yes."

"You're gonna love it," Joey said, putting on a party voice. "The clubs, the restaurants. The bars," he said.

"And the bitches. New York's got the finest women in the world."

A couple of girls, college kids, turned as they passed, their mouths gone sour at what they heard. Joey turned, smiling back at them. "Hey, baby, you wanna play carnival? What say I guess your weight?"

One of the girls shot him the finger; the other said, "Fuck you, asshole."

"Ah baby, don't be like that," Joey turned and called after them. "You know you love it. Just gotta give it up sometime."

When he turned back, the big guy wasn't smiling. He was heading for the door. Joey had to run to catch up again. "Hey, hey, man, this way," he called. "I'm parked down in short term."

They walked back to the elevator that led to the lower parking level. When the elevator doors closed, Joey tried again. "So what you say we go out, get something to eat, couple of drinks, huh?"

The elevator door opened and the big guy stepped out into the nearly deserted parking area. "You talk too much, Bonanza," he said.

Joey followed him out into the parking garage and thought about that. "Hey, ya know, just trying to be friendly."

The guy stopped, looking around the garage. "Don't try so hard."

Joey was starting to get pissed off now. Like, who the fuck did this guy think he was? The fat asshole flies in and wants everybody to kiss his ass. Well, fuck him. "Sure, any way ya want it, that's just fine."

"Which car, Bonanza?" the guy said, impatient now.

"And another thing, don't be calling me Bonanza, awright? I don't like it."

"Why not?"

"'Cause I don't like it," Joey snapped. "Ain't that enough?"

"Which car?" the guy asked.

Joey puffed out his chest a little, straightening himself inside the suit. "Over there, by the wall. The white Lincoln."

They were settled in their leather seats, Joey had the key in the ignition, when the guy asked, "Where's my package?"

"Christ, you want 'em now?"

"Yes."

Joey reached over, opened the glove box, and pushed the truck release. Then he walked around and dug out a box from under the spare tire. When he got back to the driver's door, he tossed the package over to the big guy before getting back in. If the guy recognized the insult, he didn't let on.

The big guy nodded, then started to tear away the Santa Claus wrapping paper. Joey watched, fascinated. This was unheard of. In eighteen years, he'd never seen nobody unwrap nothing out in the open—not dope, not whack-up money, nothing. Some guys he knew probably went into the crapper to unwrap Christmas presents.

Inside the wrapping was a styrofoam box. The big guy separated the two pieces, dropping the top half casually to the floor. Cradled in the molded compartments was a piece: a .380 Beretta. Alongside, someone had dug out the compartment that held the clip, making it large enough for a silencer.

Holy shit, Joey thought to himself, the guy was a shooter. "Nice piece," he said, trying to stay calm. "New York's a dangerous place, you know."

The gun looked small in the big man's hands as he dropped the magazine, examined the cartridges, then slapped it back into place. He nodded and grunted his approval.

Joey, still fighting to stay calm, said, "Better slide that under the seat, so the attendant don't see it," then started the car. From the tape deck, Sinatra began singing "New York, New York." Joey had put the tape in on purpose before he parked, mood music. But also to clue the guy in as to just what kind of people he was dealing with. He realized now that it didn't matter.

The guy didn't slide the piece under the seat. Instead, he screwed on the silencer, twisting the fat aluminum tube in his thick fingers, working it down on the threaded barrel.

"Hey, what the fuck," Joey said. "I told you to stash the piece."

The guy didn't answer; rather, he racked the slide back, then pointed the gun at Joey.

It was only then that Joey DeVecchio saw the game plan. And the moment he saw it, he went for the door handle with both hands. But the big man pulled him back by the shirt collar, his fat fingers working their way in between the custom-fitted shirt and the newly shaved neck. He smashed Joey's face into the top of the wheel twice in fast succession, flattening his nose and dazing him. Then he twisted around in his seat, gun in his left hand, and shot him twice in the back of the head.

Both bullets exited somewhere just above Joey's right eye and drilled into the instrumentation. Sinatra's voice died in mid-phrase as the digital readout on the dash clicked off.

The big guy grunted, calmly turned the car's engine off, and walked back upstairs with his carry-on and new shearling. He had no problem at all finding a taxi to take him to the city.

Two

He wasn't going to make any money. Nobody had to tell Max that. He could feel it when he walked into the bar. But then he switched on the television in the corner above the coffee machine and a local weather guy, dressed in a scarf and pretending to shiver under the studio lights, was going "Brrrr, good night to stay indoors with a glass of eggnog."

Max switched the channel and thought, what a prick. For once he'd like to see someone on television say, "Good night to go out and drink an adult beverage. And remember to tip big, folks."

A little later the carting service guy came around to get paid and said, "Naw, nobody's doing any business."

Max paid from the register and made a note on a petty cash voucher. "You want something?"

Outside the truck growled and a kid in a red sweatshirt and knit Knicks cap gazed impatiently, hanging off the back.

The garbage guy looked out at the kid, then back at the bottles and said, "Yeah, scotch would take the chill off." Max poured the house brand into a shot glass.

"So it's been slow?" Max asked. The carters, the older guys, could tell what kind of business every bar and restaurant on their route was doing from the breakage—the empty liquor bottles. And they knew how many people were out on the street. They noticed things, like a river of cabs cruising up Third with FOR HIRE signs on.

The garbage guy put the drink away in a swallow and set the glass down. "Real slow, Max," he said. "Only ones doing anything are the Blarney Stones, Treaty Stones, the green bars. Those old-timers would crawl over their dead sister's body for their Jamesons."

And then the garbage guy was gone in a blast of chill air from the door. The new waitress came in while Max was sectioning lemons and watching Third Avenue. It was beginning to snow. The small flakes drifted down in a fine powder, hit the street, and were swept uptown by the early evening traffic.

Max had cut two lemons, sectioning them off into neat slices, then decided against a third. Business would be light with all the good working folks staying home in front of the television drinking eggnog. Sometimes a strong wet snow would bring people out, couples mostly. But this was a light cold one, the kind that drove people inside.

The new waitress came over, sat on the stool in front of Max, and watched him cut fruit. "My horoscope said to avoid new business opportunities," she said. "But I got this audition tomorrow. What do you think, Max?"

He picked up another lemon, tried to remember her name, and turned the small yellow fruit smoothly in his hand against the knife, letting the blade travel from top to bottom as he made the single incision. "What paper, the *Post* or *Newsday*?" he asked, setting the knife down.

"*Newsday*," the waitress said. "It's for off-off Broadway, a showcase."

Max pulled gently at the top section of the lemon's skin, bringing it off the pulpy center in a neat yellow spiral. The waitress seemed unimpressed. Then he remembered her name, it was Julie. Lately they all seemed to be Julies or Jennifers. "*Newsday*'s bullshit, go to the audition," he said. "You want some lemonade, Julie?"

"In January? Give me a break," the waitress answered and slid off the barstool to consult with Kee, who was moving about in the shadows, a frail figure, ancient and inscrutable, and potentially better informed than *Newsday*.

He watched her walk across the room, her black jeans riding in a pleasing rolling motion, her shoulder-length brown hair tied back with a strip of black ribbon. She knew how to dress for the job at least. Tight jeans and white shirt unbuttoned just enough. In six months she'd be gone, waitressing in some better-paying place; set up by some guy rich enough to afford her; or back on a bus, or more likely a plane, to Michigan, which is where she said she was from.

When she first came in, she announced that she wanted to be a model. After all, wasn't she the best-looking girl back in her hometown? On the rally squad and almost the homecoming queen. Didn't everyone say she could be a model? When she first hit New York, someone took five hundred off her for enough shots for a portfolio, and she spent the next month trying to find an agency. Then one night she came in and announced, "I think I'd like to try film." It was the way she said it that struck Max, as if she was talking to Jay Leno. First guest after the monologue, *"And then, then I just decided I'd like to try film. I said to myself, 'why not?'"*

Outside the snow was coming down harder. Cars had begun to use their intermittent wipers. Max began cutting the yellow peel into short twists. He'd be lucky if he broke two hundred for the night. Lynn wasn't going to be happy. The night stretched out in front of him as an endless shift. Could be worse, he thought. Holiday Inn lounge in Syracuse. Airport bar in Cleveland. Any bar in L.A.

Max finished cutting the lemon peel and slid the partitioned plastic drawer back into its place above the speed rack. As he turned back toward the register, he caught sight of himself in the mirror. It brought him up short. Still the firm chin, the light brown hair, and the thin nose. It was still a face he could call his own, but no longer young. No, not young. All the sharp angles were fading ever so slightly. He was beginning to go soft and indistinct. At thirty-five an inevitable betrayal was at work. He thought of how it took him longer to get going in the mornings, then turned away from the mirror.

A little while later, a few of the regulars wandered in for their after-dinner drinks and wandered out again. There was a short flurry when the movies let out. And then it trailed off back to regulars, neighborhood people. It kept on like that until one—all regulars. Still in suits and ties, business dresses, and carrying briefcases. The bar could vanish over a weekend and they'd move down the street or over to Second Avenue.

Around two the nightclubbers drifted in for one last drink before heading home from an early evening.

By three the serious drinkers arrived, and Max was still thinking about closing early. That's when the little stockbroker fell off the stool and said, "Shit."

Max was facing the back bar, ringing up a drink on the register when he heard the thud. He turned to see an empty space where the broker had been sitting. "Dwayne, you okay?" he called, moving down the bar.

"Yeah, fell is all," came the reply from the floor.

A moment later, the girl in a leather mini and dark stockings, standing next to where the broker fell, shouted "Fuck," and kicked him in the head twice with a lizard-skin Charles Jourdan.

Max jumped the bar, one foot pushing off the ice bin. Used to not have to use the ice bin at all, he thought as he landed in the middle of it, coming between the girl, her blue-blazered boyfriend, and the bond broker.

"He put his fucking hand up my dress," the girl said, moving back as Max hauled the broker up, propping him against the bar.

The little broker had a drunken smile on his face and announced, "She isn't wearing any underwear!" The girl's shoe had opened a small cut on the side of his chin, and he was bleeding down into the collar of his Brooks Brothers button-down, but didn't seem to notice.

"Hey, what the fuck kinda place is this?" the boy-friend said, just to be saying something. He was maybe twenty-three. Still, it was a good question; Max didn't know either anymore. Then the broker swayed slightly and vomited on the boyfriend.

It took about six seconds for the boyfriend and the girl to hit the street. Still holding the broker upright with one hand, Max signaled the waitress for a little assistance.

"Not a damn thing under there. No panties. Nothing," the broker said. "Wearing red garters and black stock-ings. Must be a first date, don't you think? Still trying to impress him."

Julie came over, took a look at the broker, and eased him gently away from the bar with an arm around his shoulders.

"Dwayne's out of it again," Max said.

"No shit, Max," the waitress replied and walked him away in a lurching stagger. She had a good six inches on him. In the last three weeks, the broker had fallen down seven times.

"Get a towel for that head, then take him back and let him lay down across the back benches," Max instructed, climbing back over the bar.

"Do you ever not wear underwear?" the broker asked the waitress as they moved toward the back. "I mean on a regular basis."

"In January?" Julie said, steering him toward the back benches. "Give me a break."

Max gave last call at three forty-five and turned off the juke and the outside lights. Four or five of the regulars, hard-core drinkers from the old days, drifted toward the back of the room in a weary conspiracy. The three customers—two men and a woman at the bar, kids out past their bedtime—downed their drinks and left. Max locked the door after them, turned back toward the juke, fed it a five-dollar bill from the register, and noted the payment on a petty cash voucher. The juke was a new Rowe—all CDs. Max figured he'd have about two more months with it before the operator realized he wasn't making any money. When that happened, the guy would pull it.

Julie came by then, sliding up on a bar stool and began counting her tip money. "So, what was it like?" she asked, unfolding a small pile of bills on the bar.

He knew the question was coming. It always came once they found out about his somewhat dubious career. "What was what like?" he asked back, a reply scripted years before.

"The TV thing," she said, smoothing out a crumpled single across the wet bar. "How'd you get the job?"

She wasn't playing it cool, not even playing it tough, like a lot of the girls who come to the big city. She was just asking. She could have been fishing for something, maybe a longshot at an introduction to someone who could do her career some good. Max filled a rock glass with ice and poured three fingers of Glenlivet over the cubes. Dramatic pause. "They were casting a soap," he began. "I got an audition, didn't get the part. Six months later the casting director called back with another deal. Johnny Q."

The waitress had stopped counting; she was looking at him now. Not impressed, and more than a little cynical. "Just like that? That's all it was?"

Max took a sip of the drink, resting a leg on the ice bin, a little up bar from the waitress. "There were readings, right?" he said. "Two here and four in L.A."

"They flew you out to the coast?" she asked, trying out the word *coast*.

"Yeah, they flew me out, I read some more. Then we shot the pilot," Max said, finishing off the drink. Back then he had the kind of looks they wanted. Not too pretty; lean, and a little hungry. Now, he noticed all the heroes looked a little dazed. Shit, you want dazed, I can play dazed, he thought every once in a while. Dazed isn't a stretch, not at all.

"I never saw it," the waitress said, skepticism rising like a backed-up sink.

"They never aired it here," he answered. Then he started to say something else, but stopped. What was he going to say, they took a write-off? Aired the dubbed version in Brazil, to recoup? He never did get the full story. Oddly, he remembered the script vividly. It made "T. J. Hooker" look like Chekhov.

"Just because you got busted?" she asked, finishing the thought.

"Yeah, that's exactly why." What could he say? It wasn't as if he were a teenager and the local sheriff found a half ounce of pot under the seat. It was $410,000 worth of cocaine in a rental car from Florida. It was the kind of weight that they put on a table for display on the six o'clock news. It was the kind of bust morality clauses were written for.

The skepticism in the girl's face turned to that special off-brand pity reserved for the truly and terminally stupid. "If you have a tape, I'd like to see it sometime," she said, probably thinking it was the kind thing to say.

Out of the corner of his eye, Max saw the red Saab pull up out front. It backed smoothly into a parking place, then bumped both the car in front and in back gently. "Boss lady's here," he said.

The girl shot a panicked look out the window, where a slim older woman was coming around the front of the Saab. She was wearing a full-length fur, open to reveal the red dress underneath. The cold didn't seem to bother her. "I can leave now, right?" Julie asked, getting off the bar stool.

"I need your bank," Max answered.

The girl dug out the thirty she'd begun the night with, and dropped the bills in front of her. Max handed up her coat from under the bar along with her signed receipt for the bank. The receipts were a holdover from when the place had more than one waitress—when there had actually been customers.

As Julie reached the door, the older woman was standing there, not knocking, just waiting. The waitress slid out with a mumbled greeting, and the older woman slid in, bringing a blast of chill air in with her.

Lynn had that affect on other women—especially women under the age of thirty. They were all scared to death of her. It didn't matter if they knew her or not, though the terror was generally enhanced by having her as a boss. More than once, Max wondered what those girls saw in her that sent them retreating from a room. After a few drinks, he might say that it was a vision of things to come, if they weren't careful—peroxide hair, thin lips, and laugh lines. But deep down he knew it to be attitude—an attitude of such knowing and unforgiving female insight that cuteness, chatter, and charm withered and died horrible deaths under its illuminating glare. Lynn ate *ingenues* for brunch.

Tonight she was wearing the Blackglama that, in itself, wasn't a good sign.

Years ago they would have called Lynn "a tough broad" and said, "She's been around the block a few times." But it was more than that. She was closing in on fifty and *had* been around the block more than a few times. What she found was a neighborhood of fools, thieves, and scumbags, all looking for the main deal while they ducked out on the rent.

Lynn sat down at the bar like she owned it, which she did. The place was part of the divorce settlement. Max turned, brought down a bottle, and refilled his glass.

"Is that the real thing?" she asked, indicating the

Glenlivet. She had a voice that was husky—filtered through almost three decades of Chesterfields. Two packs a day. It was a mystery where she found them, but she did.

"You want one?" Max asked, already filling a rocks glass with ice.

She nodded and reached into her purse, hunting up a Chesterfield. "Do any business tonight?"

Max poured the drink in front of her and turned to replace the bottle. "Not much," he said.

When he turned back, she was holding a tamped-down Chesterfield in her left hand, the one with the perfect three-carat marquis-cut diamond Miles had bought her, and staring toward the small cluster of regulars at the back table—counting beer bottles and empty glasses in her head. About twenty bucks.

Max lit the cigarette off a disposable lighter and waited to see what would happen next.

She took the first sip, then a deep drag off the unfiltered cigarette, and let out a sigh. Her face seemed to cave in a little, relax. "Christ the world is filled with pricks," she said.

"Big date tonight, huh?"

"If that's what you want to call it," she said, and took another drink. "Total out the register for me, will you?"

Max turned and hit two keys. The night's total came up. It was just under three hundred.

Her eyes squinted through the smoke to read it. Then she noted the figure down in a ledger she pulled from her purse. "What are you doing, giving it away?"

"Yeah, the tips are bigger that way," Max answered blandly. Lynn was in one of her moods; it helped not to react.

She unsquinted her eyes and glared. "Maybe I'll get some young bartender in here, huh?" she said. "Some Tom Cruise-y looking guy. Young. You know what I'm saying?"

Max finished off his drink, trying not to stare back. You'd do better to outstare a laser. "So, what was he, doctor, orthodontist, lawyer, golf pro?"

"Fifty-two and an accountant," Lynn said. "A fifty-two-year-old accountant driving a Porsche, with a one-bedroom up over on Seventy-ninth."

"Sounds promising."

"Know what he told me?" she answered. "Told me he didn't usually date women my age. This from a guy who bought his place at the top of the market."

Max refilled his glass and topped off Lynn's. "What's he looking for? He could do worse, right?" he asked, more for conversation than anything else. But Lynn couldn't let it pass.

She gave him a look that mirrored the waitress's earlier in the evening. "What do you think he's looking for? Some twenty-two-year-old with a Hoover for a mouth."

Max decided to play it brave. "Showing your age there, with that Hoover line." Yeah, he thought, eight years ago it would have been a "Hoover for a nose" and realized he was showing *his* age.

"I'll tell you what he'll settle for," Lynn answered, then took a long pull on the Chesterfield. "And I'll tell you what he'll get. Some divorced thirty-six-year-old with two kids and a house on the Island."

Max knew Lynn well enough to know that she wasn't just shooting off her mouth. "Pretty sure of that, huh?"

"Shit, Max, you wouldn't believe what's going on out there," she said. "Two, three dates, and these women are asking the guys to help out with the mortgage payments. They can't sell those houses, the market sucks, and most of them are loaded with equity loans. They're desperate and they're scared."

"They could get jobs," he suggested. "It's been known to happen."

"As what, assistant buyers at Saks?" Lynn laughed. "There wasn't a day that these women ever pulled in thirty K a year. Now they got eighty-thousand-a-year lifestyles and ex-husbands driving Porsches."

"Lynn, it's been real pleasant, you know," Max said, moving away. "But I'm going to close it up."

"Getting home to Suzie, huh?"

"It would be nice, you know?"

"How long's it been for you two, almost two years, off and on?" she asked back, eyes looking for the first hint of disaster.

"About that," Max answered. He wanted to make this one work or thought he did. That was the first thing. The second thing was figuring out how to do that. They'd both been playing it by ear, Suze and him. Neither one daring to use the word "love" and both wary of the future.

"She's a good one for you, Max," Lynn said, still staring. "Don't fuck it up."

Max finished off the scotch and bit into an ice cube. "I'll try not to."

Lynn took a good swallow from her glass and a pull on the cigarette before speaking again. "The kid got another one of those postcards from Miles," she said, letting the smoke out. "This one from the Caymans. Added it to her collection."

"Yeah, she like it?" Max asked, genuinely interested now. The answer would be something to tell Miles next time he saw him.

"Tell him she liked it," Lynn said. "Pulled out the atlas to find out where the Caymans were. Just for the record, I know it's you helping him out with those."

Max didn't answer.

Lynn took another long drink. "You want to explain something for me?" she asked.

Max brought the empty glass up and bit into another ice cube, nodding.

"So far he's sent her postcards from Bermuda, the Caymans, Guatemala, Los Angeles, Thailand, and Singapore," Lynn said. "Am I missing any?"

Max shook his head. Whatever she was going to ask was going to be good.

"You explain to me how he's going to explain to his daughter why he doesn't have a tan when he gets out of the joint," Lynn said, a small smile playing over her face. "She'll be fourteen by then. She may notice."

THREE

The big man lay propped up in a hotel room bed watching television. The show was "Branded," an old black-and-white western he remembered from his childhood in Hawaii. He had remembered liking the television show about a man with few friends. The other children had called him Chop Suey, because he was not full-blooded Samoan. He did not know who his father was and his mother did not mention it. Then she died, hit by a bus filled with tourists, and he went to live with the nuns in the orphanage in Samoa. There too, they called him Chop Suey.

The big man took a long drink of the beer and watched as the "Branded" man fought in a saloon. Men toppled over chairs and tables. Outside his window, someone was yelling. The fighting and shouts brought his attention from the television to the hotel room window. It was barely dawn—a gray light leaked into the window between the worn curtains.

He stretched and flexed, then brought both broad feet from under the covers and let them touch the matted carpeting. He was staying on the fifth floor of the Howard Johnson's on Eighth Avenue and Fifty-second. His room faced Fifty-second and all night he was vaguely aware of the traffic and shouts coming from outside.

Now, someone was shouting again, cursing. This time the shouting did not subside. Padding the few feet to the window in his boxer shorts, he opened the curtains with mild, cautious curiosity.

In the middle of the street were two women. They were carrying something and yelling. Then he saw that they were not carrying it at all, but fighting over it, pulling it first one way and then the other, as each

21

one struggled to keep her tenuous grip on it. Cars were passing slowly, not so much to avoid hitting them, but to watch the spectacle.

The big man reached down, pulled the last Budweiser tallboy from its plastic ring, and popped the top as he continued to watch. The beer was almost warm, but not quite.

When the two women turned, he saw the thing they were fighting over was a television—nineteen inches at least—and that they were not women at all. They were men dressed in women's clothes—short dresses, high heels, and jackets. *Fa'afafine*.

A few people, maybe a dozen, stood lined up on the sidewalk, watching and calling encouragement.

He opened the curtains wider and tilted the can high, letting the beer run into his mouth as he stood in the window, practically filling it, fascinated. As the argument became more heated, one of the men who was like a woman released one hand from the molded plastic handle in back and pulled his fist back and swung. The big Samoan judged it to be a good punch, not what he would have expected. It connected high on the other woman who wasn't a woman's neck, snapping the head to one side and sending her staggering back on spike heels.

The television fell, the picture tube shattering with a soft pop that the Samoan could hear from his room. The two women who weren't women stopped fighting just long enough to assess the damage as complete, then continued fighting, no longer hampered by the television. As the big man drained the beer, the fighting moved east, toward the far sidewalk, scattering the onlookers, who began to form a loose semicircle. And then it suddenly stopped.

The big man stared for a moment, puzzled, then followed the gaze of the two men in dresses and high heels. A little man was running across the street. He looked to be Spanish and was wearing tan work boots, red pajamas, and a blue peacoat. He was waving a machete above his head.

The two men in dresses scattered and ran. But neither

one was a match for the little man with the machete. He took off after the one heading east. That's when the police arrived—three baby-blue police cars with flashing blue and white lights surrounded the man with the machete. The doors flew open and the Samoan saw cops, eight of them at least, draw down on the little man with the machete. When the little man in the pajamas dropped the machete and raised his hands above his head, the Samoan dropped the beer can to the floor and left the window.

The big man turned on a table lamp, then walked slowly into the bathroom, opened a plastic toilet kit, and removed from its cargo of toothpaste, shaving cream, and disposable razors, a set of rat-tailed files fitted into a plastic sleeve. He brought the files back to the bed, selected one from the center, and examined it carefully. Then he drew out the pistol and silencer—carefully wrapped in a Howard Johnson's towel—from their place between the mattress and box spring.

He hummed a song as he moved the file gently in and out of the gun's barrel. Then he picked up the silencer and repeated the process, altering the barrel markings forever. There was no need to repeat the process or alter the hammer, ejector, or clip. Bullets were all he ever left behind.

The apartment building was on East Eighty-fourth, between Second and Third. It was one of those tenement walk-ups that some guy with a little money had bought when real estate prices were low in the mid-seventies. He could have sold it in the eighties and financed a Florida retirement, but he borrowed against it instead to buy another . . . and another. Dreams of a real estate empire danced in his head.

Sixty-five units wasn't an empire, but it wasn't chopped liver either. Not in Manhattan—not in '86.

He'd painted a little, retiled a little, and put in new intercoms. This was the sole extent of his renovation.

When the market collapsed he was so loaded with debt that he forgot about building an empire and the Florida retirement. His concerns scaled back and he concentrated on beating the rent-control laws and praying that the oil furnaces would make it through just one more winter.

It was nine-thirty in the morning when the big guy in a shearling coat and New York Knicks knit cap opened the entranceway door and studied the names on the buzzers. When he found the name he was looking for, he pressed it twice.

"Who is it?" a woman's voice asked.

"Federal Express," the guy answered.

The door buzzed open.

The apartment he was looking for was in the back on the second floor. He took the slate steps slowly, pulling an empty Federal Express envelope from the inside of his coat as he moved. He held the envelope in his left hand. In his right hand, still sunk deep into the pocket, was the small Beretta.

When he reached the apartment, he held up the envelope, shielding his face from the peephole.

Inside a lock clicked open, and then another. Finally he heard the chain pull away, and the door opened an inch. Before the woman could get a good look at him, he pushed his way in with his right shoulder.

The unexpected force threw her back into the room; something made of glass broke. She let out a little cry as he closed the door behind him and brought the gun up.

He saw that she was wearing a long nightshirt. Silkscreened across its front was the double-C logo of Chanel. It was stained with coffee. A small brown puddle of coffee was at her feet, spreading across the floor from the shattered mug.

Still pointing the gun at the girl, the big man put a thick finger up to his lips, silencing her.

When she began to back up slowly, the big man shook his head and motioned slightly with the gun. She stopped. Then, in a soft, almost gentle whisper, he said, "Peter Marotte."

The girl shook her head no and began to cry; it was like a whimper.

"Peter Marotte," the big guy asked again. It was only

then that he heard the water. Someone was taking a shower.

The girl turned toward the bathroom without thinking, looking for help.

"Peter Marotte," the big man repeated.

Then from the bathroom a man's voice called, "Who is it, Pat?"

"Peter Marotte?" the big man asked, again in a whisper.

The girl shook her head no, violently.

The big man smiled and called out, "Peter!"

"Yeah," the man in the bathroom called back. "Who is it?"

He shot the girl three times, then walked to the bathroom where he found the man kneeling, dripping wet and naked in front of the sink. The first shot hit his chest, making him crumple to the floor. Then the big man lifted Peter Marotte's head by the wet hair and shot him again, this time through the left eye.

It had been one of those days. First thing that morning, her digital talking scale broke—the electronic man's voice coming out of the tiny speaker in a sputter of static, like a radio tuned between stations. It could have been all for the best—she never did like the man's voice talking up at her as she stood naked and dripping wet from the shower. But at 237 pounds, the scale had been pleasantly nonjudgmental.

Then the mail came. An overdue notice from Visa, two letters from collection agencies that handled her MasterCard debts, phone bill, electric bill, a warning from the Discover card people, and a letter from American Express telling her that the card had been terminated. The whole thing was so depressing that she was nearly out the door before she remembered that it was double-coupon day.

Roseland Tenaklowski hated double-coupon days. She hated the way the women fished through their purses looking for that one lost coupon. Funny how it always seemed to be for baked beans or coffee. And she hated

the way the older ones would try to pull a fast one,
slipping a long-expired coupon in the middle of their
ragged piles, trying to get over for forty cents. And
lately, with all those layoffs at GM and everywhere else,
it seemed to get worse.

Double-coupon days made her wish she'd left Jersey—or at least Elizabeth.

Now, as she fed the last few items of the day over
the scanner's ruby-red beam, mechanically tilting the
bar-coded sides past the reader, she was gratified to see
that the pale, thin woman standing in front of her wasn't
clutching her precious pile of coupons. But she wasn't
going into her purse either. Rosey knew the type, the
ones that waited for the total to come flashing up before
they reached for their money—like it was all some kind
of surprise they had to pay for groceries.

Two loaves of Wonder bread, two gallons of milk,
a box of Kix cereal, a thirty-pack of large Pampers.
If she thought of it at all, which she didn't, Rosey
would have known it to be the items of an emergency
run to the supermarket. Pampers for the toddler, cereal
for the morning, bread for the other kids' sandwiches
tomorrow. The things that people dragged out for in
the middle of the night when they discovered that they
needed them. All the serious shopping ended at eight or
nine; by eleven-thirty, it was just odds and ends.

The other cashiers were already cashing out. Pulling
their drawers and carrying them back to the elevated
office for the final count, where the new night manager, the latest in a long line of thin, go-getter types,
was counting the cash and matching it against his own
screen.

The woman shuffled off, out through the door into
the nearly empty parking lot. Rosey watched, noticing
that she wore bedroom slippers. Imagine that, bedroom
slippers when it's fifteen degrees.

Then the assistant manager put the key to the door
and began shutting off the lights.

Rosey pulled her drawer and carried it up to the
office.

"Roseland, right?" the manager asked, trying to make conversation as he took the drawer. The back end of the drawer was numbered with a six, which was all he had to know.

"Yeah," she answered, waiting. You had to wait until he totaled you out. It was part of the nightly ritual. At least it added a few minutes to the time clock.

"Like in the ballroom," the manager said, flipping up the spring-loaded bars that held the money in place.

"Yeah, it's where my parents met," Rosey said.

The manager pulled out a few twenties and quarter rolls to deduct the hundred-dollar bank she started the night with. "No kidding."

Rosey fished into the pocket of her gray smock and pulled out a pack of cigarettes and a red lighter. "Yeah, no shit," she said, watching him count. He counted money like an amateur. The way the kids at Burger King or McDonald's do, moving his lips slightly.

"You know how bad that is for you, smoking?" the manager said, slowing his counting to a snail's pace.

Blowing a line of smoke up in his direction, "No. How bad?"

The manager finished counting and rubber-banding the money before he answered. "Takes maybe ten years off your life, maybe twenty."

"So if I smoke long enough, I was never born, right? Do I clear for the night?"

The manager checked the computer screen again. "I know I haven't been here long. But I just wanted to tell you, I see us all working together, like a team."

From out of the corner of her eye, Rosey saw the assistant manager begin to roll his eyes.

"Do I clear?" she asked.

"That's teamwork from everyone. Work with me and we'll all succeed."

Rosey had been on checkout for twelve years, since minimum wage was around three bucks an hour. Now she was getting six-fifty and had more than a sneaking suspicion she wasn't in line to become president of the company. "Yeah, sure," she said. "Do I clear?"

The manager's face dropped at the apparent failure of his pep talk. "You clear," he said, disheartened.

Rosey turned and headed back for the time clock. The other cashiers were heading out the door, but didn't bother to say good-bye as the assistant manager locked the door after them.

She punched out, grabbed her purse and coat. The assistant manager turned the key in the door. "'Night, Rose," he said.

"Yeah, sure," she answered, and stepped out into the darkened parking lot. There were only two cars in the lot. Her '83 Buick, which was starting to burn oil, and the manager's red Honda, which was so new it still had the sticker on the back window. She was parked way the hell over by the gas station on the corner. That was the thing about working second shift, you couldn't find a space when you got to work, then when you left, you had to hike across an empty lot.

Passing the manager's car, Rosey bent to study the sticker. He'd sprung for a sporty option package: custom stainless wheel covers, removable stereo, wing spoiler, wind deflector, electric power moon roof. The sticker put it at $16,050.

It wasn't until she straightened up that she saw the guy. A big guy, looked Puerto Rican. Big though, no neck and a stomach that stretched tight against the shearling coat. He was wearing a New York Knicks knit cap pulled down tight over his ears.

"Roseland?" he asked, his voice flat and deep.

"Yeah," she answered instinctively, squinting in the darkened parking lot to see who recognized her.

"Give me your purse."

"What?"

"The purse."

"What? Who are you?" she asked. It was that he knew her name, that's what threw her. Muggers didn't know names.

Then the big guy shrugged, pulled out a small gun with a long silencer, and shot her without raising the gun from waist level. He did it so quickly and without so much as an instant of hesitation that it didn't seem real to her, at least not like on TV. The first bullet punched into her low in the stomach. It didn't hurt so much, more like a poke. She opened her eyes wide in disbelief and took a slight step forward.

The big man shrugged again and shot her three more times. The second shot hit her in the left lung and the third just below the collarbone. The fourth entered her heart.

She was dead before she hit the ground.

The big guy, who wasn't Puerto Rican, stooped down and quickly removed from her a gold-plated necklace, imitation diamond ring, gold-plated digital watch, and purse. He moved quickly, working the jewelry off and holding it in one hand. Then he opened the large purse to find four veal filets, still wrapped in plastic. He shrugged again, dropped the jewelry into the purse, picked up the shell casings, and added them. Tucking the purse under the shearling jacket, he walked quickly from the parking lot toward his Ford rental car.

It wasn't until he was far away from the city that he began dropping things from the car. He dropped the watch on the left lane of Route 1 near a store called Daffy Dan's; the purse left the car just past the Thunderbird Motel; the imitation diamond ring dropped a moment later; the shell casings he dropped at quarter-mile intervals; the wallet and canceled credit cards, weighted down with the gun, flew from the window as he crossed the Pulaski Skyway, falling heavily into the Passaic River.

This part of New Jersey smelled. Even in the cold air it smelled of chemicals. And he thought of his home and Pago Pago where the canneries lined the water. On hot days they smelled, too.

There was an airline ticket in his back pocket. He would catch the red-eye to Los Angeles, change planes, wait out a two-hour layover in Hawaii, then get on another plane for Western Samoa. Two days later, he would leave for Australia.

As he approached the Lincoln Tunnel, a light snow

began to fall. He searched the dashboard for the wiper controls, but couldn't find them. As he came up to the toll, he looked down, found the wiper button concealed on the directional lever, and turned them on. The wipers beat furiously, clearing the windshield in two swipes, then grated against the glass. He clicked the lever again and a fine mist shot up and cleaned the windshield.

He paid the toll and headed into the tunnel, checking his watch. He would take the other tunnel, the Midtown, then head to Kennedy. He still had time, if he hurried and didn't get lost.

Halfway through the tunnel, he managed to turn the wipers off. But then, as he was coming out, he saw that the snow was falling heavier in New York. It took him a second to find the controls again. When he looked up, he saw he was heading for a yellow divider between two lanes. In the center of the island was a skinny man in a sweatsuit with a box, running from the sidewalk toward a blue van that was stopped fifty feet down from the green light. In the yellow glow of the street lamps, he saw a picture of a fax machine on the box.

Turning the wheel hard to the left, he cut into the lane and heard the screech of metal on metal as his car collided with a red Hyundai. Coming down hard on the brakes with two feet, he skidded right. The sudden noise startled the skinny man in the sweatsuit, and he lost his footing on the snow as the other car, a maroon '75 Monte Carlo, hit the Ford from behind, crashing into the quarter-panel hard enough to send the little car skidding across two lanes. The man with the box fell, vanishing under the car. There was a slight bump as the Ford's right rear wheel caught him on the lower chest. Then the Monte Carlo hit him again, crushing the skinny man's legs, and smashing into the Ford on the rear wheelwell.

The big man knew immediately that the skinny man in the sweatsuit with the box was dead. He sat silently, not moving a muscle, listening to the blare of car horns and knowing that he was going to miss his plane.

Four

Max could recall the exact moment he realized that the eighties wouldn't last. It was after-hours, and he was in the back office with a young Wall Street type, the guy's girlfriend, a well-dressed gram dealer, and a stylish coke whore.

By Max's estimate, the Wall Streeter had dropped something like four hundred in five hours, which entitled him to a little after-hours courtesy from the bar. But it was Max who steered the free-spending Wall Streeter over to the dealer, so that was worth something too—a couple of bumps, at least. Such was the stuff of which 5 a.m. alliances were forged.

The Wall Streeter and the girl were decked out in Armani. They'd been up all day and all night, but were still young enough to look fresh-scrubbed and wholesome. Nobody was going to put their picture on a box of corn flakes, but they looked as wholesome as anybody could in the back room of a bar at five in the morning.

The drug dealer was wearing a Ralph Lauren suit and Luchese cowboy boots. He was a charming guy and just seedy enough to make buying from him an adventure for a young Wall Street type and his girlfriend. For all those young men with their crisp yellow ties and fresh-minted MBAs, he was an urban outlaw. As hip as a white guy could get. For the woman—one of those young girls not long out of Holyoke or Smith—he was the bad boy from the wrong part of town. Stylishly rumpled and unshaven, if he was any sexier, he would have had to have been foreign—maybe even French. Up close, Max supposed, the scent of leather, bar smoke, and Remy could harden nipples under the silk. It was a look popular in the eighties and what a screenwriter patron had called "greasy chic."

Years later, Miles mentioned seeing him upstate. He'd
lost two of his fingers and had an eye gouged out—a victim of the internecine politics of the general population.
When he first hit the cellblock someone had made him
his bitch, then traded him off in the ritualized economy
of prison commerce. Miles did say he was still charming,
though a bit dispirited at having recently tested HIV
positive.

They were sitting close, in a loose semicircle on folding metal chairs. Bally pulled down the framed eight by
ten of an autographed Jack Johnson fight photo—one of
the thousands the boxer signed in his declining years
at Hubert's Museum and Flea Circus on Forty-second
Street.

The drug dealer tapped out a generous portion of
product from the bindle, heaping it in the center of
the already well-dusted glass. Then he began chopping
and sectioning it into precise lines with a gold Amex
card. That's what the eighties were, gram dealers with
gold cards. The Wall Streeter's girlfriend pulled the
Moët bottle from the ice bucket, then made a little
show of tipping it up to her mouth and drinking. The
drug dealer smiled and finished sectioning off the eight
identical lines and passed the framed photo clockwise.

Suddenly everybody got quiet as Max leaned down for
the first toot. Then the Wall Street type, who couldn't
have been more than twenty-five, said, "You know,
it's really hard to have a good time for less than a
thousand dollars in this town." He meant a thousand
a night.

As the blow dusted cooly up into the back of Max's
sinuses and throat, the truth of it hit like a jolt. *The kid
wasn't joking*. Max stayed frozen for what seemed like
a long time, head down, the rolled twenty-dollar bill—
fresh and crisp from a bank machine—to his nose. Then
the gram dealer tactfully took the framed photo and the
coke whore took her toot.

"Reagan saved this country," the drug dealer said.
Max could feel his face tightening and hoped the dealer
was playing to his customers; the Wall Streeter looked

like the Young Republican type. But Max sensed it as sincere.

"Market economy," the girlfriend began, then cut her thought short as she took her turn.

A little while later the conversation declined into coke babble—all big plans and bright futures. Everything would get better forever. Why wouldn't it? The dealer was looking to rep some bands and get a record label. The Wall Streeter was optimistic about his impending move to Drexel. Even the coke whore was scouting patrons for a clothing line she would design.

Max just sat there, the sniff singing in the circuitry of his head as the mask of his face numbed over. And suddenly he felt a tightening in his chest—like a belt pulled down to the last notch. At first he thought it was his heart—exploding from the blow—then he realized it was fear. Something, *maybe even everything*, was terribly fucking wrong.

Max, waking up, rolled over and felt Suze's hair under his cheek. Inhaling, he smelled herbal shampoo and cigarette smoke. Occupational hazard, you worked in a bar, you smelled of cigarette smoke.

When he opened his eyes, he saw the back of her head and how the long blonde hair was spread out across the pillow. Reaching an arm out under the blanket, he felt her breast under the nightshirt. She made a little noise in her sleep and snuggled in closer.

It was a good fit, he thought, thinking of the way her rear cradled into him. Then he realized he also maybe meant the way they were together. What was she, thirty, soon to be thirty-one? She'd been in the city six or seven years. And they'd both been through a lot of the same bullshit. The cocaine thing, the after-hours thing, the bad-relationship thing. Everything.

Easing up on one elbow to see her face, he noticed, not for the first time, the beginnings of lines around the eyes and mouth. She was getting a little heavier, the weight creeping on slowly, pound by pound, mostly around her middle and thighs. Max knew he could do temporarily better. Though what were the alternatives? Hook up with a twenty-three-year-old office worker who finds bartenders attractive. That would last, how long? About six months, if he was lucky. No, he'd wait this thing with Suze out a year and see where it went.

Suddenly she opened her eyes and rolled over into his arm. "What's happening?" she asked, voice still sleepy.

"Gotta go to work," Max said quietly. "Grab an hour. I'll set the alarm."

She closed her eyes and snuggled down into the pillow, mumbling, "Excellent idea."

The whole thing was just comfortable as hell and it scared Max more than a little. Scared him that something would come along to fuck it up and that something wouldn't come along to fuck it up.

He slid his arm out from under her head and slipped out of bed. The clock was on the other side of the room. He set the alarm for another hour. She had class another hour beyond that, which gave her plenty of time.

Max didn't have to turn on the weather channel. He already knew what it was from walking the six blocks from his apartment. It was cold and windy. What he needed was a calendar—because the days were starting to blend together again. He was pretty sure it was Wednesday, but was hoping for Thursday. The closer to the weekend, the better. At least he'd see some business on Friday and Saturday night.

He was doing the monthly inventory, checking the bottle levels and noting them on a legal pad, when Julie came in.

"We gotta talk, Max," she said.

His back was turned to her, and instinctively, he checked his watch—six-thirty. An hour early, which meant she was either quitting or asking for the night off.

Max turned and asked, "There a problem?"

Julie was standing at the end of the bar by the door. Next to her was an older woman. She was maybe fifty, but not an Upper East Side fifty, and not a Scarsdale suburban fifty, either. Maybe Levittown or Paramus. The type who watched the food budget—cut coupons and knew what macaroni and cheese tasted like. She wore a blue cloth coat and a dark red cloth scarf. Bundled inside the coat and scarf she seemed tiny, but didn't make a move to take them off, as if she wasn't sure if she was going to stay. It had been a long time since she frequented a saloon, if ever, and wasn't quite sure what to do next. Behind a pair of thick, large-framed glasses, her eyes were red and moist.

"This is Mrs. Brimmer, Max," Julie said, leading the woman to the bar.

It didn't sound good, that Mrs. part. Nobody was a Mrs. anymore, not even the ladies who lunched. Max set down the pad and moved to the end of the bar, smiling cautiously.

"Remember Pat, my old roommate?" Julie asked.

"Yeah, sure," Max answered, not having a clue. They all had roommates, these waitresses. He held out his hand, and the woman shook it, hesitantly and without taking off her mittens.

"There's a problem," Julie said. The ends of her mouth twitched down. Her eyes were red, too.

Max waited, leaning against the back bar. The woman was looking straight at him now—staring unblinking behind large thick glasses. Then she started blinking, fast, and a tear leaked out from the corner of her eye. She lifted the glasses and wiped it away with a mittened hand. The gesture made her look like a little girl—afraid and trying to be brave.

"Look, Max, somebody uh, murdered Pat yesterday morning," Julie said, then grabbed a quick look toward the woman.

It took Max a second on this one. "Oh, no," he managed, coming away from the edge of the back bar. Who the fuck was Pat and what was her mother doing in the bar?

The older woman nodded her head in confirmation. With the last nod, her head stayed down, staring at the wood.

"Would you like a drink?" Max asked.

The woman nodded again.

What do you serve a woman whose daughter's been killed? Brandy is what they gave the distraught in the movies. Max poured her two fingers of peach brandy in a rock glass. The woman drank it down in a gulp, mittens still on.

"The police came by this afternoon," Julie said. "Asked me some questions. I called Mrs. Brimmer. The cops had her over at the precinct."

Max poured himself a drink, three fingers of Remy. He gave Julie a questioning look, bottle halfway to the shelf, but she shook her head no.

"Here's the thing, Max," Julie said. "They won't let Mrs. Brimmer into the apartment. She can't get any of Pat's things, you know? They won't tell her anything."

Max took a long drink of the Remy. "Do they know who did it?"

"They won't tell me," the woman said, her voice breaking a little. "They, the detectives, won't tell me anything. They keep telling me to call back."

"Have they caught the guy?" Max asked. If it was street crime, a mugging gone wrong or a rape gone too far, then they'd have the guy by now or would never get him. After twenty-four hours the odds turned bad.

"They won't say," Julie answered. "I went down there. I couldn't get anything out of them."

"They've got a job to do," Max said, feeling stupid the instant the words were out of his mouth. Next thing, he'd be saying something about how he was sure justice would be done.

"But they could tell her," Julie said, angry now. "They could tell her something . . ."

Max took another drink of the Remy and set the glass down on the corner of the back bar. He began to ask how it happened, but held back. He'd ask Julie later, after the woman left. Probably some maniac or crackhead on the subway. "Look, there's the Victim's Rights Board or whatever it is and that other one, the Survivors of Violent Crime thing."

Julie stepped closer, elbows on the bar. "I thought maybe you could ask around, you know."

"Ask who?"

"People you know," Julie answered. "At least find out when we can get her things out of the apartment."

"They said they'll release her tomorrow," the older woman said, her voice weirdly calm now. "They showed me a picture—her face was the same, almost. You know, everyone there was very nice, considerate." The woman was staring down into the worn mahogany. She was still in shock. It might be a couple of days, maybe even a week or more before it sunk in. But right now, she was being dragged around the Upper East Side by a waitress-slash-actress reciting the facts of identifying her murdered daughter at the morgue.

"Mrs. Brimmer," Max asked. "Where's your husband?"

"He's home," Julie shot back.

"Should I call him? He can come pick you up," Max answered.

The woman shook her head. She was still staring at the mahogany.

"He can't," Julie said. "He's . . ."

"My husband is housebound," the woman finished. "He's in a wheelchair. I don't have much money with me, but I can go to a cash machine or if you'd take a check. I'm sorry, I'm just not very good at this sort of thing. There's been arrangements to make. The detectives asked questions . . ."

Max watched as she began digging around in her vinyl purse, working through the contents awkwardly with a mittened hand.

"Look, Mrs. Brimmer, I'm sorry, but it isn't a money thing," Max said. He wanted to reach out and shut the purse. "But we should let the police do their job. I wouldn't know where to start . . ."

"What about all your cop friends?" Julie shot back.

Max offered her up a look that would send a normal person running for the door or at least for a quick reality check. His cop friends were a trio of retired neighborhood guys who did their twenty and were pensioned off at forty-five. Sean Murphy did private security work around the city—supervising ex-cons, misfits, and cop wannabes who worked as minimum-wage security guards. Tony Cosillini watched monitors in the lobby of a midtown office and read paperback westerns. The third was an actor, playing First Cop and Second Cop on soaps and television dramas. When they weren't casting cops, he played cabbies, counter guys at delis, food vendors, and First Hood or Second Hood. Back when there was a film industry in the city, he was a fixture at extra calls.

It was through the third, Pete Betano, that he met the other two. Depending on their schedules, you could usually find one or more of them drinking coffee at a diner down the street. Max, when he joined them, acted as audience.

The woman was staring at him now, just peering up at Max with big, watery eyes that looked like they were going to cry again. "There's a dress, a blue dress, that if you could get," she began. "And some jewelry, a charm bracelet, a ring, and a necklace. I think that Pat would have liked to . . ."

She didn't have to finish. Max knew why she wanted the dress and jewelry. "Have you made arrangements?" he asked.

The woman's head came up; the eyes were wide with the horror of it. Two days ago, her daughter was living in New York, probably going on EPA and open casting calls, taking acting lessons, voice lessons, dance lessons, and phoning home four times a week. Everything was exciting for her. Now she was dead.

"They gave me a number to call," she said. "The detectives said that since it's a murder case . . ."

Max didn't want her to finish. He knew that the number was for the medical examiner's office. Murder victims were sent down there for an autopsy. That is where she would have identified the body. Nobody came out, pulled open a door, and lifted a white sheet anymore. Now the loved ones waited in an office and a detective or assistant M.E. came out with a Polaroid in one hand and an identification form in the other.

A year ago, a detective came around with a Polaroid; it was the picture of a bouncer Max knew from the after-hours circuit. The guy was found in a parking lot near the West Side piers between two cars. Somebody had stabbed him with a serrated steak knife, the kind that comes attached to a strip of cardboard and they sell at Grand Union or Food Emporium. The only thing in his pockets was a book of matches from Barmy's.

Max wasn't sure whether he should lean toward her or away. Julie solved the problem by coming up and putting an arm around the woman. "Look, I'll ask around," Max said. "You'd probably do better to talk to the detectives on the case, I'm telling you that right now. But I'll ask around and see what I come up with."

Julie looked up from the woman and gave him a small smile that said he'd maybe done the right thing for once. The woman nodded slowly and started to get up from the stool; she moved mechanically.

"I'm going to take Mrs. Brimmer home, okay," Julie said. It wasn't a question. "So I'm taking the night off."

"Sure," Max answered. It wasn't going to be busy anyway.

He watched as they went through the door, Julie's arm still around the woman's shoulder as they moved slowly across the sidewalk. They stopped at an old Ford Horizon with Jersey tags. Julie took the keys from the woman and opened the door for her. A moment later, they were gone, vanished into the Third Avenue traffic.

FIVE

The next night before work, Max found Sean, Tony, and Pete sitting at a back table of the Grace Coffee Shop, drinking coffee. They could have been in those seats for two minutes or two hours. There was no way to tell, though they looked dug in.

Sean and Tony were swapping sections of the *Daily News* and *Newsday* sports sections. Pete had the new *Variety* in front of him. He read it with a pair of half-glasses riding low on his nose, holding the paper far away in both hands.

Max couldn't remember the last time he read *Variety*.

"What you say, kid?" Tony asked, as Max slipped off his coat and sat down. He was scanning *Newsday*'s sports section, the sleeves of the plaid flannel shirt rolled up halfway to his elbows. The USMC tattoo on his right arm was badly blurred, but still large. He was a short dark guy, with a pitbull stance and arms like Popeye on steroids.

Pete turned the page with careful deliberation. He read the trades with the enthusiasm of a true convert, all of them, every word, column by column. *Variety*, *Backstage*, *Hollywood Reporter*. He read the list of names of unfair producers on the back page of *New York News Reel*, SAG's magazine. He retired as a homicide detective. Max now saw the same thoroughness in the way he went about acting, never missing a word or opportunity, never counting on luck, but always ready for it. And remembering everything, as if he'd be testifying under oath. You could see him in the early morning, talking up the kids in line at the open calls, kibitzing with the other actors, the director, even with the production assistants during shooting breaks. If he had a free half hour, he'd spend it in the lounge at the SAG offices, gossiping and reading the bulletin board.

"What's the word?" Sean asked, putting down the paper to take a sip of tepid coffee, then picking up the Marlboro from the black plastic ashtray and taking a pull. He was wearing a supervisor's white shirt with square patches with the name of the security outfit and uniform pants with a blue stripe down the side. The black clip-on tie hung from one side of the opened collar. Sean Murphy had spent the better part of twenty years on the night shift and it showed in his hollowed, deep-set eyes. He was thin, and proud that he could still get into the uniform he wore on graduation day from the police academy, which didn't surprise Max. He'd never seen Sean eat. For all he knew, the guy existed on Marlboros, coffee, and the occasional shot of Irish.

Then Sean raised the paper up again, all but his bony knuckles vanishing from view as a small cloud of smoke rose from behind the newsprint shield.

The waitress brought Max a cup of coffee without being asked, then topped off the other three cups. Max added milk and took a sip. "I need a favor," he said, trying to drop it casually into the silence. It was best not to jerk these guys around with small talk. They could smell bullshit half a block off.

The three ex-cops stiffened, but didn't answer. All cops welcome citizens in need of an unofficial favor the same way that most people look forward to the discovery of a dead rat in their bathroom. Only ex-cops hate favors more.

"Little favor," Max added, not knowing if it was little.

"How little?" Pete asked, putting the *Variety* down in front of him and pushing the glasses up on his nose.

"How long does a crime scene stay sealed?" Max asked.

"Depends on the crime," Sean answered, letting out a lungful of smoke behind the paper, but still not committing to anything.

"Homicide," Max said.

Tony made a sound that was like a laugh, but not quite, then turned the page to hockey scores, keeping his eyes glued to the numbers. Sean put the paper down, either sizing up the situation or going for another sip of coffee.

Pete leaned forward then, studying Max. After about three seconds, he tilted his head, just a little. Nice gesture, Max thought, good for television. "Go ahead," he said.

"Waitress got murdered up on Eighty-fourth," Max started. "My waitress brought in the mother. The mother wants some stuff out of the place to bury the girl in."

Tony brought the sports section up in a perfect impersonation of Sean and said, "It's that double."

Max took another sip of coffee. "You know about it?"

"Two white kids get whacked on the Upper East Side, it makes the papers," Pete said. "Shit, didn't you read yesterday's paper, kid?"

Max shook his head no.

"Made the news," Sean said. "All channels, five, nine, and eleven, led with it."

Max shrugged. Was that why the days were blending together, because he'd missed the papers and the television news for a few days?

"Young talented actress and her boyfriend victims of the city. That's how they played it," Tony added. "Like there aren't any victims above Ninety-sixth."

"It's high profile," Pete said. "There'll be heat on the detectives."

"What do I tell her?" Max asked.

"Who caught it?" Sean asked.

"Paper quoted Haloran and Tanza," Tony answered, still hiding behind the sports section. He was interested but intent on sitting this one out.

"Now there's a pair," Sean said.

"Anything you could find out, you know?" Max asked.

"What? You got your sights on this other waitress, the live one?"

"Know the difference between a waitress and a '57 Chevy?" Tony put in.

"Not everyone's had a '57 Chevy," Max answered, finishing the ancient joke. "So nobody's gonna make a call for me?" Max asked the question to all three, but looked directly at Pete.

The two divided halves of the sports section came down slowly. Pete eyed the other two, who shrugged, then he rose heavily from the table, finishing off the last of his coffee as he came up. "Get a refill on this for me, will ya?"

"It's appreciated," Max said, then watched as Pete walked to the front of the diner where the pay phone hung. He made two calls and was back in ten minutes.

"Day after tomorrow," he said, sitting down. "Have her go through the DA's office. They have control of the crime scene now."

"Not the cops?" Max asked, taking a sip of coffee.

"Not on something like this," Pete answered. "It'd be the DA and the crime scene guys, but not the detectives."

"You want some advice?" Sean said. "Don't let the mother go up to the apartment alone. Really, don't even let her go, not even with a relative or one of those victim advocate people. Have her get a friend or your waitress to fish out what she needs."

"Yeah?" Max asked. This was a new one. "How come?"

"It's a tough scene," Sean finished. "The techs would've been all over it. Stuff from the drawers lying around. Fingerprint dust over everything."

"There'll still be blood," Tony added, cutting to the point.

"It isn't how she'd want to remember her kid's place," Pete said in a soft voice.

"I get the idea," Max said.

"They'll send a detective or a uniform up with someone," Pete said. "Have the parents call. She might have to sign for the possessions in a memo book."

"If the landlord isn't a prick, he'll have the super or

someone tidy up," Sean put in. "For a few bucks, he can send the stuff to the family. That's the way to do it."

Julie came through the door half an hour early. Max was finishing a take-out burger and drinking draft. The beer tasted like shit, which meant the coils were shellacking up again. He'd have to flush them out soon, or have the beer distributor find a guy to do it.

"What'd you find out?" she asked, walking past Max to hang her things in the back room.

"You can get in day after tomorrow," he called. "Call the DA's office, they'll send a detective or somebody up with you."

When she came back, he noticed that she was wearing the same clothes. "Yeah, that's good," she said. "Pat's folks are real upset. You know?"

Max thought, no shit. Their daughter gets blown away, you wouldn't expect them to shake it off. "Someone suggested that you go up and get the stuff," he added. "The place is going to be a wreck."

"I stayed out there last night," Julie answered, sitting at the bar. "Real heavy scene, you know?"

Max worked the angles through his head. What was it? Did she get off on inserting herself in the center of the murder? To be on the inside of something, even a fucked-up thing like a murder, was better than being on the outside of everything. Just the idea of it made him think he'd been in New York too long.

Kee came out of the bathroom then, carrying the empty ten-gallon bucket he used to dump ice in the urinal. Max and Julie watched him cross the floor, place the white plastic bucket under the side of the bar near the ice machine, and come around the front. "Thursday," he said. Thursday was the day he got paid.

"Thursday, already?" Max asked. It was part of his ongoing crusade to engage Kee in conversation.

"Yes, Thursday," came the definitive response.

Max counted five twenties from the register and handed

them over. Kee had been paid a hundred a week for as long as anyone could remember. No paperwork, no social security number, and no 1099s.

There were four keys to the place: Max had one, Lynn had another, one sat in a property envelope of an upstate prison with Miles's number on it, and Kee had the last. For a hundred bucks a week, he swept up, dusted, washed the rest rooms, took out the trash, emptied the ashtrays, and cleaned whatever stray glasses were left around the bar. The whole thing took an hour and a half a day.

Kee counted the money, put it in his pocket, and headed for the basement where he kept his plaid lumberjack jacket.

"He's a creepy guy," Julie whispered before Kee made his reappearance.

"Kee? He's okay," Max answered.

The old man shuffled back out and headed toward the door. Max and Julie watched silently as he paused at the door to zipper his jacket.

"See you tomorrow, Kee," Max called.

The old man raised one hand in weary acknowledgment that could have meant "sure," "maybe," or "fuck you," before vanishing out into the cold.

"That his first name or his last?" Julie asked.

"Don't know," Max answered as he pulled a petty cash slip from the register and began filling it out under the office and bar supplies heading. If the IRS ever got wise, Kee's five grand a year would look small. Lynn's accountants wrote off and depreciated everything but the ice. And that was *after* she gave them the second, *official*, set of on-premises books.

"How does he live on what you pay him?"

Max finished the slip and put it under the partitioned money tray. "He makes more than you or me," Max said, smiling. "He's got five bars on his route. Five that I know of."

"You're kidding," Julie answered, amazed. "He's making five hundred a week?"

"That I know of," Max said. "I'm taking a cab down to Tory's one night, this after-hours place that closed, and I see him coming out of this dyke bar on Thirty-second. So, it's probably more like seven or eight. Tax free."

"Holy shit," Julie said.

"Wanna hear a great story?" Max asked. Then he began telling it. "Back in like '86, we're packed every night. People standing in line for the bathroom to do blow, drinking like crazy. It was like a blizzard in August. One Thursday, Kee comes up to me and lays a bundle on the bar. I say, 'Hey, where'd you find that?' He says, 'Bathroom floor.' You know, some dealer probably dropped it. 'Well, I better take that,' I said. And do you know what he does?"

Julie shook her head.

Max smiled, "Real quick, he slaps his hand down on it and says, 'One hundred and twenty-five.' I say, 'For a gram?' He comes back, 'Gram and quarter.' "

Julie walked away, shaking her head slightly.

Lynn came in early, a little before closing, and set herself up at a back table. She wasn't wearing the mink, which was a good sign. She had on a knee-length down coat over jeans and a man's pink button-down. The place was empty, except for two regulars who left ten minutes after she sat down.

Julie waited on her cautiously, delivering a scotch, then took up a position near the window, watching the traffic.

"Got time to lean, you got time to clean, honey," Lynn called out from behind a haze of cigarette smoke.

The girl turned, only slightly panicked, her eyes going from Max to Lynn, then back again.

Max came away from where he was leaning, and said, "Why doncha split? We're not doing any business."

"Sure, split," Lynn said.

When the waitress's eyes shot back to Max, he motioned with his head toward the end of the bar for her to get her things. She was out the door in about ten seconds, but not before saying, "So, see you tomorrow, right?" Just to make sure she had a job.

"Same time, same place," Max answered, then poured himself a scotch and joined Lynn at the table.

"So, you banging her or what?" Lynn asked, stubbing out the butt of one Chesterfield and lighting another.

"Is this like a work-related question?" Max asked back, taking a sip of his drink and leaning back.

"Just like to think one of us is getting something out of her," came the answer. "I know I'm not getting a waitress. Maybe you are, huh?"

"Wrong, Lynn," Max said.

"If I'm wrong, then you're slipping," Lynn said, exhaling a cloud of smoke. "I'd figure you're about due for a split with Suzie."

"Maybe I'm just getting older, wiser, or something."

"Yeah, okay, whatever you say," Lynn said, her voice heavy with disbelief. "We do anything tonight?"

"Two hundred and change," Max answered. "You want me to total out for you?"

"Later," she said. "Anything going on on the street?"

"You hear anything about a double murder?" Max asked. "Couple of kids."

Lynn set the cigarette down, picked up the scotch, took a drink, then set the glass down again on the Dewar's coaster. "You mean that thing on Eighty-fourth?" she said. "Just what I read in the papers. The guy wasn't a kid."

"What was he?"

"Thirty-six," Lynn said. "What's the matter, you don't read the papers?"

Max was going to say something about thirty-six still being a kid these days—they kept raising the age limit on that. Nobody seemed to grow up anymore. "No, no newspapers, magazines, no television."

"You got a personal interest in this or what?"

"The girl was a roommate of Julie," Max said. "She brought the mother in last night."

"Christ, what for, happy hour?" Lynn asked. "That girl really doesn't have any kind of sense, does she?"

"Wanted me to ask somebody about getting back into the apartment, is all," Max said, then finished off the scotch. "The mother was real shaky, she could have gotten the same thing from the detectives."

"I don't like it," Lynn answered. "You putting your nose in a big-time felony like that."

"Fuck it," Max said. "It's done. I was just wondering is all."

Lynn sat there for a few seconds, drinking. "I got the paper from yesterday in the car, if you want to look."

Max got up, to get away from Lynn more than anything. "Yeah, you got the keys?"

Lynn slid the Saab's keys across the table and he headed for the door. The *Post* and the *Wall Street Journal* were in the backseat of the Saab. He grabbed the *Post* and headed inside. He was halfway to the table where Lynn was sitting when he thumbed through, looking for the story. He didn't have to look far; the *Post* put it on pages four and five. A double-page spread with COUPLE MURDERED IN UPPER E. SIDE APT. headline. Underneath were four or five photos, the outside of the building, the closed door of the apartment, and a head shot of the girl, who looked vaguely familiar. But it was the photo of the guy, not a head shot, but an amateur photo, that caught Max's eye. It was the same guy who said you couldn't have a good time for under a grand a night, so long ago. The guy looked older, a little more worn, but it was the same guy, smiling into the camera. In the background, at his left shoulder, was the slanting trunk of a palm tree and a section of striped beach umbrella.

Max sat down and began reading. In the second paragraph they mentioned his name, Peter Marotte. It also mentioned that he'd once worked for Drexel Burnham. It was the same guy.

The big man had spent two nights in jail, the first in a precinct, the second in a holding pen at the court house. At the precinct they gave him hamburgers and french fries to eat. The courthouse served only baloney sandwiches.

It was past nine at night when they finally released him. They had kept his passport, plane ticket, and two thousand dollars for bail.

The grand jury date was set for six weeks. The assistant district attorney had told his free lawyer that they would probably acquit on all charges, the most important one being vehicular manslaughter.

The skinny man in the sweatsuit had been identified as a drug addict. The box, which was covered in shrink-wrapped plastic, contained two red bricks taped to the styrofoam packing mounts that had once held a fax machine. It was, his free lawyer explained, a common thing for addicts to sell shrink-wrapped packages with bricks in them to cars from New Jersey. The drivers believed they were purchasing stolen fax machines and camcorders for forty dollars. The skinny man, the free lawyer said, had it coming. His own sister had paid thirty dollars for a brick that was supposed to be a CD player not two weeks before.

The big man grunted and thanked his free lawyer. Then he walked uptown, through Chinatown, the wind biting his face, cutting through the shearling jacket and numbing his legs. When he reached the video arcade, he went in and fed three five-dollar bills into the change machine, then walked out. At a pay phone near Houston, he dialed a long-distance operator and deposited thirteen dollars in quarters.

He'd been in the system nearly fifty hours. His people would be worried. The phone at the other end, halfway around the world, rang once. The big man mumbled a few words, repeated the number of the pay phone, and hung up. Then he waited, guarding the phone, one meaty hand on the handset, pushing the receiver down. In his mind, he could clearly see the old man he called. He could picture him leaving the tiny grocery store, mounting the ancient three-speed British bicycle, and pumping his way down the dirt road in the afternoon heat. It would be at least an hour before the phone rang, but that did not matter; the big man was nothing if not patient.

While he waited, he thought of the skinny man in the sweatsuit, selling empty boxes and bricks to people from New Jersey. It would be a good story to tell when he returned home.

Six

Max lived at a good address. A very good address. The sole tenant of the brownstone in the heart of the richest zip code in America. His junk mail was just outstanding.

His immediate neighbors were an Argentinian jewel broker to the east and a Wall Street analyst to the west. The analyst made frequent sonorous appearances on financial talk shows. Both viewed Max with surprising good cheer. Each one, Max knew, had a healthy respect for luck, which is what landed Max in the brownstone in the first place.

In truth there was some luck, but mostly it was a trust funder named Denny Mcbride. Denton "Denny" Mcbride, who owned the building, had never worked. At fifty, he was short, bespectacled, and soft-looking beneath his Anderson & Sheppard Savile Row suits. Even if he hadn't been an alcoholic, Denny was pretty much unemployable—a fact that afforded him moments of a peculiar reflective amusement and never anything like anxiety or shame. Luckily, his grandfather made a bunch of money somewhere, then his father made a bunch more. Denny, his sister, and his brother probably decided at some point—prep school or puberty, perhaps—that there was plenty of money and kicked back forever. The brother moved out to L.A. The sister married Oklahoma money, which she had somehow shrewdly discovered buys more than ostrich-skin boots and Resistol hats. Twice, sometimes three times a year, she proved that it even spent in Paris, Gstaad, and Milan.

Denny spent his days painting watercolors. He painted mostly gin bottles, scotch bottles, and old checkered cabs. The taxis he painted from memory. The gin and scotch still lifes he worked on between sampling his models.

He was a harmless kind of alcoholic. He drank, painted, and drank more. He loved his liquor, and he loved muscular men, two at a time. Denny lived his life in a mild alcohol haze, confident that there would always be enough of everything. He had neither watched the news nor read a newspaper for fifteen years, not since coming to the unquestionable conclusion that both were instruments of scoundrels with sour dispositions determined to depress him for no good reason whatsoever.

Max had a genuine fondness for Denny. He liked him as much as any bartender could like a monied alcoholic patron who regularly tipped thirty percent. One night Denny came in with a Food Emporium bag containing six frozen mackerels. He carefully arranged the seafood on a bar stool like a teepee, ordered a Ritz Fizz, drank it slowly, then left with his fish. Another time he announced that he had memorized every city named for a U.S. president.

When Max complained to him one night that he was looking for a new place to live, Denny chirped right up that there was an apartment on the top floor in the back. "Servants' quarters you know, but awful cozy."

Max moved in with a two-year lease. Halfway through the first year, Denny died of a coronary. Then came the lawsuits. Brother and sister went to war in earnest over the remainder of the estate. When Max's lease ran out he got a letter from the brother's attorney, quickly followed by one from the sister's lawyer. It was all very seedy to them, a bartender/actor living in the servants' quarters. No doubt just another manifestation of their dear dead sibling's eccentricities. That was, of course, after they conclusively established no claims of palimony would be forthcoming.

Then Max pointed out that there was maybe a couple

hundred thousand in antiques in the house. Nine hundred and forty-eight thousand, one of the lawyers corrected. A risky proposition, leaving them alone, Max offered. Pipes freeze, roofs leak, guys with criminal intentions, maybe even family members, get ideas. To empty the house into storage would be an expense—particularly the added insurance of a bonded warehouse.

"I see, you're proposing then to act in effect, that is, in the capacity of, a groundskeeper," one of the lawyers, the sister's, said. "And to continue paying the present rent."

Six years later the lawsuits were still crawling through the courts as one of New York's classiest white-shoe firms began slugging it out with a crafty good-ole-boy $450-an-hour Okie lawyer. Max paid rent, $425 a month into an escrow account held in trust by a bank. Twice a year the brother and sister arranged separate New York vacations, staying at the place. Such is the stuff of apocryphal New York apartments.

But now, with Suze in the picture, things had changed. In another couple of months there'd be talk of moving in together. And that was the acid test. Max knew deep down in his gut that both sides would throw him out at the first mention of bringing Suze in on a permanent basis. He suspected they already knew about the three nights a week she spent there. But full time was another story altogether.

Max woke from a sound sleep to the sound of voices. First there was Julie, calling him to say she'd be in late. Then came Lynn, complaining about some bill from a liquor distributor. And finally, a call from Todd Manion, a bar owner down the street.

Max let them all play out on the answering machine, then rolled over, half-expecting to feel Suze, and disappointed when he realized it was her night at home. A vague picture of her studio apartment flashed in his head, and he wondered if he could live there. Three hundred and fifty square feet with a convertible sofa for a bed and a view of an alley.

He rose wearily. The digital readout of his clock said two-thirty. Outside the sky was the color of dull aluminum. A chill came from the general direction of his window.

"Fuck it," he whispered to himself, knowing that in itself was a bad sign. But then he reached for the phone and ordered breakfast from the diner on Lex. Having breakfast delivered at two-thirty in the afternoon was a worse sign.

Where were all those days that bartending was supposed to free up? No standing in line for the movies. Grocery shopping in uncrowded stores. Acting classes. *Auditions.*

No sooner was the thought out of his head when his agent's assistant, Babs Binindi, called. He sat on the edge of the bed, half-awake, drinking tepid coffee and listening to her through the answering machine's speaker.

"Max, it's important, call the office today. Gil has to speak with you. We need to schedule a meeting. So call. Okay?"

There was something in her voice, an edge. It wasn't an audition, that much was sure. No hint of opportunity, not even a thank you or good-bye. No, this was *the talk*. The one where Gil Pontero sat somberly behind his glass-top desk and said something about goals no longer being mutual, and perhaps, wouldn't a change be appropriate at this stage of things? And don't let the door hit your ass on the way out, kid.

Max ate the omelette out of the round aluminum container, drank the remaining take-out coffee, and dressed for work. White shirt, black jeans, black high-top Converse All-Stars. Out on the street, another cold wind was blowing. He could feel it through the entranceway's door and through the grommeted air vents of his Chuck Taylors.

So far, it had been one of those snowless New York winters. A few late-night flurries that don't leave a trace by morning. Snow, a real snowstorm, would help offset those mean gray skies and brighten the streets.

Stalling, he opened the mailbox. Two letters, the phone bill, and a business envelope from SAG. Opening the SAG letter, he discovered that his health insurance was about to be canceled because he hadn't earned the five-thousand-a-year minimum.

Max harbored a secret nightmare: an image of himself behind the bar at a Blarney Stone near Times Square. He's maybe fifty, wearing a white short-sleeve shirt and black knit tie. In front of him are five or six drinkers, every one of them knows his name. Behind him on the back bar is his white porcelain cup filled with an off-brand vodka. Lately there had been a frightening vividness to it. The jukebox is playing "New York, New York."

Now the nightmare was coming true, piece by piece. First the call from his agent, then the SAG letter. An evil and unpleasant future was beginning to show its teeth. Max knew this to be true, and not just for him. There was the feeling that truly desperate and ugly times lay ahead, waiting.

But he had Suze. There was maybe a future for him with her, though they were still doing some slow wary dance, both afraid to rush into anything. She'd been hurt before. Kicked to the curb, as they say. But who hasn't?

Max had a different problem. He kept thinking about the next best thing. What if someone, something better, did come along? A better body, a big bank account, a more comforting love, then he'd be screwed. Commitment felt like surrender. Any kind of serious commitment meant closing the door on a world of possibilities. That was one fear, and it was a big one. The other fear was that maybe Suze *was* the one. There just wasn't a way to know.

The city was filled with guys, women too, all waiting for that next best thing to come along. The next best job, the next best apartment, the next best meal, the next best piece of ass. All of them always looking to trade up, grasping toward the next level. Just working like hell at it.

You could read it on their faces. It came across as a dull expectancy, desire, and desperation. And Max knew, just by watching them, that they'd turned something critical into reflex.

Just thinking about it was like poking at a bad tooth. But talking about it—one of those endless relationship talks that stretch into hours—was worse.

Max reached Third Avenue and headed uptown. Two blocks away, he was already feeling for the bar's keys in his pocket. He could see Suze's face in his mind's eye—large brown eyes, small nose, and a mouth that was maybe just a little too wide. It was a pretty good sign, he thought, seeing her so clearly. There was a time, before her, he couldn't picture a woman ten minutes after he said good-bye.

He thought about what she'd be doing right then, and saw her in the restaurant uniform, white shirt, blue men's tie, and dark slacks, setting up for the dinner rush at the midtown restaurant she worked. Later, she'd be sitting by the door, checking reservations in the book and answering the phone.

Crossing the street, he thought about her at school, slogging through her college degree, finishing up at NYU after a seven-year vacation, and wondering what all those kids from the suburbs thought of her.

He decided to give her a call when he got inside.

There was a dark red 525 Mercedes parked outside the bar. Max knew who was in it. Todd Manion. He could see the bar owner's curly blond head bobbing slightly as he talked on the car phone, the *Wall Street Journal* spread open across the steering wheel.

Max walked past the Benz without looking in its direction. By the time he had the key in the door, Todd was out of the car and coming up behind him at a stiff cold-weather trot.

"Max, whoa, Max," Todd called. "We gotta talk."

Turning, Max eyed him more carefully. Nice winter tan, Burberry coat, dark blue suit underneath, and a tie just ugly enough to be expensive. The guy almost looked legit—that is, not like a bar owner.

"Yeah, I got the message," Max said, fighting the key into the lock. "Come on in."

Todd came up short and began to stammer. "Is uh . . ."

"Lynn's not around," Max said, stepping into the bar and holding the door open.

Todd put on a smile of small relief at the news, nodded, then walked into the darkened room.

Ten years ago Todd was bartending over on First Avenue, at one of those places that served blue margaritas and Seven-Up shooters to kids who lined up two deep at the bar and thought the city was just an extension of college. Every month or so he'd buy a half ounce, take out his two or three grams, step unmercifully on what was left, then sell it off to people he knew were solid. He was also stealing pretty good from the bar—seventy-five or a hundred a night. Nobody knew what Todd did with his money until he made a move.

Todd's move came at eight-fifteen in the morning. Max remembered it, because he was there. They were in the high-rise apartment of a woman with a serious coke problem. The woman was sitting in front of the television watching the Home Shopping Network with a mirror in her lap. She'd been going for almost two days and showed no desire to stop. Every time the product changed, she lowered her head for a toot. Todd was sitting across from her, drinking a glass of Armagnac, and Max was talking up some waitress whose name he'd forgotten forever.

"Why do you watch that?" the waitress with Max asked the woman.

On the screen, a model was poking at a glazed porcelain pup with a knitting needle. Now they all watched, eyes fastened to the screen as she lifted the ceramic dog's collar and tags up with the needle.

"It's interesting. Sometimes there's a bargain," came the answer. "Good stock, too."

"That's traded?" Todd asked, setting his glass down and turning his full attention to the television.

"Selling at nine and a quarter," the woman said, then took a toot.

Todd lifted himself very carefully from the chair and went to the phone. When Max heard him give a broker account number to the discount house, he followed him into the kitchen.

"Hey, man, you know what you're doing, right?" he asked. Not an unreasonable question after a night of partying.

Todd was smiling. Not grinning, but smiling, showing a full set of teeth, right back to the molars. "Yeah, I know what I'm doing," he answered, then ordered two thousand shares at the market opening price.

For six months he rode the stock up to sixty, buying more and more along the way on margin. By the time it was up to the high sixties, he was in for almost fifty grand. Then he sold, shorting the stock with half his profits. A couple of weeks later, the thing fell like a stone.

He took enough out of the deal to buy out a lease on a bar, lure in a group of limited partners, and open the doors. Now he was wearing a family-crest signet ring, Sulka tie, and Bermuda tan.

"You want something?" Max asked, moving around the bar.

"OJ, no ice," Todd said, slipping out of the coat as he climbed up on a bar stool. "Yeah, and could you let me have a couple of bottles of schnapps 'til tomorrow. Delivery didn't come in."

Max poured him an orange juice in a white wine glass and made one for himself. "Peach, huh?" Max asked, knowing Todd needed the schnapps for Woo-Woos. Guy probably went through two or three bottles a night.

"Yeah, peach," Todd answered. "No rush."

Max pulled two unopened bottles from the cabinet, hoping he wouldn't get a run on Woo-Woos. Ever.

Todd eyed the bottles like he was paying for them, then said, "So, what's going on?" and took a sip of the orange juice. "How's Miles? How's Suze?"

Max drank down half his juice and moved back around

the bar, taking a seat next to Todd. "This like a social visit?"

If he was surprised by the question, Todd didn't show it. Rather, he lit up a cigarette with a gold Cartier. "Hear about that waitress? The one that got killed."

"Yeah," Max answered. "Miles's fine, by the way. Suze, too."

"I heard that you knew her, that true?"

Max took another sip of the OJ. "No, she was a roommate of the waitress here. Maybe she came in once or something, you know."

"She worked at my place," Todd said. "A good kid, nice ass. I was going to put her behind the bar. Then she quit."

"Yeah?" Max asked, waiting for the punch line.

"See, here's the thing," Todd said, making a point to look Max in the eye. "I'm a suspect, I think."

Good punch line, but his timing was off, Max thought. "No shit."

Todd brought up his cigarette, took a long pull, let it out in a thin stream, then took a drink of the juice, figuring how to lay it out. "See, we kind of had a thing going," he said at last. "Nothing serious, just a little thing."

"Janey find out?" Max asked. Janey Bowdritch was the woman watching the Home Shopping Network. Todd later married her. The joke was he married her because he wanted to get rich off her television viewing habits. The truth was, he married her because she *was* rich. She was old money. Fishers Island: Newport. The Spence School. A mother that dabbled on committees and ate lunch at Le Cirque twice a week. And a daddy, poor darling, who died at a Sotheby's stamp auction. The *Times* ran a tasteful five-inch obit. In the Bowdritch circles, you were mentioned twice in the press. Wedding announcement and obit. The old guy didn't disappoint.

"Janey's out of town drying out and avoiding scandal," Todd said. "She knew. Now the police know. They kept asking if she was trying to blackmail me. Shit. You know what they say, 'It's just as easy to marry a rich girl as a poor one'? It ain't true."

"I think that was 'Fall in love with a rich one,' " Max answered. It was an odd feeling sitting next to a guy who maybe killed two people.

"Really?" Todd answered, a little surprised. "Well, whatever. Now the cops think that Pat was trying to blackmail me."

"Was she?"

Todd gave Max a long look, then said, "No, as a matter of fact she wasn't. It was just a thing in the spring. She was living with this guy, Marotte. A good guy. I'm married. We'd go out once a week and do the nasty at a hotel. Order up room service. No big deal."

Max kept looking, staring at Todd, as if a sign that said "killer" would appear on his forehead. Maybe he'd start twitching around an eye like some villain from a thirties movie.

"What, you're shocked?" Todd said, annoyed now. "A bar owner boffing a waitress. Quick Max, better call '60 Minutes' and 'Nightline.' "

Max took a long drink of juice. "So, what do you want from me?"

"I want you to look around, you know?" Todd said, serious, eyes drifting from his OJ to his own reflection in the bar mirror. "Keep your eyes open. Maybe get a look at the police files."

It was beginning to fit into place. "You haven't been talking to Julie, by any chance?"

Todd smiled pleasantly. "I saw her at the wake today, out in Jersey."

"You went to the wake?"

"Look, I'm not a complete asshole, you know? Besides, I can't make the funeral, Janey scheduled me for some charity thing the same day. By the way, that girl, Julie, treat her nice, okay? She's a good kid."

A thought took hold in Max's head. "What? You nailed her? At a wake?"

"Yeah, well, in a manner of speaking. You know, we stopped, on the way back. So, what about it? You going to do it?"

"Just count me out, okay?"

"I was going to pay you." Todd tried. "How about two grand?"

Max got off the stool and moved around the bar. "Thanks, but no."

Todd was quiet for two beats. "What's the big deal? It's not like you never did a favor, right? That's your thing. Find an apartment for someone who needs one. Find the bookie with the best spread. And, correct me if I'm wrong here, but wasn't it you who found that waiter when his parents came to town worried about their kid?"

Max stayed quiet. If he stayed quiet long enough, maybe Todd would give up and leave.

"Hey, remember when you made the home video of the guy with the soft-tissue and nerve damage chasing twenty-dollar bills down Park? Now, that was a fuckin' classic. America's funniest home video."

Max had dropped five twenties behind the guy on a windy day. The insurance investigator, a regular customer, paid him a grand, plus expenses. But the thing that made it a really great film was the lead-in—the establishing shot—before Max approached the guy, he was in a Mercedes showroom, studying stickers and talking up the salesman. Max nailed him just as he came out through the door. The jury ate it up. A junior-high English teacher with a negligence trial two weeks away, shopping sixty-grand cars, drew a nice picture.

"A long time ago," Max answered. Max had to think back to put a year on that thing. Must have been '83 or '84.

"As I recall you've also handed out your share of subpoenas," Todd persisted. "Process-server extraordinaire."

How could he remember? Max hadn't thought about that stuff in years. Paying off a maitre d' so he could put on a waiter's jacket and serve a real estate developer court orders for child support before the entree. The sneakers should have given it away. Never accept a wine list from a steward wearing Chuck Taylors. "Todd, where do you get this stuff?"

"It's legend," came the answer.

"It's over," Max said. But it was never over. What started out as a little sideline, a way to pay for acting classes and a weekend out of the city, fueled a reputation. He got known as a guy who had contacts. Someone to call in a pinch. The rumors and gossip about him were all out of proportion, but in truth, he did nothing to bring them back into reality.

"Come on, I really need some help on this thing," Todd whined. "What have I ever asked for, huh?"

"Whyd'nt you hire some investigator? Get a pro. Maybe someone you could bring into court."

"Won't work," Todd said. "I gotta keep this real low profile. Just find something for me, and I'll hand it over to the lawyers. Look I got to get this thing settled, fast. The granny's on me like a bad suit."

So that's what it was, the grandmother. There's always a grandmother, Max thought. They keep them tucked away in some pre-war condo. Pull 'em out and dust 'em off twice a month for lunch at the Palm Court or an early evening at the Carlyle. Tough old WASP broads, they remember cafe society like it was yesterday. And they're holding a good chunk of change. For every privileged wild-child coke fiend on the Upper East Side, there was a grandmother who kept them safe from the evils of pro-letariat marriage and scandal. On one side they have the family and on the other a kindly gray-haired man of the cloth, usually an Episcopalian, with a twinkle in his eye, squiring them around town and talking obliquely about the needs of the parish. And all the while, there's a law-yer, pen poised like a dagger, above the old dame's will.

These old women knew the game. They played their hands like Atlantic City dealers standing behind a hundred-dollar table. And Janey's grandmama was a grande-dame classic. Apartment on Fifth Avenue and Seventy-second. Talked about "that horrible Mr. Roosevelt" and "those people," with the assured voice that God was indeed a Hoover Republican. Max met her briefly at the wedding. She stared intently like a statue witnessing the end of the world. "That old douche bag's got two Picassos and a Chagall hanging in her place,"

Todd reported to Max during the reception, and then he
went to work on her in earnest. It took two years to win
her over.

The whole deal hit Max in a flash. "I thought you had
her in your pocket?" he said.

"Some fucking fag cousin ratted me out. I go up to
see her, and she looks at me like I stepped in shit."

"Look, she'll forget about it," Max said. "She's gotta
be, what, eighty?"

"Eighty-two," Todd answered. "And she doesn't forget anything. She's still going on about how Dali pissed
in her potted plant in Paris in nineteen-fucking-thirty or
some shit. 'Simply a dreadful man, never cared at all
for the Spanish.' "

"Forget it," Max said. "It's over my head. Get a
professional."

"Come on, it has to be low profile."

"What were you going to do, put me on the payroll
as a bartender?"

"Consultant," Todd answered.

"Wrong guy, wrong job," Max said.

Todd turned, studied the traffic out on Third and
played his last card. "How about a part in a picture?"

"Come on, this is just fucking bizarre, you know?"

"Janey's got a cousin," Todd said. "Head of production for an independent producer. Nice girl. They're
shooting a made-for-television in the city next month.
You still got the same agent?"

Max froze, the pull of it like a magnet. "What, extra
work, right? A day player?" he asked, hoping for the
worst.

"Lines, I can promise you lines," Todd said, smelling
blood. "Say yes and I'll have you signed on in two days.
No bullshit, no audition."

What was the choice, keep on going like he'd been
going? Let the days blend together like they had been?
Wait for Lynn to finally fire his ass?

"You still got your SAG card, right?" Todd asked.
"It's a lock, you know, a solid lock."

"Know what I think? I think you're bullshitting me,"
Max said. "It doesn't work like that."

Todd shook his head sadly, still smiling. "It works exactly like that."

"Why don't I believe you, Todd?" Max said. "Tell me that?"

"Because you don't know that I'm boffing Janey's cousin," came the answer. "Or that the cousin is married to the agent who packaged the deal. Look, don't do a thing until you get the contract."

"What do I have to do?" Max answered, walking cautiously down from the end of the bar. Just thinking about it he could feel himself in over his head. Alarms were going off like crazy. And just as quick, he was shutting them down.

"Give it a month," Todd said. "Ask some questions. Just put your nose in it a little. Find something to knock me out as a suspect."

"Like what?" Max was hooked and knew it.

"Like maybe she was banging someone else," Todd said. "Like maybe her boyfriend was dealing, whatever. I'll tell you flat out, if I get nailed on this, I'm gone. *Fini.*"

"Just out of curiosity, you have any kind of alibi? You got anybody you could bring in?"

"The best," Todd answered, smiling.

"Yeah?"

"I was at Sixty-four and Park, all night and all day, rubbing belly buttons with a rich widow."

Max refilled his glass from the plastic jug. "Call her in," he said.

Todd smiled his most ingratiating smile, a little boy done wrong. "Might be a little hard just now."

"Yeah?" Max said, taking a sip of juice.

"Yeah," Todd answered, still smiling. "It was Janey's mom."

Max nearly gagged on the OJ. "Is there anyone, anyone at all you won't fuck?"

Todd's smile faded, his face gone sincere as a Payment Due letter. "Yeah man," he said, his voice level. "I wouldn't fuck a friend. You know what I'm saying?"

SEVEN

The call came in the morning. Max was reaching for the phone to order breakfast, his hand six inches from the receiver when it rang. He picked it up like you'd pick up a broken wine glass.

"Max! Max boy!" came the exuberant voice at the other end. Gil Pontero. A rare event, his agent placing the call direct, not using his assistant. Even more surprising, he wasn't on the speaker phone.

"Gil?" Max asked, stalling until he could shake off a little drowsiness. From the bathroom, Max heard the shower running.

"Max, Max boy!" Gil boomed into the phone. Gil tended to repeat himself when he was excited, like he was getting residuals or trying to push the line count up.

"What's up, man?" Max asked, already knowing the answer.

"Got you a part is all," Gil said. "Not even noon and I'm busting my balls for you. Appreciate it."

"I do, really. When's the audition?"

Suze came out of the shower, hair plastered down her long neck, breasts hanging perpendicular as she bent down to dry off her legs with a towel. Somewhere they had passed a point of comfortably naked, though he could not remember when.

"No audition," Gil said, the smugness of his counterfeit triumph oozing through the phone. "No audition. I sent your reel over and they loved it. I'm holding the fucking contract in my hand."

"A commercial?" Max asked, his voice flat.

Suze stopped drying and smiled. Behind her in the doorway a cloud of steam leaked into the room. She smiled assuming good news and stopped drying to listen.

"A made-for-TV feature," Gil laughed.

"No shit."

"No shit."

"No lines though, right?"

"I count twenty-eight," Gil boasted.

"No shit."

"No shit. It took a little doing, you know. Called some favors in. Played a little hardball. But there's some real meat on it."

A little doing? Played hardball? A couple of days ago Gil was probably calling him a washed-up prick to his assistant. "What's the part?"

"The lead's neighbor," Gil answered. "A scene with her and a scene with cops one and two after she's raped, murdered, and mutilated."

"Comedy, huh?"

"Don't be a wiseass," Gil shot back, his mood suddenly shifting at the scent of trouble. "These guys didn't want to touch you. We had to go high up to get you green-lighted. You hear what I'm telling you? Don't blow it."

"Yeah, maybe," Max answered and checked the clock. It was a little before noon. Suze had a class at one or one-thirty. "So, what's the gist of it?"

"It's a great story. Yuppie hooker. Psycho pimp. Big budget. You get killed—second to last to die."

"Send over the script, and I'll look at it," Max said, looking from Suze toward the window. A light snow was falling into the barren garden.

"You'll look at it? What're you saying here, you'll look at it? *NG*. No good. No fucking good," Gil Pontero boomed into the phone. "I busted my fucking balls to get you this part and you're going to *look at it?*"

Max could picture him, coming forward in his chair to rest his elbows on the glass desk as he yelled. "Okay, send over the script and the contract."

Gil took a long cleansing breath on the other end of the phone. "You'll have them in an hour, have them back to me before close of business today. You hear what I'm telling you?"

"Yeah Gil, I hear," Max answered, then hung up. Gil might have been an asshole, but at least he was Max's asshole, as the saying went.

Suze wrapped the towel around her, so that it covered her breasts and extended down to mid-thigh. "Good news, huh? A part?"

"Yeah, maybe," Max answered, studying her. She still looked good. Years ago Miles told him, "All pussy wears out. One day you're all nice and secure, then ba-bing, in walks some twenty-year-old with a bogus ID and one of those smiles. You don't stand a chance."

"Max, what's up, you're looking a little funny," Suze said, sitting down on the bed next to him. He could feel the damp heat coming off her.

Max tried to shake the thought, but couldn't. Where would they be in a year? Maybe taking apart their lives like Miles and Lynn had done. Staying together just long enough to keep torturing the other with bad lies. Really trying to wound each other until neither could stand it anymore. For Miles, the wounding and ugliness lasted longer than the pussy.

"Max, Max," Suze called.

When he felt her hand smooth down his hair, he snapped out of it. "Yeah, I guess I just spaced there for a second," he said.

"What's going on?" she asked, moving in closer and tilting her head to look at him. "You okay?"

"Gil called to offer a part," Max lied, thinking, it's beginning, right? That's how it starts, with lies like that.

"Yeah? That's great, huh? I don't see the problem."

"Just thinking, you know," he said, getting up. There was no use ordering in breakfast now.

"Yeah?" Suze said, getting up.

And he thought, what was the point in starting some kind of discussion now? She had a class in an hour. What would he say, "Miles said, 'All pussy wears out'?" Now there was an opening to a discussion. Finally he said,

"It's nothing, Gil's got me a shot at some made-for-TV thing."

"That's it?" she asked, her face still concerned.

"Yeah, I was just thinking, you know it's been a long time between parts."

Her face relaxed and she turned back toward the bathroom. "Well it's not unheard of," she called back.

"No," he said. Then added, "Want to go out for some breakfast?"

"Can't, I'll grab something downtown," she called from the bathroom.

Max, relieved, mumbled something, showered as she was dressing, and dressed as she gathered her books together. And that was another thing: what was it with this Ozzie-and-fucking-Harriet domestic bullshit? The both of them running around the bedroom and bathroom, bumping into each other as they got ready, was just bad staging.

"Walk me to the subway?" she asked, gathering her books.

Max picked up the change from the dresser, pocketed the bar keys, and said, "Sure."

He'd go out, eat at a diner. Buy a couple of papers and read them through.

By the time they hit the street, the snow was coming down in great wet flakes. He walked her over to the Lex line, got a quick kiss on the cheek, then headed uptown.

Max had seen Suze around for maybe three years before they hooked up. She was one of those women who bounced around the edges. Never right in the center, always attached to some guy. From what she and other people told him, the first guy was an East Village art dealer who made his money downtown and spent it uptown. There were a couple of others after that, but when Max first talked to her, she was living with this guy who sold downtown lofts to the new rich. If he sold three a year, he was into six figures on commission. That year he sold seven and was doing maybe three grams a day in blow. Suze wasn't far behind.

"So, what do you do?" she said, easing up to Max at some party. Probably scouting prospects for the real estate boyfriend. The host may have been the boyfriend, but he wasn't sure. He arrived in a crowd that had long vanished into the night.

"I'm an actor," Max said. He'd just gotten the role of Johnny Q. Things were looking pretty good. And everyone was telling him lies.

She eyed him suspiciously, trying to sense bullshit, sniffled a little from a recent trip to the bathroom, and said, "What have you been in?"

"There's a network series," he answered. "Airs next season."

"Interesting," she said, suddenly looking past Max toward her boyfriend who was talking up some fashion model in a black strapless number.

Six months later, the boyfriend threw Suze out and took up with the black strapless model, and Max's bust with Miles was history. So was the series. And nobody was telling him lies anymore. She came in the bar late one night attached to a guy who was busy handing out cards for his after-hours place to the clientele. Max tossed the guy out so fast that he didn't have a chance to collect Suze from the john, where she was doing up the last of his toot.

"Where's my friend?" she asked when she came out.

Max leaned over the bar and said, "Your boyfriend's a fucking scumbag."

She thought it over for about three seconds and answered, "Yeah. How about an Absolut, rocks?"

A year later they were nearly living together.

Max discovered it was Friday by checking the top of the *Newsday* he bought. If the snow kept up, then maybe he'd see some business. He could use it.

He walked the half mile up to Eighty-fourth, thinking of his deal with Todd and wanting a cup of coffee. The cold air did little to wake him up as he crossed the street and passed the apartment house where the dead waitress lived. It was nothing special. A renovated tenement, large apartments broken up into smaller ones.

Max was three or four doorways beyond when he turned back and stepped into the alcove. A new intercom system with a couple of names from the fourth floor removed from the occupant listings. Beyond the wire screen over the glass of the inner door was a narrow hallway and tiled floor. Inside he could see the banister at the foot of the stairs and the line of aluminum mailboxes. The whole thing was morbid as hell.

Max thought for a moment about what they would do in the movies and the answer came back, fuck it, get a cup of coffee. He walked two blocks to the first diner he could find.

The place was into the lunch shot. Not many businesses up here, few office buildings made it up this far. But most of the counter and all the booths were filled with store clerks, uniformed doormen from high-rises, bank tellers, store security guards, and a few old timers who spent their days in coffee shops. At night, around two or three in the morning, the place would be empty except for a few old timers and stray couples eating breakfast before heading home to bed.

Max squeezed into a seat at the counter between a woman and one of the Yorkville old timers, which meant German. You could still hear stories about how some of the Germans marched in brown shirts back in the thirties. Arrests of Nazi collaborators in the forties. Even die-hard fascists in the fifties and sixties.

Ten years ago, Max ran into a building's super who found a trunk packed with pre-war Nazi memorabilia— including a box of breakfast cereal with Hitler's picture on it. He lugged it into one of the better auction galleries that discreetly found a Texas buyer who paid enough for the super to put a down payment on a house in Midwood and take a course in air conditioning repair.

Max was halfway through a daily dose of the city's woes when he heard the woman next to him complaining to a friend, "I swear there must have been twenty calls to 900-HOT BABE, 976-BIG SLUT, and 976-TOTAL

BITCH. And the bill's got two pages missing."

"Bitch has too many letters," the friend replied, through a mouthful of food.

"Well, you know those numbers. First I thought it was Al, you know. But two hundred dollars."

The friend, bored, asked, "What you do?"

"I called the phone company, they sent out another one. I tell you, when I saw those charges . . ."

"So was it Al?"

"No, it was Kevin," came the answer with a disgusted finality.

"He's only fourteen!"

"Fourteen and a little pervert," the woman said. "I swear I thought I raised a perverted kid. I went down to the school to talk to the shrink—not that it would do any good. I get out of the car and see these little cards, printed up like money all over the sidewalk."

"What? At the school?"

"Two blocks away. A block away. The people that do it throw them out of cars, two in the morning near schools. On purpose. That's what the assistant principal said."

"That's something," the friend said, sliding off the stool with her check.

The woman followed, saying, "I tell you, I want to get out of this city, out of Queens."

"I don't blame you, I don't," the friend said, as they moved to the register, checks in hand.

Max turned to watch them leave, sizing the pair up as store clerks, forty and overweight. It was the scam that caught his attention—the deal with distributing 900 number cards near schools. The city was filled with enough latchkey kids to keep it going indefinitely.

He thought about it for another thirty seconds, idly running it around in his head. Then it hit him like a bolt. Dropping a five on the counter, he gulped down the last of his coffee and headed for the door. Max walked quickly down Second, thinking.

Two blocks later, he had a plan. Stopping at a pay phone, he dialed information, asked for the number of

Peter Marotte, and found the phone had been disconnected. He hung up and dialed information again, this time asking for Brimmer. The operator gave him the number for P. Brimmer on East Eighty-fourth. Bingo. The apartment had two phones.

Max already had a quarter out of his pocket and halfway to the slot before he thought better of it. Calls from pay phones might be flagged at the phone company, and street noise wouldn't help either.

He found what he was looking for a few blocks down in the lobby of a new condo. The building was half-empty, the condos about to go to auction. Six floors or more already taken over by the bank and rented out. But the guy working the door was someone he knew, though wouldn't admit to it. The doorman was a bartender who got caught stealing so often that there wasn't a decent bar in New York that would hire him. Now he was wearing a burgundy uniform with gold braid and waiting for tips that would never come.

As Max came up on the lobby, he saw Derek sprawled out on a seat behind the stanchioned ALL VISITORS MUST BE ANNOUNCED sign. A burgundy topcoat was draped over the back of the chair, and he was reading a paperback. Max opened the door and watched Derek's eyes fly open. Cheap reflex brought him halfway up before he saw it was Max.

"Derek, how's it going?" Max asked.

The guy had a dark lean face and black hair that was combed straight back. Everything about him cried out weasel. "Whattaya want?"

"You still bartending?" Max asked. He couldn't remember the last job Derek held, though a motel lounge out near Kennedy sounded about right. What he remembered most was the time Derek clocked some little Columbia coed in the ladies' john of an after-hours joint. The coed had spilled half a gram of sniff he'd just bought.

"You know, here and there," Derek answered with a casual lie. "I got a few things going. Wouldn't believe the action I got in this building."

Thing was, Max would believe it. The job looked like a horror show. He could see it in the lobby—the way it was done up in polished brass plate and a veneer of cheap marble. It was the kind of place where kids from Westchester and the Five Towns lived out their three-year New York fantasies in cut-rate condos subsidized by their parents. The face-saving line went that their parents bought it as an investment. A hundred thousand financial consultants in the city and the best investment their parents could find was a $180,000 one-bedroom condo.

Used to call those kids twenty-sixties, because they made twenty and lived like they made sixty as additional cardholders on their parents' American Express accounts. Max could smell it on Derek; he had the distinct odor of petty abuse and brass polish.

Yeah, there is justice at work in the universe, Max thought.

"Anything big time?" Max asked, knowing that Derek wouldn't know big time if it came up and bit him on the ass. His idea of big time was clipping thirty from the register on a Saturday night.

"You'd be surprised how many of these yuppies—the women—are lonely. Whole building of lonely fucking women. The video store delivers. Wouldn't believe what these chicks are ordering up for Saturday night entertainment."

"Yeah?" Max said. He'd believe anything.

"You looking for someone?" Derek said, suddenly forgetting about the door job as thoughts of stealing behind a bar did a slow tango behind his eyes.

"Maybe, you know, for when it gets busy, around March," Max said. "I might have a few shifts opening up. Two, three months."

"Need someone with a little experience, huh? Yeah, well, I'm around," Derek said. "Look, I'll give you the number. And I'll tell you. I got a following here. I can definitely bring in some people. Lotta women."

Derek walked back to the empty concierge desk and scrawled his name and number out on a yellow Post-It.

The writing had the quality of a graffiti tag on an abandoned building. "Give me a call," he said.

Max pocketed the number. "Could I use the phone? Local call."

Derek needed to think this over. He'd be granting a favor without a sure payoff. "Yeah, sure, man," he said after a good ten seconds. "Behind the desk."

"No concierge?"

"You're looking at him," Derek answered. "Dial nine to get the outside line."

Max walked behind the desk, found the phone, and dialed nine. Derek stood over him, watching and listening. "Hey, it's a private call, okay?"

Derek took a half dozen steps to the door, still listening. When a young woman in a fur approached the door, he reluctantly went to open it for her. Max dialed the customer service number. A young woman came on the line. "Yeah, I have a question about a bill?" Max said.

"Billing number please," the woman said.

Max repeated the P. Brimmer number and the woman said, "Yes?"

"The bill came with the last three pages missing," he said. "And I'm just showing all these message units."

"I'm showing sixty-four message units," the woman said.

Max took a breath, let it out, and said, "Hold on a second," then he waited, just long enough to make the customer service person believe he was digging out the bill. The woman in the fur passed by the desk, staring with mixed hope and dismay that Max might be the new concierge. "Okay, I'm showing sixty-four," he said. "That's way too many."

"That's what's indicated, sir," the woman said. Max suspected that like information operators, somewhere in her system a clock was ticking, measuring the time of each call. Now he was screwing up her average.

"Okay, okay, I got a question," Max said. "All the numbers—most of them any of these?" And he read the number off the concierge's phone, miraculously remembered an ex-girlfriend's number, and threw in Gil Pontero's number.

"Sir, I can't go through all sixty-four," the woman said. "And I cannot give out that information. I can send you a detailed bill."

"Okay, but can you tell me what the last two are?"

"Sir, I cannot give . . ."

"Sure, I get you, but could you send them to my office?" he asked.

"The bill will arrive at your home," she said curtly, then hung up.

"Okay, time's up," Derek said, coming around the desk.

Max hung up the phone. "All done."

"Okay, so you'll give me a call, right?"

"In a couple of weeks."

"Great, I'll be waiting."

Max headed to the bar to take care of the liquor distributor Lynn was bitching about because he had nowhere else to go. Probably the distributor wasn't coming through with the napkins and coasters. Under law a bar was allowed something like seventy bucks a year, per brand. Lynn pushed it past the limit, extorting all she could out of the distributors. And now he was heading to work to give some distributor grief because he had nowhere else to go.

That's what it narrowed down to after a few years, the bar became your life. Bars, bartenders, waitresses, waiters, chefs, and a few of the regulars were your friends. Put in the eight or ten hours behind the bar, then go out to some other bar. Or an after-hours club. Or a private party in some apartment. Or an all-night diner for burgers. Then one day, sooner than expected, it's four in the morning and there's a scotch rocks in front of you, and you realize you're forty-three with six hundred in a checking account.

When he got to the bar the small bond broker was waiting at the door, shifting from one foot to the other nervously.

"What's up, Dwayne?" Max asked, unlocking the door.

"Got laid off today," the broker said, following Max into the darkened bar. Kee had already cleaned; the stools were upturned on the bar, legs in the air.

Max brought a seat down and walked around the bar as the broker peeled off his topcoat and threw it into one of the booths. The cut on his chin where the young woman kicked him was masked by a Band-Aid. "No shit," Max said, genuinely sorry. "That's a shame. Fucked up."

"Fuck it," the broker said, leaning his elbows on the bar. "You know, just fuck it."

"Absolut rocks?" Max said, making up the drink.

"Yeah," Dwayne answered. He was already drunk. Probably spent the day working his way uptown, bar to bar.

"So, what happened?" Max asked, setting the drink down in front of the broker and waving off the proffered cash.

"Went in early this morning and my terminal was shut down," came the answer. "They take you off-line, it isn't to give you a promotion."

"Could be the computer was down."

"About ten minutes later security was watching me clean out the desk. Shit, I went to Wharton, I'm not going to steal pencils."

The broker drained the drink in a swallow and set the glass back down, nodding for another. Max poured him another over the old ice. "That's a real fucking shame," Max said, making room for the bottle in the speed rack. "So, what are you gonna do?"

"I still have some money, maybe go down to Phoenix and dry out. Do the detox thing," Dwayne answered. Then he drank half the vodka in a slow gulp. "Come back, look for another job. Won't be easy this time. Not with Drexel on the resume."

The name caught Max's attention as he topped off the glass. Again the broker offered money, but Max waved it away. "I didn't know you worked there?"

"Those were the days," Dwayne said, then raised his glass in a toast. "To Drexel, Burn 'em and Churn 'em."

"You know that guy that got blown away?" Max asked, as Dwayne brought the glass to his lips.

The question elicited a coughing laugh. "Peter! Peter-goddamn-Marotte!"

"You knew him?" Max asked again.

Dwayne finished the drink in a hurry. "Oh yeah, I knew him," he said. "Since Wharton. I could tell you stories about that guy."

Max fought hard to contain himself. It took him a full five seconds to get the excitement under control. "Tell me a couple."

"First off, the guy was brilliant," Dwayne said, suddenly almost seeming sober. "I mean you wouldn't know it to talk to him, but he was a genius. He only had one problem."

"Blow?"

"Naw, he did his share, but wasn't into it," Dwayne said. "What it was, what he had and had bad, was a taste for shit. Here's this guy, zooms, zooms through Wharton without breaking a sweat. Every Fortune 100 company kissing his ass to join the team, and he takes a year putting together venture capital deals for some outfit, then goes with Drexel. Fair enough, Drexel was hot back then. Just before the shit comes down, he splits. World tour. Two, maybe two and a half years."

"To where?" Max asked.

"Who knows. All over," Dwayne answered. "But he's clean. Not indicted, subpoenaed, nothing. He comes back, know who he goes to work for? Dobbin, Witlin, and Caffrey."

"Never heard of them," Max said.

"Never heard of DWC?" the broker laughed. "How 'bout Fielding, Richards, and Hogan?"

"Nope."

"Chop houses, bucket shops," the broker said. "Boiler-room deals."

"Fill me in a little here," Max said.

"It's like this," the broker began. "These guys . . ."

"Fielding, Richards, and whatsit?"

"No, there isn't a Fielding, Richards, or Hogan,"

Dwayne shot back. "They just pick the names because they sound classy. *WASP*. Now, don't interrupt and I'll tell you about them."

Max nodded.

"These brokerage houses, and I use that term loosely, cold-call from lists," Dwayne began. "They'll get a secondhand list —American Express, Mercedes, who knows where they get them. Some of them even use a TRW list. You know, credit ratings, income, that kind of thing. They don't subscribe to the service, some firm out in Jersey specializes in selling them secondhand."

"Is that legal?"

"Hey, it's done," Dwayne said. "Or maybe they'll get a list of doctors on Long Island. Some of them, all they have is a reverse phone directory. But they know the exchanges. The money neighborhoods."

Max refilled Dwayne's glass again, and the broker took a long swallow.

"So they get the lists and start cold-calling," Dwayne said. He was warming to the topic, motioning with his hands. "Doctors and dentists are best. Not enough cash to have full-time money managers, but say, ten or twenty grand earning five or seven percent. Once a year they run around like crazy, finding some way to keep it from taxes. They've got liquidity. They get these guys on the phone and start offering them discount services for blue chips. Maybe they say they're an old established firm that just lowered its minimum account from two mil. Makes them sound like Morgan Guaranty, but more discreet. So discreet nobody ever heard of them."

Max was beginning to see the light. "That's the bait, right?"

Dwayne beamed, like a teacher at a proud student. "Then they switch. By the end of the call, sometimes even after they sell them a hundred shares of IBM, they move them from blue chips into some unlisted company, an initial offering. Microbreweries were hot for awhile. Robotics. Silver mines. Software. Genetic engineering. It doesn't matter. All high-risk garbage. Very high risk."

"Do the companies exist?"

"Probably, maybe technically," Dwayne hedged. "Are the investors going to see the twenty- to forty-percent return? Fuck no. If they're lucky they'll get a couple of Xeroxed quarterly reports. But by then Dobson, Dogshit, and Dingleberry are out of business, moved, defunct."

"People give these guys money?" Max asked, astounded. "Big money?"

"They didn't sell this shit to pension managers. Not even the S&L guys were that lame, bless their greedy midwestern hearts. But if you want to call ten or twenty K big money, sure," Dwayne answered. "The guys working the phones hook them pretty good. And commissions are high. Come on with a line like, 'Don't tell your broker, it'll drive the price up.' Or, 'They're talking merger,' 'The company's definitely in play.' Used to be they hooked them by promising insider information. Used to call it 'trash bagging.' Fill 'em up and throw 'em away."

"So what happened to the guy, Marotte?"

"Don't know," Dwayne answered. "He was working the chop houses like crazy. Then there were some rumors he was managing a boiler room in Vegas. The kind that promises you a free gift if you buy ten bucks worth of vitamins for a grand. Those guys send out postcards saying, 'You've Won a Car' or a ranch mink. They hook them like that. The guy had a taste for shit."

"But those guys don't kill you, right?"

Dwayne smiled. "What? A housewife in Tampa is going to go gunning for the guy who sold her nine hundred dollars worth of vitamin B on the family Visa card? Not likely."

"What about the other thing, the stocks?"

"Come on, some orthodontist from Syosset is not going to come after a guy who took ten grand off him," Dwayne said. "What he's going to do is take the write-off, not give his staff a raise, and bounce the price of little Johnny's braces a few bucks higher. That's the beauty part. It's like stealing with no legal recourse."

Max ventured another question. It looked as if Dwayne

was about to fall off his chair again and he wanted an answer. "So, who killed him?"

Dwayne looked up bleary-eyed from his drink. "Who killed who?" he asked back.

"The guy, Marotte."

"Somebody did, right?" Dwayne said. "Sometimes you just have to say fuck it. He gets killed. I get canned. You just have to say fuck it."

Max took the empty glass away and put it down on the side of the sink. "You want to lay down for awhile, Dwayne?"

"Yeah, sounds like a good idea," the broker answered, then climbed carefully down from the bar stool.

When Max was sure that Dwayne was sleeping across the back bench, he walked to the phone and dialed Suze's number at work. If the trains were running good, she'd have finished class and would be at the hostess desk.

She answered on the second ring, her voice crisp and professional.

"I have a party of thirty, name's Donner," Max said. "What's good?"

She giggled a little, recognizing his voice, and said, "The ribs. And we have some nice liver."

Suze was quick, Max had to give her that. "No, I'm having some family and friends for dinner," he answered in the voice of a reluctant patron. "I think I'll pass."

She could have said, "Donner, Pass," but didn't. Instead she turned serious and answered, "Max, try to get home early tonight. I'll wait up."

Her bullshit detectors were out, Max was sure of it. Worse still, she might want to talk about the relationship.

"Sure," he said, fingers tightening around the phone. "No problem."

He stopped thinking about Suze by thinking about Miles. He'd head downtown in a couple of days to pick up some postcards. Maybe someplace European this time; Ireland or Scotland. England, maybe. But someplace a tan would fade. He'd try the travel agencies this time around. They usually had some on hand.

The thing he dreaded wasn't taking them up to Miles to fill out, though that was always more than a little sad. The guy had spent his entire life lying to women, now he was lying to his daughter and coming through like a pro. The messages on the cards were always upbeat and very often funny. No, the worst part was standing around the International Departure gates at LaGuardia, trying to talk someone into mailing them when they got off the plane. Clergy were the best, college students almost as good. Families on vacation or businessmen were the worst.

Every time he'd come up with some new line of bullshit. Anything and everything but the truth, then offer twenty bucks to cover the postage and trouble. Still, no matter what he paid or said, only two out of five cards ever made it to the kid.

Max was taking his time prepping the bar when Julie came through the door at a quarter to seven. She walked in just as the messenger from Gil's office was leaving with the signed contracts.

She spotted Dwayne crashed out at a back bench and made a sour face. "He's starting early," she said.

"He got fired today," Max answered, slipping the plastic drawer with lemon and lime sections under the bar. "So be nice."

"No shit," she said. "He tipped good, too."

"End of an era."

She gave Dwayne another look, almost maternal, then looked away. "Real fucked-up thing happened today."

"Yeah?"

"I came in with Pat's mother," Julie said, her voice dropped to a tone of pure gossip. "You know, to get Pat's stuff."

"You didn't let her up there, did you? You went up and got it, right?"

"No, she wanted to do it," Julie answered. "It was something she wanted to do. And the cop wasn't any help. He kept asking me out, you know? Did you know all the cops, like most of them, are from Long Island?"

"That's real romantic, getting picked up at a murder scene," Max answered.

"It's not like I'd go out with him or anything," Julie snapped back. "Besides, we were out in the hall."

"I guess that's okay, then," Max said. "Being out in the hall and all."

"Give me a break, will you," Julie answered. "Anyway, Pat had all this jewelry. Necklaces, rings, broaches, beautiful stuff, Peter gave her. She kept it in the boxes. Under the sink, in the wall. You know, Tiffany's, Harry Winston, Cartier."

"That's great," Max answered, not all that interested, but listening anyway.

"She has to sell the things, to pay Pat's Amex and Visa bills. You know they were over eight grand, just for one month."

Max couldn't help but raise an eyebrow. Something was wrong; waitresses didn't spend that kind of money. "They should get a lawyer, see if they even have to pay it."

"No, she wants to," Julie said. "So, we check out the stores, see if they'll take the things back. And guess what?"

"No idea."

"Peter didn't buy them there," Julie beamed. "The man at Cartier said that they were all probably bought on Forty-seventh Street, you know, the diamond district."

It didn't surprise Max. Guys had been doing that for years, giving women jewelry in boxes from exclusive stores. They charged something at the store, then returned it, *sans* box. Or just found a store clerk willing to make a quick twenty for handing over the box and wrapping. Sometimes a good line of bullshit would work too. "Same stuff on Forty-seventh," Max said at last. "Costs about half what you'd pay in the big stores."

"Yeah, but it's just so, I don't know, creepy," Julie said, then turned her voice suddenly perky. "But guess what?"

"What?" Max answered, mimicking her slightly.

"I'm a spokesperson."

"A commercial, no kidding. What's the product?"

Julie made another face and took off her coat. She was wearing a dark wool sweater underneath. "Well, you know, it's kinda fucked," she said, carrying the coat to the back. "The way it happened and all. But I'll be helping out the family, you know. And if I thought about it at all, I guess it's exposure."

When she came back out, Max asked cautiously, "What're you selling?"

"I'm the spokesperson for the Brimmers, you know," she said, edging up to the bar. "Pat's mother can't handle it. So, I'll be dealing with the media and all."

"Dealing with the media," Max repeated.

"Yeah, you know, giving interviews and all," Julie said. "Keep the thing in the public eye." She was smiling as she sat down. "They need somebody. I've got this friend. A guy I met. He says he can book me on some talk shows."

Max walked down to where she was sitting. "You mean, like Joe Franklin? Got a song picked out yet?"

"You're always such an asshole, you know. No, like serious news shows."

Max saw it then and it disgusted him—like catching sight of himself in a mirror at the end of a two-day coke fest. "But it's exposure, right?" he asked in numb sarcasm.

Julie's face turned to stone. For just an instant, she looked like Lynn at three in the morning—the way her features coalesced into ice beneath the makeup. "You're just the guy to start talking, right?" she said in a soft whisper. "I know about that deal you're running with Todd. So give me a break, will you?"

Bull's-eye, Max thought. She's knocked it out of the park. "That's over," he said and walked away, back to the office for no purpose whatsoever.

Julie came off the stool and stood in the center of the bar. "Yeah, since when?"

"Since right now," Max called back and slammed the office door behind him.

Through the closed door, Max heard her yell, "Todd won't like it. He's going to be really pissed off."

Max lowered himself into the chair and creaked back. In front of him, scattered over the crowded desk, was a stack of pink, blue, and white invoices. "Fuck him," he said softly. Then he saw the second button on the phone light up. Julie was making a call.

Twenty minutes later there was a soft knock on the door. It could have been Julie, or a liquor salesman, or a soda vendor. But Max said, "Come in, Todd."

Todd came through the door in a camel-hair coat that must have run more than two grand at some Madison Avenue boutique. The coat looked Italian, and Todd just looked pissed. He shut the door behind him and stood, staring.

Max pretended to sort invoices by color. He could feel the guy's eyes burning into him with undiluted hate.

"Eight minutes," Todd said, at last. "That's how long it took me to find out you'd signed the contracts. It won't take that long to cancel the deal."

"Cancel it," Max answered, looking up from the bills. His voice was calm, under control. He felt moral as hell. Mother Teresa of the Upper East Side.

Todd looked around the office, letting his eyes go narrow with disdain. Here was a guy throwing something away. Not even trading it off. He pulled the metal folding chair over from a corner and studied it, judging the dirt factor against the price of dry cleaning the camel hair. "You're a real piece of work," he said, scraping the chair against the concrete floor and sitting down. "A real fucking piece of work."

Max shrugged. What could Todd do to him? It was hard letting a guy whose motto was "Always give the Quaalude to the guy," stake out the higher ground.

"You fucked me, big time," Todd said.

"So, you fucked my waitress," Max shot back. Bar wit.

Todd's eyes went more than a little nuts. He was out of the chair and across the small room in three steps, camel hair flying behind him like the cape of some stylish comic-book super hero. "You think this is a fucking game!"

Max went for the army surplus machete in its canvas sheath held to the underside of the desk by yellowed, brittle tape. He could whack him with the thing still in the sheath. But Todd was too fast; he was on Max before he could get a good grip on the weapon. The tape gave way, and the knife fell from his fingertips.

"You tell me if you think this is a fucking game!" Todd yelled, one hand coming around Max's throat, the other striking out hard, crashing through Max's upraised hands and catching him in the chest.

Max punched out, his fist catching a length of coat. Then he stomped the heel of his sneaker down on Todd's Guccied instep. The little brass harness must have hurt like hell, because the grip around his throat relaxed. Max punched out again, this time hitting Todd just below the sternum and knocking the wind out of him.

Todd stumbled back as Max came out of the chair, fists low and ready. "Come on, let's do it," Max said, closing in, his toe catching the sheathed knife. With a casual kick, he knocked the big knife to the opposite wall. He was starting to feel like John-*fucking*-Wayne as he moved in and Todd inched back toward the door.

Todd brought a hand up, palm out, and began shaking his head, slowly at first, then as Max moved in, faster. He held his stomach with his other hand. He was in a half-crouch and gasping slightly.

"Come on, you don't want to go?" Max asked, closing in. He was about to push Todd out the door when the hand holding the stomach vanished inside the dress jacket. When it came out again, it was holding a gun. A shiny little automatic.

"Back the fuck off," Todd said, waving the gun in the general direction of the desk. Max was so close he could read the name "L.W. Seecamp Co. Inc." across the side of the barrel.

Julie came in the door as Max began backing up. "Now, you boys play nice," she said. A line she probably thought up as she crossed the bar. But one look at the gun in Todd's hand and the big machete on the floor knocked all the motivation out of her delivery.

"Get in here," Todd snapped, motioning with the gun. His voice was strained, full of panic.

Julie stepped into the room, her eyes wide as saucers.

Todd closed the door and waved the gun so that she stood next to Max.

"So, what now, you shoot us?" Max asked, sitting down in his chair.

"Don't be an asshole," Todd said. "For once in your life, try."

"I'm not the one holding the gun," Max said.

Todd looked down at the gun, as if he just realized he was holding it. "It's legal, I've got a carry permit."

"Okay, sure," Max said. He was trying to keep very still.

"Oh God, please don't kill us, please," Julie cried, begging.

Todd turned toward her; she was beginning to cry. "I'm not going to shoot you," he said, to no effect. His voice was almost pleading.

Max knew that the thing had escalated beyond anything Todd had in mind when he walked into the bar. "Look, give me the gun, and we'll talk about this, okay?"

Todd thought about this for a moment, then took the gun in both hands; it made a clicking noise. Julie let out a small gasp and closed her eyes tight. The magazine slipped from the grip and Todd handed the gun to Max.

"A fucking gun?" Max said, tossing it gingerly on the desk. "You come in here with a gun?"

"It's licensed," Todd said. He was leaning against the wall, both hands jammed in the pockets of the camel hair. "I have a carry permit."

Max didn't doubt it. Not a week went by that he didn't get a flyer from some outfit guaranteeing carry permits to bar managers and owners. Cut-rate lawyers filled out the forms in a way that assured approval. Usually, there was mention of night deposits, large amounts of cash, that kind of thing.

"That's a relief, really," Max said. "I wouldn't want to get shot with a unlicensed piece."

"Look, I'm in this thing and looking for a way out," Todd answered.

Julie moved so fast that Max didn't have time to react. She was across the room and on Todd. "You scumbag, you fucking scumbag!" she shouted as she pounced, knocking him back against the wall.

Max came out of the chair and pulled her off Todd. When she cursed, wriggling out of his grip, he wrapped his arms around her, locking his hands just below her breasts, and hauled her off, feet dragging on the concrete floor. She kept on cursing, then started kicking. Todd judiciously moved to a corner, where he was protected by a gray metal file cabinet.

"That bitch is crazy," Todd said, trying not to look like he was cowering as he moved further into the corner.

When Julie stopped kicking, Max released his grip. "Okay, it's over," he said. "Let's all get a-grip here, okay."

"Fucking scumbag," she muttered, shooting Todd a look of pure hate as Max let go.

"Julie, listen to me, will you?" Max asked. "Go out and bring back a couple of beers from the cooler, okay?"

"I'll take a light," Todd said.

Julie shot him a drop-dead-asshole look and walked through the door. It was only after she left the room that Todd ventured out from behind the file cabinet. The way he moved was arrogant, like he was walking into a four-star restaurant where he knew the owner. "That's one tense bitch," he said, straightening his tie. "She been taking lessons from Lynn?"

"You pointed a fucking gun at her."

"I wasn't gonna shoot anybody."

Max took a deep breath. The stupidity of it was astounding. He'd just come *that* close to being a headline.

"Okay Todd, no hard feelings, we're still friends," Max said. "But really, I'm not doing the job, and please, get out of the fucking bar."

Todd didn't leave. He smiled, picked up the metal folding chair, and sat down. "What can I tell you? What can I say that'll make it right? Name it."

"What? I'm not speaking English here? Leave."

Todd reached down and picked up the knife, and handed it to Max.

"Thanks," Max said, tossing it under the desk. "Now really, you have to go."

"Well, at least you can tell me what you found out," Todd said.

"Then you'll leave?"

Julie came back in with two beers, neither of them light, set them down on the floor between Todd and Max, then left. When the door closed behind her, Max started talking. "Okay, that Marotte guy was probably dirty," he said. "He ran stock scams over the phone. Went to Wharton and his phone was disconnected."

Todd picked up the beer from the floor and said, "That's it. That's all you found out?"

"That's it," Max said.

"What about the girl?"

"She really was trying to be an actress."

"So it was the guy they were after, huh?"

"Seems like maybe he burned someone in a stock deal."

Todd got up to leave, setting the beer down on the chair. He buttoned his coat. "Thanks for nothing," he said, and walked out.

When the front door closed, Julie came back in and said, "He forgot his gun."

Max turned, saw the piece sitting on the desk, the magazine gone. "He'll be back," he said, knowing that he left it as an excuse to come back. Like a woman who leaves something—earring, underwear, diaphragm, at an apartment, needing an excuse to call.

"Can I see it?" she asked, her eyes glued to the little automatic.

Max lifted it up, feeling its solid weight in the palm of his hand, then put it in the desk's center drawer. "No."

"It's not loaded," she said. "Just let me see it, please."

"We have to open," Max said, then shut the drawer.

"Please, just let me hold it."

Against his better judgement, he opened the drawer and handed it to her.

She held it lightly, awkwardly, then grabbed it around the grips, moving her finger into the trigger guard. "It's cute, isn't it?"

"Yeah, it's adorable," Max said, reaching out for it.

Julie pointed the gun at him and peered down the barrel. "Now, about that raise."

"Quit screwing around and give it to me," he said. His palm was up and his fingers were motioning for the piece.

"Maybe I should get one," she said, moving the barrel away from Max toward the wall, which was plastered with emergency numbers and vendors' business cards. "For protection. I saw a special on the news about how women should carry guns a couple months ago."

Max came up out of the seat and began reaching for the pistol. "Julie, give me the gun."

A small smile played across her face as she pulled the trigger.

The blast was deafening in the small room as the shell in the chamber discharged. Max felt the heat of the bullet whiz by his arm as it drilled into the wall.

Julie dropped the gun in horror as the thing bounced up from the floor. Both of them stood numb, ears ringing as the acrid smoke filled the office. Then the same thought hit both of them. "Holy shit, Dwayne!" Max said, rushing past the woman and out the door.

Dwayne lay sprawled out on the bench directly in front of the office. He looked dead. The bullet could have caught him in the back, anywhere.

Max ran to the broker and carefully lifted his head. It was then that he saw it, the small splintered groove of exposed wood where the bullet had plowed into the bench not four inches from Dwayne's ear.

"Oh, God, God, God, is he dead?" Julie asked, keeping back a few feet.

Max righted the sleeping broker on the bench and began slapping him lightly. The eyes came open slowly, unfocused and confused.

"He's okay," Max said, looking behind Dwayne for traces of blood.

Julie sighed and sat down on a nearby chair.

"Hey, how's it going?" Dwayne asked.

"Fine," Max said.

Dwayne focused on Julie. "How's it going?" he asked.

"Fine," Julie said, trying to smile.

"Just let me sleep for a little while," Dwayne mumbled, lying back down.

"Sure," Max answered and let him lie back down.

"I got shit-canned today," Dwayne said, and closed his eyes.

"It's the luckiest day of your life," Max answered.

Eight

The big man needed to leave the Howard Johnson's. The daily room charge was quickly melting away what was left of his money. Soon he would have to sell the Rolex President on his wrist.

He found what he was looking for on the Upper East Side, not far from where he shot the man and woman. An ad in the *Village Voice* led him to a high-rise condo sublet.

The doorman, a short, dark-haired man in a burgundy uniform, phoned up to the apartment, then pointed toward the elevator. The apartment was on the twenty-third floor, facing west.

The woman who met him at the door was dressed in a gray flannel suit and was perhaps the angriest woman he had ever seen. He could see the anger shooting out from her eyes, see it in the way she walked, her heels coming down hard on the floor with each step. Her face had a immovable grimace on it that pulled the ends of her mouth down. She looked, the big man thought, a little like the carved masks they sold to tourists on his island.

"So, this is the place," she spat, turning her back on him and clicking across the parquet floor in high heels. "Eleven hundred a month. Two months minimum. If you want to buy after that, then we'll see, won't we?"

It sounded like a challenge to the big man, but he brushed it aside. The apartment was not big, the size of a small hut. "Yes," he answered, shutting the door behind him.

She turned to face him and began pointing to furniture, a bookcase, breakfront, and sofabed. "That, that, and that go into storage. Would you believe this hutch cost two-eighty-nine back in '87? Two hundred and eighty-nine thousand."

"Dollars?" he asked.

She smiled a bitter smile. "It wasn't *pesos*, babe."

He had seen similar apartments in Japan. But that was Tokyo. "It is very nice," he offered, to be polite.

"They're all cocksuckers, you know?" she said suddenly. Her hands were still on her hips. Her mouth was set into a thin sneering line of lipstick.

He was not accustomed to women speaking in such a way. The words, the way she spit them out, took him aback. "Who?" he asked finally.

"All those motherfuckers in their ties and attitudes," she answered. "God and I'm out of Prozac."

"I'm sorry," the big man said. He was squinting slightly with puzzlement. Behind the woman, in the small cubicle that was the kitchen, was a row of long-bladed knives held to the wall by a magnetic strip. If she moved closer to the knives he would leave.

The woman's face softened, but not much. "You don't know what I'm talking about, do you?" she asked, shaking a stray strand of dark hair from her face with a violent throw of her head.

"No."

"I got laid off eleven months ago," she said, her voice rising again. "Ten years working my fucking ass off and they canned me. Well, fuck them."

"I'm sorry," the big man said. "Laid off is fired?"

"Yeah, that's exactly what it is. What do you do, anyway?" the woman asked, her voice softening now.

"Import/export," he answered, hoping she wouldn't ask any more.

"That's another thing, those fucking Japanese!" she said, pointing her finger at him for emphasis. "You don't import anything Japanese, do you?"

"South Seas," he said, moving back a step. He was fearful that he was talking to a crazy woman.

"Ten years with those pricks, writing press releases, and they fire me, like some secretary," she explained. "Like a fucking secretary! And now I'm out of Prozac. Dammit!"

She moved then, turning her back on him and walking to the window to look out over the roofs of buildings. It was near dusk and the sky was a pretty shade of pink, like a shell. "I would like very much the apartment," the big man said. "I can pay by cashier's check. Tomorrow."

She turned so suddenly that the movement startled him, tensing from fist to elbow, the muscles bunching up across his broad back. "Look, you're just a guy off the street," she snapped. "If I asked you something, would you give me an honest answer?"

He thought about this for a moment, then nodded.

"How old do I look?" she asked. "I mean I'm all strung out now. Six interviews in two days and not a bite. *Nada*. But I don't look thirty-five, do I?"

Pretending to examine her closely, he shook his head gravely before saying, "Twenty-seven."

A little smile played across her face. "Okay, you got the place," she said. "Come back by ten tomorrow morning with a check. That's first, second, and a grand security deposit."

"Good. Ten."

The woman sat down on the sofabed and stared off into space. "Thirty-five years old and moving back to Armonk, shit."

The big man paused, wanting to turn to the door, but not able to. "Armonk no good?"

Her eyes shifted slightly so that she was staring straight at him. "Armonk is where my parents live. I'll be living with my parents, if you must know. I suppose you should."

Wanting to say something nice, he said, "Good to live with parents. Find nice man, marry. Have children."

Her face changed, moving through seven or eight expressions of varying degrees of hate, anguish, disgust, and fear before settling on a compromise that included all of them. "Maybe where you come from. But not in New York," she whispered. Her whisper was like a hiss. "Listen, if anyone calls for me, just say that I left for Europe, okay?"

"Not Armonk?"

"No, not Armonk under any circumstances," she said more loudly. "Then call me with a number, if that's not too much trouble."

"Not trouble."

"And if the broker calls, you'll let her in to show the apartment?"

"Yes."

"Good then, we have a deal," she said, coming up off the sofa to shake his hand.

When he left, she was sitting back down on the small sofa, hands up to her face. All those years and all that bullshit for nothing. Where was she now? A consultant? Shit, half the guys standing on the unemployment line were consultants. It was something to put on the resume. Nobody believed that line anymore. Nobody. If you were lucky you could hustle a few hundred a month writing press releases for old clients. But what was a couple hundred a month? Nothing.

Even subletting was worthless. Three grand and change wouldn't make a dent in the debt. She was four months behind on mortgage payments and two on maintenance. The letters began arriving months ago. First from the bank that serviced the mortgage, then from the building management.

At first she was just going to sweat the bastards out. Not pay up on the mortgage and let them come to her. The last thing the banks wanted was another fucking unit on their hands. They'd go out of their way to restructure, anything, just so long as they didn't have to foreclose and take the thing to auction. She figured she could maybe go into a work-out situation and knock a couple hundred off the monthly charge. But with her bank account hovering precariously near the cutoff for free checking, a couple hundred a month wouldn't mean shit. Plus, the condo's market value was sinking like a stone; ten percent a year since the fall of '87. Even if she sold the place tomorrow, the bank would still come after her with a deficiency judgement. She didn't even have enough equity to borrow against.

She was just tired of the entire fucking thing. The place was like a stone around her neck, dragging her down. And now the doctor wouldn't renew her prescription for Prozac. Well, she'd just see how much he liked getting those insurance forms back in the mail. Her coverage expired two months ago.

She moved from the sofa to the breakfront, first thinking that maybe there was another prescription in the drawer, then finding the last half dozen letters from the bank.

"Fuck 'em," she said aloud. They want to get nasty, she'd show them. Get all the furniture out tomorrow morning. Take the foreign guy's three grand and move to L.A. It would fuck up her credit rating for seven years, but she could get an Amex off her mother's card.

Very deliberately, she took the six letters and paperwork on the condo, tore them up into very small pieces, and put the pile into a manila envelope. Then she took the spare set of keys and dropped them in the envelope. She'd FedEx it from L.A. to the bank president.

* * *

Delbert Kray drove a dark blue '84 Plymouth Fury
with dark wheels and no hubcaps. It looked like a
government car, which is exactly the effect he desired.
Fifteen years with the FBI had taught him nothing if not
what kind of car to drive and how to dress. He wore a
dark suit, white shirt, fifty-seven-dollar Florsheims, and
a five-dollar polyester tie. He also wore a pair of white
calf-length socks for no other reason than he knew
J. Edgar Hoover, the little dick-smoker, had hated white
socks. If there was a hell, Delbert often thought, the
joint was run by guys in white socks with J. Edgar in
the middle, spitting and snapping like a rabid cat.

All of Delbert's—or Del's—as he liked to be called,
248 pounds fit nicely along the bench seat that sagged
dramatically toward the driver's side.

His oversized head of curly rust-colored hair was in
perfect proportion to the rotund body. Though he had
gained weight over the last ten years—maybe seventy
pounds—his face still had the startling look of being
added as a hasty afterthought. The small, deep-set eyes,
crooked nose, and small mouth with a too large pair of
lips gave the appearance that it had been assembled from
scraps left over from Nixon.

Kray was an insurance investigator. Maybe he wasn't
the best one, but as he himself would admit, there weren't
many better. Not for the price.

Now he was on his first job since the weather turned
cold and worrying over it. The thing that bothered him
was why the lawyer had called in the first place. The
lawyer, one of those skinny Ivy League types, didn't
want him up at the office. They met at a bar downtown.
Didn't even tell him who put him up for the job. Named
three insurance companies and a state pol that he'd
worked for. Said he came highly recommended. Well,
shit, that's all well and good, but it'd be nice to know
who's talking about him.

"You understand, we require a very discreet investigation," the lawyer said, sipping his scotch.

Kray understood.

"We would simply like to know the circumstances of his death and of his life immediately preceding."

"Anything else?" he'd asked.

"We would also like to be informed of anyone who has expressed interest in the case. Journalists, for instance, who may be thinking of writing a so-called true-crime book focusing on the murders. Investigators that perhaps the young woman's family may have retained. We understand that you also have contacts within the police department. We would like to be apprised of the investigation's progress. Needless to say, any so-called breakthroughs would be of interest. Is that within the realm of what we might reasonably expect?"

"Sure," Kray said, lifting his own drink, a beer. "Mind if I ask who exactly your so-called client is?"

"I'm afraid that's privileged information. Just as your association with our firm is confidential," the lawyer answered. "Now, understand this, although you are in the employ of the firm, all payments will be made in cash. You'll report to no one, absolutely nobody but myself. Is that acceptable?"

Acceptable? It was hinky as hell and maybe even illegal. If anything went wrong, there was no way to trace it back to the firm. "Yeah, sure," Kray said. "How 'bout a card?"

The lawyer reached into his breast pocket and pulled out a Mont Blanc ballpoint. "You can reach me at this number. This is my home; I'd prefer if you call during business hours. The machine is monitored closely," he said, scribbling a number down on a napkin and handing it to Kray. "Are there any other questions?"

"Just one, who's gonna carry the envelopes?"

"I'm not certain we're on the same page here," the lawyer said, taking off his gold wire-framed glasses and examining them in the dim light.

They were on the same page, just that this guy didn't think Kray could read. "The envelopes with the money in them," Kray said. "For whoever knows more about your client than you want them to."

The lawyer didn't answer. Instead, he kept on examining his glasses.

What Kray had going for him was the methodical cunning that comes from fifteen years with the FBI and the dark cop certainty that human nature was pretty much a cesspool. Newspapers and newscasts were the holy writs by which he sought affirmation of this private truth—that every man, woman, child, and pooch was a thief and a liar. The only variables, he knew, were skill, intelligence, and fear.

Delbert Kray's single vice was comedy albums. Cigarettes, he craftily concluded, were not a vice. Not even three or four packs a day. Now, as he pulled onto the BQE, the car thick with gray smoke, he listened to one of his favorite Henny Youngman performances. It was a bootleg tape recorded at a Catskill resort in the mid-sixties.

Edging out a blue Nissan into the left lane, Kray began to laugh. He laughed loudly and long, each one-liner feeding the wheezing laughter built by the one before. His mouth opened up in curled lip mirth around a Lucky Strike. The woman in the Nissan shot him a panicked look that turned to horror when she saw the fat man enshrouded in smoke, laughing for no apparent reason. The Nissan faded back into traffic, the woman cautiously putting four or five cars and a cement truck between her and the fat laughing lunatic.

Inside the Plymouth, Kray beat the wheel with the palm of one hand as his shoulders hunched up in phlegmy merriment. The funnyman's voice and accompaniment of applause and laughter emanated from eight high-end speakers. The only luxury item included in the car was a state-of-the-art CD player. The system was new, as was the twenty-two-thousand-dollar home unit on which he was in the process of re-recording his album and tape collection. The home stereo system was his pride and joy, a high-tech miracle that inscribed perfect digital sound on blank CDs. It was an audiophile's dream, which was strange, since Delbert Kray owned not one recording of music. Not a single song. His entire six-hundred-piece collection was made up entirely of comedy material.

Delbert was now driving into Manhattan to look into this guy's murder. Find out just what he was into before he got whacked. Drugs probably, that's what they were all into these days. He would give it two weeks at two hundred a day, plus expenses. When he told the lawyer his price, the guy didn't even blink. With any luck at all, he could pad the expenses out for two-fifty or two-seventy-five and hope the guy didn't start screaming. But it was hard to tell with those people.

NINE

The week crawled by with one two-hundred-dollar night after another. There was a flurry of kids in the middle of the week, ten or twelve of them, who wandered in at two in the morning and dropped two hundred, doubling the night's take. Lynn arched an eyebrow when Max totaled out that night, but said nothing.

Max knew it wouldn't be repeated. Barmy's wasn't their kind of place. It was an antique to them. A museum. And secretly, he wasn't sorry about it. Whatever success Barmy's once had, that audience was long gone, vanished—aged past the nightlife.

All week, Julie came in with a new theory why Todd did it. The reasoning was loosely based on the logic that Todd was an asshole, but then fell apart when she made the jump about Todd and that guy, Marotte, both having a thing for Pat.

For guys like Todd and probably Marotte, the city was filled with Pats. And Susans. And Maries. And Karens. They were a renewable resource. Jealousy was not in their emotional vocabulary.   .

Janey, on the other hand, was not replaceable. She

was the long shot that paid off, the winning Lotto ticket, a full scholarship to a lifestyle. And Max couldn't help but wonder if maybe this Marotte guy hadn't threatened Todd's free ride.

It was a week after the gun incident when Julie came in from the cold and said, "Did you hear about Todd?"

Max was sitting at a back table, feet up, reading a day-old paper and drinking a take-out coffee. "What about him?"

"He's dead," she said. "Somebody shot him."

Max brought his feet down and tossed the paper on the table. "No shit?"

"They found him last night. I really thought he did it, killed Pat and Pete. I guess not, huh?"

A silence filled the space between them as each judged the other's reaction. Max could see nothing in her face. He wondered what she saw in his. Maybe now she thought he did it?

A half hour later he found out. Two detectives, a fat one and a skinny one, came in to ask questions. The questions started slow, easy. Then one of the detectives, the fat one, moved toward the back of the bar—just a guy checking the joint out. The act wouldn't get him into the semifinals of Star Search. He headed straight for the back bench and the bullet hole. Max had dug out the slug and filled in the chip in the bench and the hole in the wall with Plastic Wood.

After that, the questions came a lot faster and harder.

They weren't ready for an arrest, but the detectives told Max to stay handy. He wasn't sure if it was a blessing or not that he had dropped off the gun with Todd's doorman three days before. He'd wrapped it in cardboard from an empty Dewar's case and sealed it with duct tape.

Max had no doubt, none at all, that Julie had ratted him out. But there was nothing he could do about it. Firing her would only attract suspicion.

He worked on the angles through the entire shift, turning them over in his head. Todd had his share of people who'd like to see him dead. Waitresses. Bar owners.

Bouncers. Probably stockbrokers, real estate agents, and relatives. All over the Upper East Side, people were greeting the news with small satisfied smiles. And Max was one of them.

Time and again, he found himself mildly elated that Todd wasn't walking around. The guy was a menace. Without money and on the hustle, he could be charming. New York always respected a tasteful portion of hungry charm and eager hustle. It was only after he landed in the big money that the monster revealed itself.

Lynn came in earlier than usual and tossed the last of the regulars out. She was wearing the mink. Locking the door, she turned to Max and said, "What's this I hear about you killing a guy?"

"I didn't kill anyone," Max answered and moved down to her end of the bar.

"Well, there's a guy dead," she said, tamping a Chesterfield down on the corner of the mahogany.

"A lot of people are dead."

"You spend the whole shift thinking that up or what?" Lynn asked, sitting down.

Max reached over with a disposable lighter and caught the end of her cigarette in the flame. "Just came to me."

Lynn inhaled deeply on the cigarette, let the smoke out in a thick cloud, and smiled. It was a cold, totally in control smile. "Well, this just came to me," she said. "You bring heat into this place, and I'll rip your fucking lungs out."

It was the way she said it that chilled Max right through to the marrow. "What, a threat Lynn? You know better than that. Besides, you might break a nail."

The juke was playing "Heartbreak Hotel."

"I know this," she answered. "One auditor, one ATF guy, one more fucking cop through that door who doesn't order a drink he doesn't expect to pay for and come-on to the waitress and you're history."

"You are, you're threatening me," Max said, trying to brazen it out.

"You think I'm threatening you," she said, her voice

low. "You do anything to jeopardize my license, and you'll be on the street so fast you wouldn't believe it. This joint, this lousy fucking joint, is what sends the kid to private school. Puts food on the table. And pays my bills."

"I understand," Max said, and found himself backing up slightly.

"No, I don't think you do," Lynn continued. "Now, you're a good guy. We've had some laughs. But one hint that the kid won't be able to go to college—Sarah-fucking-Lawrence or whatever, and I'm driving upstate to pay a visit. You understand *now*?"

Max understood. All she had to do was pass word to Miles that the future was shaky, and the next two goons paroled out would slice him up in some alley. Miles would do that, not for Lynn, but for the kid.

"Yeah, I get you Lynn," he said.

"You better fucking well get me," she answered, bringing the cigarette back to her mouth. "Now total out my register."

TEN

Max woke around noon next to Suze, thinking about Todd's murder. He lay there staring at the ceiling, turning over the options in his head. Maybe she'd been watching him for a long time, but he didn't notice until she said, "I know what'd make you feel better." And her head vanished under the covers. "My patented hangover cure."

And he thought, yeah, I can see how it starts to fall apart. All those misconnections. You see something or feel it, and it's something else. You never know what's in the other person's head. Can't ever know it. She thought he had a hangover from too much scotch and too few customers.

Soon she was digging a hand in the nightstand for the condoms. Then she was on top, breasts bouncing slightly, her hands down on Max's shoulders, bracing herself. Eyes closed in the noon light.

And all Max could think about was Miles saying, "All pussy wears out. Gets stale."

A little while later, Suze said, "Well, that was just a whole lot of fun." And then she rolled over.

Max, feeling mean and a little wounded despite the truth of it, said, "It's never like it is that first time, huh? Maybe it's just getting a little old."

She was about to say something, probably something good, but stopped and said, "What's up?"

"Remember that guy Todd Manion," Max answered, rolling over to face her. She was very close, her face resting on the pillow next to him. "Somebody killed him."

"Really? Well, I can't say it's a loss. You know how he interviews waitresses?"

"On their knees?" Max answered, raising up on one elbow. At least for Todd, it was what it was. Did any of the waitresses think it was anything else? Going down on Todd in the back of his bar meant maybe getting a job. And often he came through with one, sometimes adding staff just to accommodate a girl. Sometimes he made a couple of phone calls. Usually, he hooked them up with work.

"Who told you, one of the waitresses?" she asked.

"He did, actually," Max said. Then added, "I think I'm a suspect. The cops were around."

She was quiet for a long time. "Well, he was an asshole."

"Does that mean you think I didn't do it?"

"Sorry, but it's not your style," she said. "Unless he was annoyed or angsted to death, I'd rule you out as a suspect."

And suddenly he wanted to unload everything on her. It was an urge so compelling, it was frightening. This isn't like you, he thought to himself. But it was like him, exactly.

When he was done talking, she slipped out of bed and headed for the shower. "Know what I think?" she called, turning on the water.

"What's that?"

"I think a woman did it," she said.

"Yeah? It would be nice karma, huh?" he said, not expecting an answer and thinking that's what she really wanted to believe. She wanted to believe in some justice at work in the world. Another missed connection. If there were mystical forces at work in New York, the city would sink like a stone under the weight of bad karma.

And from under the hot water, she yelled back. "You know, it's just a feeling I have."

Max was in it and big time. The way he saw it, he had to find something to give the cops so they'd turn the heat down on him. He didn't have to rat anyone out, just offer up a clue that would send them off in another direction. That's the way it worked.

The detectives probably found Julie's name in Todd's address book and paid her a visit. Might have taken maybe all of five or ten seconds for Julie to offer Max up. Now, all that Max was sure of was that Todd and that guy, Peter Marotte, were tied in somehow.

The papers said that Todd was killed in an apparent robbery attempt. They listed him as "proprietor," and "bar owner," until the last graph, which ran in the *Post*, *Daily News*, and *Newsday*. The *Times* didn't run a word and none of the papers ran an obit. Instinctively he felt the force of Janey's money in the omissions. The family would want to keep the thing quiet. It wouldn't do to be involved in a murder, even on the receiving end.

Max found the back issues of papers in the library on Fifth Avenue. What he was looking for was in the first news stories published after the murders of the guy, Marotte, and the Pat Brimmer girl. The actress had been from Jersey, Paramus. The woman at the downstairs desk gave him enough quarters, and he dialed Jersey information. The Brimmers were listed. The woman's voice picked up on the second ring with a tentative, "Yes?"

He recognized the voice; it was the same woman that Julie had brought into the bar. "Mrs. Brimmer?" Max asked.

Again the tentative, "Yes."

"I don't know if you remember me; Julie brought you into a bar a few weeks ago." He spoke softly, only partly because he was on the second floor of the library.

"Yes, I remember," she said. "You helped us with the clothing. I thought it was another one of those calls . . ."

"Calls?"

"Since, since it happened, you know we've been getting the strangest telephone calls. These men, they call, they say horrible things about Pat," she said, her voice small and brittle. "I swear, I don't understand it. Why would they do it? Why would someone call like that?"

Max felt his chest go a little tight. He wasn't surprised. Any name in the paper was fair game. Suddenly he felt guilty as hell for calling. "I'm sorry to hear that," Max said. "Have you called the phone company about it?"

"I have. They told me to press seven and say, 'Did you get the trace?' but it didn't help. One man called and said he was a police captain. He began asking obscene questions. I hung up on him."

Max took a deep breath and pushed on, "Mrs. Brimmer, have you been getting Pat's mail?"

The woman paused for a long time, her voice again turning suspicious, "Yes."

"Was there a telephone bill in it?" he asked. "Not a regular bill, but a thing called a Local Usage Detail?"

Again a pause, then another, "Yes."

Now it was Max's turn to pause. What're you gonna do, huh? Are you gonna lie to her? And the answer came back, yeah, you're gonna lie your ass off. This shit makes Todd look like a saint. "Look, a friend of mine needs to see the bill," Max said. "He thinks maybe it'll help find the person who did it."

The silence lasted so long that he thought maybe the line went dead. When the woman finally spoke, it was in a very soft voice. "Have you told the police? Have you spoken to the detectives?"

Max felt himself sinking deeper into the lie that could come back to haunt him in ways he could imagine in vivid detail. The police would be curious as hell as to why he was calling. "Look, I'm acting as a sort of intermediary," Max said. "If he could go directly to the police . . . I'd just like to show him the bill. If he can do anything, I'm sure he will."

"Does your friend, does he think it's something to do with that other murder? That bartender?"

Max took a deep breath. "I don't know, Mrs. Brimmer. Really, the police would know more than me."

"Julie seems to think they were connected," the woman said. "That it's all one thing. That they were in business together."

"Really, I don't know. The police, they would know more than Julie. Believe me. I'm just trying to help out a friend with this phone bill thing."

"I can fax it to you," the woman offered. "My husband has a fax machine."

Max reached for his wallet and dug out a card from a postal service in the East Eighties. "Great," he said. "Here's the number."

The woman read the number back to him in her soft brittle voice of grief. He thanked her and hung up, feeling nothing but guilty.

Max found Pete up at the SAG office over on Broadway, kibitzing with a couple of young kids in the lounge across from the receptionist. It wasn't much of a lounge, an alcove with three walls covered in glass bulletin boards and another bulletin board running down the center. The boards had the usual stuff on display: what's being cast, warnings about checking registration of student films, union notices, sublets available in the city and L.A., used exercise equipment, furniture, pets, and bargain airfares to L.A.

The lounge was a hangout of last resort. It was a good place to use the pay phones, if you happened to

be in the neighborhood. Mostly losers, fifty-year-old
ingenues, out-of-work character actors, and the really
truly desperate were the regulars. Still, every once in a
great while you could maybe pick up some extra work
from a posting or hear something. But those were the
long shots, and that's what Max figured Pete was doing
there, playing a long shot.

The old cop was telling a story, something about a
location shoot near the docks where the second unit
director armed the production assistants with pockets
full of twenties to keep the hookers away during night
shooting. Max knew the story. In the end the unit ended
up hiring five of the girls as "special technical advisors"
and extras. The kids stared wide-eyed. Show biz!

Pete was facing the receptionist as Max came in to
check out where he stood with insurance. His chin came
up in acknowledgment, but he didn't move toward Max
until he finished the story. It was three steps from the
elevators, and with each step Max took, Pete's smile
faded, reading a problem on his face.

"What's happening?" Pete said. With a lot of actors
on the wrong side of fifty, youthful phrasing dropped
into their conversation at odd moments. But with Pete it
was different; he used language from the film business
the way street cops do—as a weapon to fend off bullshit. It didn't matter if it was an assistant director with
attitude or a kid from East New York who took down a
liquor store.

"Got time for coffee?" Max asked.

The three kids filed past them toward the elevators.
Pete plastered on a temporary smile and nodded them
out. "What kind of trouble?" he asked, turning back to
Max, his face grim.

"Big time," Max said.

"We can talk here," Pete said, looking around for
potential witnesses. A couple of middle-aged women
were using the pay phones on either side of the lounge.

The SAG office was about as confidential a place as
the second chair on the "Tonight Show." In an industry
where gossip is construed as power, everyone had an ear

open for the stray tidbit. "I'd rather find someplace else," Max said.

"I'm meeting someone," Pete answered in an obvious lie. "Come on, lay it out for me."

Max focused at a point on the wall, staring over Pete's shoulder into a notice of some movie cast long before the flyer was ever printed. If you're in the city more than six months and still thought there was an chance of getting a part from those notices, then it's time to start asking for directions back home. "I'm a suspect," he said.

"For what?"

"A murder," Max said.

Pete groaned slightly, took an involuntary step back, then worked a kink out of his neck with a twist of his head. "That double you asked about?"

"Another one," Max said. "But it's connected, I think."

"Christ," Pete said. "That bar owner?"

"Yeah."

"Tell me about it," he said, without sympathy.

Max told him about it, right up to that afternoon, just before he decided to go into the library. "So, what do you think?"

"Walk away," Pete said.

"I can't. What if they nail me for it?"

Pete began scratching his chin thoughtfully, but his eyes were fixed on Max, looking for some giveaway to the guilt. Finally he said, "If you did it, then fuck you."

"I didn't do shit," Max snapped back, keeping his voice to a whisper.

"Then you got nothing to worry 'bout," Pete said. "Walk the fuck away from it."

"The jails are filled with innocent guys," Max said.

Pete's eyes narrowed, locking onto Max's like lasers. "What? Is that some fucking ACLU fairy tale? Go upstate, you'll see nothing but scumbags. Next time you see Miles, ask him how many innocent guys they got locked in cages up there."

The sudden outburst was shocking in its intensity;

somewhere deep down in Pete's cop soul, something stirred, rippling across the surface. It was the kind of performance that Joe Friday looked for when he got pissed. Only with Pete, it wasn't an act.

"Man, I'm scared," Max confessed. "I mean really fucking scared."

Pete's face relaxed again, the eyes crinkled, the mouth unset. "Look, if you didn't do it, you didn't do it and you got nothing to worry about," he said. "But if you start bumping around an investigation, then you got plenty to worry about."

Delbert Kray always began with the paperwork. He'd begin with the courts, then the property records, move on to the county clerk's office. In small towns, out in the suburbs or Queens even, you talked to neighbors, merchants, the kid who delivered the papers. They'd have his life story. But in the city, nobody knew nothing, and what they did know was usually total bullshit. But it was almost impossible to live in the city without creating a paper trail.

Later he'd get a look at the police reports, personnel files, traffic violations. But those could wait. Police reports told him about a dead guy; what he was interested in was a live one. And from his understanding, the personnel reports were ten years old. As he moved up the courthouse steps, plastic Samsonite briefcase in hand, Kray took a last drag on the cigarette and threw it to the ground. It would be a long day.

Eleven

The bus company that ran service to the upstate prisons was started and run by ex-cons. You could take a train, but then you had to worry about taxis. The buses were easier, door-to-door.

Max boarded the new charter bus and settled into a back seat. The faces were familiar, young mothers with kids and guys who looked like they'd done some time themselves. Then there were the older people, parents of cons, who always looked vaguely ashamed and pissed off to be on the buses. Often, Max was the only white guy. Most of the visitors were black and Spanish, though once in a while there was this ancient white woman. Old and frail, she walked with a palsied gait and sat in the front seat next to the driver. For the first couple of years, Max ran down a list of who she was visiting—aging Mafia don, thirties gangster, a geriatric jewel thief. During each of the two dozen times he saw her negotiating the stairs to her seat, Max resolved to speak to her. But the old woman's eyes put him off. Her eyes, yellowed and clouded over with age, blazed with the most intense hatred Max had ever seen. Once a little kid, around five or six, worked his way up and down the aisle, talking to people as his mother slept. When he reached the front of the bus, he stood frozen, mouth agape, toy plane hanging at his side, next to the old woman's seat, until the driver shooed him away. The kid had been maybe riding the bus to prison his whole life, playing blissfully in the visiting room among murderers, arsonists, and drug dealers, but that old woman had scared the shit out of him.

*   *   *

For most of the ride, Max thought about the bust. He always did. It was a *there but for the grace of a plea bargain go I* kinda thing.

Miles was just back from vacation down in Boca. He'd driven all night and looked it. When he pulled up in front of the bar, Max was wandering out with the new bartender. He was soon to be a star, feeling pretty good about spending a night sitting on the other side of the bar, and wearing a pair of two-hundred-dollar sunglasses against the morning glare.

Lynn had owned the bar maybe a week, part of the divorce settlement. And Max suspected that Miles would pump him for information about what kind of business the joint was doing. The deal was, they'd hit a couple after-hours places for a nightcap, return the car when the rental place on Forty-third opened, then have breakfast. Max had done up a few lines an hour before. He was up for it.

It wasn't until they pulled into the rental place that the DEA team made their move. And it wasn't like TV. The agents came out of nowhere, ten of them. Fast and professional. They were like a force of nature, the kind of natural phenomenon that seeks out trailer parks in Kansas. Thinking about it later, the phrase, "never knew what hit him" sprung to mind.

Miles took the full weight of the bust and Max pleaded out on a possession charge for a tiny glassine baggie with residue. He got probation from the feds and cancellation of his contract under a morality clause from the producers. It wouldn't do to have Johnny Q, fearless, wisecracking DEA agent, busted for sniff.

Max never knew if Miles had put the dope in the door panels or not. He never asked. Years later, he didn't even think about it, knowing he'd never get a straight answer.

Two hours after grinding out from the Port Authority, the bus rolled into the Eastern Correctional Facility gate. The place was maximum security and built at the turn of the century by inmates. It was a prison right out of central casting. Large granite blocks, guard towers, and razor wire around the wall's perimeter. You could not approach it without knowing what the place was.

Max came into the reception room and waited at the back of the line. It took twenty minutes for the line to work its way up. Two guards processed the incoming visitors, one searching visitors and monitoring the metal detector, the other working a computer terminal. Max had Miles's eight-digit number memorized: 88A, the year he was busted and the fact he was over twenty-one, followed by four digits and a T. It was the T that always brought Max up short. The T suffix meant that there were over ten thousand inmates sentenced that year. They had run out of numbers and had to start again.

Max completed the Xeroxed gate clearance, handed it to the guard, and moved through the metal detector. No alarms; he was careful now not to wear anything to set it off. No keys. No belt buckle.

The guard behind the computer screen punched up Miles's number and checked for access. If Miles had discipline problems or health problems, Max would be waiting out front for the next bus back.

"Okay, go through," the guard said, after checking that the cigarette packages Max brought were factory sealed.

The sally port's door buzzed open, and Max stepped through with three women visitors. Only after the door clicked locked behind them, was the second door buzzed open.

The inside of the visiting room was surprisingly cheerful. Light blue walls, murals done by inmates, overhead fans. If not for the one-way mirrors of the control room that covered two walls, it looked like nothing so much as a junior high cafeteria or a bus station in some small town. The neat clusters of molded plastic chairs were filling with inmates and family. On one side of the room the children's section was filling up and a Disney cartoon was playing loudly on the television. A guard sat behind a desk on a raised platform at the front, like a teacher, his eyes moving steadily around the room, then up to the convex mirrors mounted in opposite corners.

Max staked out a seat near the rear door; outside a light snow was beginning to fall over the manicured lawn. Even upstate it hadn't snowed heavily all winter. In the summer, inmates and visitors could walk in the small park. There were umbrellaed tables and monkey bars for the kids.

As more visitors and inmates arrived, the din rose, sounding like the background noise of old movies—where the two principals are eating dinner in a crowded restaurant while the extras talk quietly among themselves.

Pictures were passed around, and men and women were hugging cautiously. Max felt a slight chill run through him. Who would visit him if things turned bad?

Miles came through the door in a stiff inmate walk, paused, spotted Max, and strolled over. It was always startling to see him come through the door. Max had always thought of Miles as the most relaxed guy in the world; it took about two months for prison to set his face into a perfect mask of indifference. And his black hair, cropped close, had grayed to steel.

Miles sat down stiffly and rolled his shoulders. "What's the story?"

"I got some problems, man," Max said, trying to ease into it.

"You got a cigarette?" Miles asked.

Max pulled out the two unopened boxes of Gitanes and handed them over to Miles. "I think I'm being set up for a fall."

"Yeah," Miles asked with mild interest as he cracked open a blue package and stuck a cigarette in the corner of his mouth. "What kind of fall?"

"Murder," Max said.

Miles raised an eyebrow and lit the cigarette with a match. "Who'd you kill?"

"I didn't kill anybody."

Miles smiled a small guarded smile. "Who died?"

"Remember Todd?"

"Hot Toddy? Somebody whacked him out? No shit?"

The smile had spread, if not into outright pleasure, then at least halfway to mirth.

Max figured that mirth was about all you could hope for in maximum security, on a good day. "Somebody shot him."

"I remember that asshole when he first hit town," Miles said, exhaling a lungful of smoke. "Boy, was he a prick."

Funny, Max always thought the two had a lot in common. He leaned forward a little, hands on knees. "Yeah, what was he like?"

"The same. That guy was a prick from the jump. He was bussing tables at some lunch joint in midtown. Used to fold the tablecloth back, use plates, napkins, anything to hide the waitresses' tips. Then he'd bang the waitresses after work."

None of it surprised Max. It was, as they say, in character.

Miles inhaled again and let it out. "That guy was some piece of fucking work."

"So, who would kill him?" Max asked. He wasn't expecting a name. He wasn't sure what he hoped for.

Miles let out a short laugh. "Take all the people he knew, and you couldn't find a person who wouldn't want to whack the guy. Tell me why you come up as suspect."

Max told him pretty much the same story he told Pete and Suze. It took less than six minutes. He was getting better with practice.

"Shit, you know what's gonna happen, don't you?" Miles asked. "The DTs—detectives—are going to go around to the wife, the friends, the staff, business partners, they're gonna be crying like babes about it."

It didn't sound good. "Yeah?"

"By the time they finish the first round of interviews, Todd'll come out looking good," Miles said, his face now set in concentration. "It ain't like TV, where everyone says, 'Yes, I hated him, but I wouldn't kill him.' It's like, 'He was so bright,' 'He was such a good husband,'

'He was the best boss I had,' yada-yada-yada-yada. All bullshit."

"So, what's my options?" Max asked.

Miles dropped the end of the cigarette to the floor. "Right now, I'd say you're fucked."

"Thanks," Max answered.

"Listen, listen to me carefully," Miles said, leaning forward. "Don't bring any heat down on Lynn."

"She's on me," Max confessed. "Cops have been around."

"She's on you, I don't fucking blame her," he answered, his voice very low and hard. "Do anything that puts the license on the line, I'll fucking be on you. Get it?"

Max felt a chill go through him and flashed on an image of L.A. It would be warm and away from all the bullshit about murder. But it wouldn't be like last time. No hotel room on Wilshire. No leased convertible. It would be an apartment in Hollywood and hustling for a bar job. And probably no Suze. The thought brought a quick flash of excitement and panic. "What about Todd?" he asked into Miles's hard stare.

"Look, he wasn't a citizen," Miles said. "I know a couple of the bent-nose boys that are in; I'll ask around."

"They'd tell you?"

"Probably not, but what could asking hurt?"

"While you're at it, ask about this other guy, Peter Marotte," Max added as an afterthought.

Miles dropped the cigarette and ground it out on the floor. "What's the deal on him?"

"A guy that got killed a couple weeks ago," Max said. "Todd asked me to check him out. They're probably connected."

"Sure," Miles answered easily.

Twelve

Suze had off the next day and woke early to cook breakfast. As Max wound his way down the narrow servants' stairway to the kitchen, he could smell the bacon and pancakes. When he pushed open the door, the smell of coffee hit him.

More than six months into it and she's still cooking breakfast every so often. Well, that would end soon. Another two months, tops, and he'd be back to eating at diners full time. But he never expected Suze to be big on the domestic chores anyway. She didn't have much of a role model.

The way she told it, her mother lit out from some small town outside Canton on the back of a BSA motorcycle. That was in '55. She was sixteen and *The Wild One* had finally made it to Ohio. The guy on the front of the bike was seventeen and had two hundred dollars in his pocket. They were heading to L.A. and made it as far as San Diego.

The Tijuana marriage lasted five years, and when the Tijuana divorce came through, her mother was three months pregnant. There were a bunch of jobs waitressing, and by the time her mother finally made it to L.A., the sixties were starting. She lit out again, this time in a VW with Suze, and landed in a commune outside of Fresno.

Suze remembered eating the stunted vegetables, goat cheese, and windfall fruit. Nothing ever seemed to grow the way it was supposed to; not the orchard, or the garden, even the few animals. The place was a collection of unfinished projects, all doomed from the start by bad planning. Sometimes the kids ate Milk Bone dog biscuits or chased the scrawny chickens around in the dust. Suze was eight and had maybe two years of school.

Sometime around '69 or '70, it started turning bad. The bikers started rolling in from San Francisco and L.A. Next came guys who weren't even bikers, just mean, with bad teeth and prison tattoos. Then came the speed, then smack. A few of the women were raped. Two of the original members were so badly beaten they never fully recovered.

Some money came in, by way of a Mendocino cash crop, but it didn't matter. The scene had turned unredeemably ugly. Suze's mother took to sleeping with a sawed-off .410 between them.

Her mother married again in '72 to a guy called Derby, who by Suze's accounts was a good guy, even after he started calling himself Dennis Melman. He finished his degree in architecture at UC Berkeley and bought the house in Marin.

They lived pretty good until '81 and the divorce. And Suze's mother still lived good. She got the house in Marin, a job as a legal secretary in San Francisco, and was active in the League of Women Voters and the local chapter of NOW.

Thinking of all the victims of failed relationships, Max edged into the kitchen and saw Suze turning pancakes on the stove. Denny had equipped the place with the kind of kitchen that could serve a mid-sized restaurant. Maybe four hundred square feet, larger than Suze's apartment and filled with top-of-the-line stuff. The kitchen had been one of Denny's projects. He dropped over a hundred and fifty grand to upgrade the place. He wanted the kind of kitchen where a catering staff of seven or eight could come in and whip up a dinner for fifty, which happened maybe a dozen times. In the end, it was just him and a housekeeper/cook.

Max pulled the coffee pot from the Braun and poured himself a cup. "What's the occasion?"

"Does there have to be one?" she asked back, coming away from the stove and forcing a smile.

Okay, he thought, she's either manipulating me toward something or it's another missed connection. "No, guess not," he finally said, and grabbed three pancakes off the stack near the stove.

"Want to go somewhere this weekend?" she asked, grabbing the remaining stack and joining him at a butcher-block table. "Drive upstate or something?"

He spread out a thick layer of margarine across the pancakes and said, "I was just upstate, remember?"

"Then out to Montauk or something," she tried, going for the knife and margarine. "You know, we could get a good off-season deal."

Briefly he flashed on a hotel room by the beach. Fireplace going, the slate waves rolling in on the other side of the window. He could smell it, the ocean. Then he heard the talk—hours of discussing "the relationship." It would be endless, and with no place to run. Trapped, Max knew, he'd turn mean. The whole thing could get ugly in a flash. And he didn't want that, either. "Gotta work," he said finally, pouring syrup.

"You could get someone to sub for you," she tried. "There's this guy at work I could get."

"Can't, Lynn's on me," Max answered quickly. "All this shit coming down. It's not a good idea."

She reached out and took the syrup. "You know, whoever heard of a bar with one bartender?"

"I have," he said, cutting into the stack. "Every night. Every fucking night." And thought, whoever heard of a monogamous bartender under forty?

She was chewing then, slowly. "You know, maybe you're just burning out a little," she tried, talking around a mouthful of pancakes. "You know, that place is depressing."

Max put his fork down carefully. "And serving a bunch of corporate assholes expense-accounting sixty-buck lunches isn't? Come on, give me a break."

She put her fork down, her face turning suddenly serious. "What's up? You're acting really fucked up."

"I'm a suspect in a murder investigation, isn't that enough?"

"No, it was even before that," she said. "I just feel like you're drifting away. Shit, you don't even talk anymore."

"Maybe I don't have anything to say," he answered and started eating again to avoid it, eyes fixed on the yellow margarine-covered pancakes, a thin layer of syrup running across the white plate. The whole thing was falling apart in front of him. They should have been together a month, maybe two, then drifted away, everyone friends. But now they were dragging it out. Mouthing the lines.

Nothing ended quick enough. The word "tedious" sprung to mind.

"I guess that's your problem, isn't it?" Suze said, pushing her plate forward and rising. "You just never know what to say anymore."

And then she was gone. Out, not through the servants' door, but into the main house, where she never went.

Max sat there, watching the margarine not melt on the pancakes, thinking of what Miles had told him. "They all fall apart on you, kid. Sooner or later they all fall apart," he said. "Marriage? Half don't last. That's fifty percent. It's a coin toss."

He could see the way it was all coming apart. Just thinking about it made him ache, right at his center. Looking ahead, he saw nothing but crying, and sobbing, and talking, and fucking. After a half dozen bad psycho-drama relationships, it doesn't even hurt anymore—not like it used to. You're thinking strategy and manipulation. Storing up ammunition, looking to salvage something from the ugliness and come out the winner in a future that was wreckage. Finally, when it had fallen beyond all hope of repair, and even the bitterness was burned out, everything would be reduced, not even to drama, but small stupid cartoons. Every long-shot plan at putting it back together, no matter how elaborate, blows up in someone's face. Max knew that at four in the morning, desperate and hopeless, we all take our cues from Wile E. Coyote.

*   *   *

It was nearly five when Max reached the storefront
mail drop and the clerk, an ill-tempered weasel, pulled
the two-page fax from a shelf and asked for ten-fifty and
ID. Max slid his driver's license across the counter with
the money.

"This is expired," the guy said, reading the license
carefully.

Max took the license back and passed him a bankcard.

"No picture on this," the guy said, stabbing the plastic
card with one finger. "You got anything else with a
picture?"

Max took the license and card back. "Forget it, man,"
he said. "I'll have it sent again down the street."

Behind him a middle-aged guy in a black raincoat
stuck a key into a lock on a box and began to furtively
pull out a handful of thick manila envelopes.

"Suit yourself," the guy behind the counter said. "I
can't release nothing without valid ID. Expired ain't
valid."

Max was halfway to the door before he turned and
walked back. By the time he reached the counter he had
two tens out of his pocket. He slid both of them across
the counter. "Look, I need that fax."

The guy took both tens, making them disappear under
the counter. "Let me see that license again," he smiled.

Max pulled it out, and the guy took it.

The fat man in the raincoat came up to the counter,
envelopes in hand. "There are photos in here," he rumbled. "I got important photos in here. You people always
bend them."

The weasel behind the counter looked up with mild
annoyance. "Get a bigger box; we got package-sized for
a couple bucks more," he said.

"Can't you put like a sign up or something?" the guy
asked, whining now. "Hold them behind the counter."

The guy set Max's license down with great care and
leaned into the fat man, both palms on the counter. "I
told you last week, all mail goes into the box. You want a

bigger slot, rent it or order smaller pictures. I ain't gonna discuss this with you every week."

The fat man grunted dissatisfaction and left, the clerk's eyes fastened to his back as he pushed out the door.

"Fucking motherfucker," the clerk muttered.

"Do I get the fax?" Max asked.

"I guess this looks like you, alright," he said and slid the curled sheets over the counter with the license.

Max took the sheets and leaned against the wall of aluminum mailboxes, reading. There were sixty-four calls. He recognized Julie's and the number in Jersey. The dead girl had called home three times a week. None of the calls lasted more than ten minutes.

"Hey pal," the clerk said, after about twenty seconds. "This ain't a library, you know."

Max began calling the numbers from the bar. It was the kind of list that charted the dead couple's life. Chinese food. Chinese food. A movie theater on Third. A no answer. Take-out burgers. Time and weather. Lotto info. A fax machine. Another fax machine. More Chinese food. An Italian restaurant on Park—which they probably called for a reservation. Two more no answers. And then, on the last call, he hit.

A young woman picked up the phone and said, "Seymour Answering."

"You're an answering service?" Max asked. He was calling from the office, staring at the bullet hole in the wall.

"Yeah, whattaya think, huh?"

"Sorry, wrong number," Max said, and hung up.

Julie showed up an hour late for work, beaming. "Did you see me on the tube?"

Max shook his head and went back to cutting lemons.

"They were doing a thing on the murder," Julie said, walking past him toward the office to stash her coat. "I got more air time than the cops."

When she came back out, Max saw why. She was wearing a tight-fitting black turtleneck, tight gray slacks. Her hair was pulled back over her ears.

Max set down the knife and lemon. "Been talking to Lynn, huh?"

"We had lunch the other day, you know," Julie said, offhandedly. "She's really nice, once you get to know her."

"Who picked up the tab?"

"We went dutch," Julie said. "She's like really smart. She wants to do things with this place. Like decorate. Make it hot again. I thought maybe we could start serving Jello shots. What do you think?"

Max finished with the lemon before answering. "And Woo-Woos, too, huh?"

She made a kind of nasty face and said, "You know, this place could be hot. Market it. We got a good location. All you have to do is get a good idea for it, you know?"

"You mean, like a theme?" Max asked, leaning against the back bar.

"And a name," Julie said. "Look at the place down the street."

The place down the street was called the Gumball. A kiddie bar from the day it opened, it packed in the under-twenty-five crowd and served the kind of drinks that tasted like anything but alcohol. The place held onto its liquor license only through the kind of luck Lotto players hope for. The joint was history with the first nineteen-year-old from Long Island that wrapped his car around a tree after too many sweets. But that didn't matter to the owners. Word on the street was it was owned by a consortium of doctors up in Westchester. It was set up in a Cayman Limited Partnership or something with a front man's name on the license. They could kill off the whole senior class of Roslyn High with Seven-Up and tequila shooters, and they were untouchable, except for the license, which didn't mean shit to them anyway. They'd earned the investment back in the first eighteen months. After that it was gravy.

"I figure that we can do it for two-fifty," Julie added. "New interior, a new sound system, some neon, and advertising. I could make this place hot."

She's using her, Max thought. Lynn wouldn't put two hundred bucks into the place if she didn't have to. The joint was like an annuity for Lynn and the kid. There'd always be business for a dark, neighborhood joint on the Upper East Side. Lynn wasn't going to roll the dice with two-fifty and her liquor license.

"Just out of curiosity, how'd you come up with that two-fifty number?" Max asked.

Julie approached the bar with no little enthusiasm and condescension. "I read it in a magazine," she said. "One of the trades that you never bother reading. They had this story about a place outside of Chicago, in Rosemont, just like this. And they trebled business by doing what I said."

Shit, Max thought, somewhere Lynn was laughing her ass off with that bitter little laugh she had. In places just "outside of Chicago," they went to a fifties theme bar in the airport Holiday Inn and thought that was *hot*.

"What about acting?" Max said. "You got to have some dedication to your craft and all of that."

Julie took a deep breath. The punch line was coming, Max could feel it. "Look at those models downtown. They opened that bar, they're doing great."

The punch line was a doozy. Julie hadn't done her first day-player role, and she's already looking at bars as chump-change investments. "That's a restaurant," Max corrected.

"You know, you're the most negative guy I ever met," Julie said, turning her back on him. "Maybe that's why you never went anywhere."

Max watched her go and said, "I went to prison yesterday."

She knew what he meant, but answered, "Big deal, a lot of people go to prison."

Thirteen

The big man was eating cubes of pork and sliced chicken from a stick, and watching "Donahue" on a thirteen-inch black and white. He'd bought the pork, six sticks of them, from a street vendor on East Eighty-sixth. He'd finished the beer, two six-packs of Budweiser tallboys, an hour ago. Now he was starting on the last of the pork. The inside of the meat was bloody, the outside burned dark brown. Donahue was running up and down the aisle of an enthusiastic audience, throwing the microphone to those in the center of the row so that they could talk about the men and women onstage. The men and the women onstage were smiling. Phil Donahue was smiling.

The big man's stomach growled and rumbled. Leaning forward, the stick in one hand, the big man turned the channel. Oprah Winfrey was three stations up. He preferred Oprah Winfrey to Phil Donahue. She reminded him of the teachers who taught in the schools on the islands. American and Australian women who came for a year or two to teach in the schools. When they first arrived on the islands they were like Oprah, full of energy. By the end of two years, they all got bored and left. Now he was bored and wished that he could leave.

He thought of his grandmother and the saying, "Catch the bird, but watch for the wave." That was the Samoan way. *Fa'a Samoa.* He had caught the bird, but this entire city for him was an unthinkable wave of people, buildings, noises. Why would people build such a place and then live there? He could not imagine. Even Hawaii, where he spent a few years when he was young, would be better.

He missed the sun. It was hard to understand how

people in this city could live without the sun. For all these rushing about *palagi*, he thought, the television was like the sun. It was the light they basked in. Like the fat, pale Australian tourists who came to the island and lay on the beach until their pale skins burned and peeled.

The big man finished off the meat from the stick, cracked it in two, and placed it in the greasy wrapper that it had come in. Then he turned off the television. So much television and beer had given him a headache. His ears pounded. He felt a little dizzy from it.

Outside it was already darkening. Soon, the streets would be crowded with people coming home from work.

He rose heavily from the chair and walked toward the windows. His stomach growled again; deep in his bowels there was a twinge and movement. The apartment was beginning to close in on him. Suddenly it seemed to grow much smaller.

Sliding the glass window open, he walked out onto the balcony, a tiny square of concrete just large enough to accommodate two tiny lawn chairs and a small table. A cold, sharp wind was blowing off the river. But he needed the air. The warm breeze that blew through the vent ducts on the floor was stale and he mistrusted it. The warm air came from some great furnace in the building's basement and was blown up twenty floors with fans. He thought that he could almost taste a metallic odor in it. Warm air that traveled so far through the center of a building could not be good.

He was beginning to sweat; the cold air cooled the sweat and made him feel a little better. Even the cold air was better than the metal air that blew up from the center of the building. As he stood on the balcony shivering, he looked down on the tarpaper roofs of the buildings below. Off in the distance, the lights of other apartments flicked on. He could see the distinct glow of televisions through curtained windows.

These are strange people, he thought. People who choose to live one on top of each other and breathe metal air.

He was sweating more now, he could feel it run down

his back and across his forehead. When he began to shiver, he stepped back inside and shut the door.

Another great chill ran through him and something deep in his bowels began to move. The bathroom was across the entire length of the living room, which suddenly looked like a mile run down a beach. He knew he wouldn't make it. And he didn't.

The next day, Max woke alone, oddly, even after their fight, missing Suze. The jukebox still jangled in his head from the night before. Some maniac had come in just as they got a little busy and fed the machine fifteen bucks to play the Rolling Stones's "Miss You," for something like an hour and a half straight. Nobody seemed to notice except him, and he couldn't get out from behind the bar to reset the juke.

He walked home at dawn, thinking about how to tell Suze about it. Whoever did it was a definite threat, but it was funny. When he got home, all he found was a note saying she had to work late on a paper and couldn't make it uptown. Something in him shifted lower.

And he thought, now what the fuck is this? A couple of hours ago you wanted her gone and the thing ended. That *was* you, wasn't it, kid? Save the story and tell it to someone else. But the answer he got back was, *Who?* You would have to know the bar. Know the circumstances. Know *him*, to think it was funny. By the time he explained it, well, it wouldn't be funny anymore. With Suze, it was like automatic.

Max took the bus downtown in rush hour, feeling odd around the suit-and-tie crowd, and thinking how simple it would be if everything were like tending bar. After twelve years it was instinct. Take the order, grab a glass, and throw in the ice. Turn and find the bottle where you know it should be. Pour for a three-count, turn, reshelf the bottle, and slide the glass over the bar, bringing back the money.

That's what he longed for with Suze. Something he understood and was comfortable with. Something more than the grim mechanics of Miles and Todd, but less complex than the slow maze that he was stuck in now.

What was it Miles had told him about women? There's only two kinds: those that say "Why?" and those that say "Why not?" After that, it's ten minutes of chatter to figure out which kind you're talking to and half an hour to prove you're not Ted Bundy. But that was bar wisdom. Take it out of the bar into your life and you've got some problems.

Max got off the bus on Forty-second and walked down, thinking that he was going to be late for work and that he'd been using Miles to cover what he really wanted for too long.

Miles had fucked himself, seduced himself like he'd done maybe five hundred women. Todd was the same way, but a younger version. Like records stuck in the same groove. Like a guy who feeds the small change of his life into a juke to hear the same song over and over. Now Miles was in prison and Todd was dead.

Seymour Answering was in the East Thirties, above a Korean deli and a flower store. The building was the kind of place that was maybe once an apartment, but now rented office space to collection agencies, discount travel agents, and companies with names like American Continental Ltd. and Trans-Consolidated Brokers, Inc. Their blandness alone fostered suspicion. It was the kind of building that didn't house companies that needed to impress anyone.

Seymour Answering was on the second floor; its door, marked by a plastic sign the color of brass, was held up precariously by four yellowing strips of scotch tape. On the other side of the door, he could hear the phones and murmur of voices.

No point in knocking, he thought, and pushed through the door.

The place was done up in plastic paneling painted to look like wood grain, except that four or five different shades had been used and nailed up with flat-head roofing nails. Above, from a stained drop ceiling, the bare tubes of fluorescents, those that weren't burnt out, sputtered and flashed. Eight or nine women, most of

them black, but a few Hispanic and white, sat around
three long tables that were arranged roughly in the shape
of a T. In front of each woman was a flesh-colored phone
console with ten lines, and a two-foot plastic wall of
cubbyholes. Strewn around the table was a collection
of take-out food containers, liter bottles of soda, and
steadily filling ashtrays.

The woman closest to the door looked over her shoulder at him and announced, "Who the fuck left the door
open again?"

A few of the other women shot Max a look, but
continued working. He was maybe three feet from the
tables, close enough to see the Post-It-note memos that
read, "7456—Dr.'s off.," "8741—route to page," and
"4573—route to 1, 2, 4, page in seq."

A large woman disengaged herself from the table and
walked over. She was white, and wearing a blue jogging
outfit that was maybe three sizes too small. Her thick
black hair was tied back behind her head. She was fat,
but big too, in a sloppy kind of way. Six feet and two
hundred and fifty pounds.

She studied Max as she approached, her face turning
from worried to bland to relieved, and finally settling
on annoyed. She had a face like an apple about to go
bad—pale in the kind of way that years of night work
make you pale. And bitter, the way that a lifetime of
bad jobs makes you bitter. The sweatsuit was scarred
by hundreds of small cigarette burns up and down the
front, melted into the polyester.

"I was wondering if you could help me?" Max asked.

"I doubt it," she said, hands on hips. "What'd you
want?"

Max tried for something authoritative. "You the supervisor?"

The woman eyed him again, checking to see if she
made a mistake, and decided that she hadn't. "No, I'm
the fuckin' den mother," she said. "What'd you want?"

"My cousin used your service," Max said, turning on
the charm. "I was wondering if I could get some of his
old records."

"Why don't you ask him?"

"He's dead," Max said, switching to grief.

"Oh, your cousin was that guy, huh?" she stretched out the word cousin, just to make sure Max knew she didn't believe him.

"Yeah, you know who I'm talking about?"

"You better talk to one of the Seymours," she answered.

"There's more than one?"

"There's a young one and an old one. Cheap fuckin' Jew bastards," the woman said, bored now. "But it don't matter. 'Cause you ain't gonna call."

A couple of the women at the table were staring now, interested or just grateful in a small way for a break in the routine. They had vague looks of expectation on their faces, like maybe there'd be a fight.

"I just got into town," Max tried, pushing on. "And, I'd like to know who some of his friends were, you know, to talk to them."

"Yeah, I'm gonna believe that bullshit," she said, rolling her eyes slightly.

Max tried another tactic. "What's your name?"

"What? You gonna report me to the Seymours?" she laughed. It was a thick, dismissive laugh. "Go get yourself a reality check, pal."

The women at the table, bored, had gone back to the phones.

"Okay, here's the deal," Max said, lowering his voice to a mumble. "You get me some numbers. I'll get you some money."

She considered this for a moment. "How much we talking about?"

Max made a move like he was going for his wallet. "You tell me how much we're talking about."

The woman walked past Max into the hall. When Max was out on the landing with her, she shut the door and said, "So where you from? And don't give me that cousin bullshit. That don't play."

"Does it matter?" Max asked.

"It matters," she said, holding her ground, back to the

closed door. "It matters if it's gonna get me canned from this shit-hole."

"It won't."

She thought hard on it for a second. "Two hundred and I'll tell you what that guy was up to."

Max backed off, "How about fifty?"

Her eyes narrowed with contempt. "You have a nice life," she said, edging back in the door. "I think I hear my phone ringing."

"Two hundred," Max conceded.

She halted, halfway in the door. "Meet me at the Blarney Stone in twenty," she said. "I'll be there on my break."

Max hit the bank machine on the corner then headed for the Blarney Stone. Inside it was like hundreds of other green-fronted bars around the city. Long bar along one side, steam table for the lunch and dinner crowd across the other, and maybe a dozen heavy tables in the back.

A small cluster of drinkers spread out along the bar, their heads craned toward the news on a television above the window. He'd just gotten a beer and was sitting down at a back table when the woman came in. Max guessed that she was probably a regular. The bartender had a Seven and Seven on the bar before she was halfway into the room.

She took a healthy drink from the glass and walked back to Max. "I want to see some money first," she said, sitting down heavily.

Max pulled out the twenties, folded over. She reached out with her free hand, and he pulled them back. "Let's talk first," he said, but didn't put the money away.

"Sure, what you want to know?"

"What do you know about the guy?" Max asked.

"Marotte, you mean, don't you?" she said smiling. It was the smile of an insider knowing a password.

"Yeah, Marotte and the girl," Max said.

She took another drink, eyed the clock over the bathroom doors. "What are you, like a reporter or something?"

"Yeah, I'm a reporter," Max said and began tapping the bills on the table.

"I heard the *Enquirer* paid five K for a picture of Elvis," she said.

Max made to get up and brought the crisp roll of twenties under the table, like he was putting them in his pocket.

"Okay, sit, sit," she said, taking a drink, then pulling up the sleeves to the sweatshirt. "What'd you want to know?"

"What were they up to?"

"The girl was an actress," she said, nodding now as if confirming some long-suspected truth. "You know, auditions, appointments, that kind of bullshit. Two messages a week, usually from her mother."

Max started putting the money away again.

"But the guy, he was a thief," she said. "Or on the hustle."

"How do you know?"

"I'm telling you, he was a thief," she insisted. "What, you want reasons how I know?"

"Yeah," Max said. "Give me three."

She let out a long sigh. "Okay, I'll give you more than that. First off, I do the mail in the joint. That guy Marotte paid by cashier's check every month," she said. "That's one. We got three guys running whores outta there, they pay the same way. Yeah, and he only came down once, you know. Okay, number two, his address was a suite number on the West Side. You know what that means or do I have to tell you?"

Max knew what it meant. The guy was using a mail drop. Instead of a box number, you could list the address as a suite number or office number. It would maybe fool about three people, all of them in Utah or someplace like that. "And what's the last thing?"

"He was using a bogus name, Mr. Grayson, and a company name called Ambassador Credit International."

"Anything else?" Max asked.

She finished off the drink, draining it to the ice, then

began scratching at her arms, raking bitten nails up and down, first one arm, then the other. When she'd scratched her arms enough, she held up the glass, signaling for the bartender. Then she looked Max dead in the eye. "I been in phones for fifteen years," she said, then looked away. "I worked boiler rooms out in Vegas. Conversation lines. Sex lines. I was a dial-a-psychic, if you believe that. Telemarketing, I sold every fucking thing you want. Vitamins. Health clubs. Beauty school. I sold *Daily*-fucking-*News* home delivery, and polled two presidential elections. I did a *voir dire* survey for a Wall Street trial. When someone's dirty, I know it."

The bartender, a fat guy with a pink face and gray hair, brought her drink over and set it down in the center of the table.

"What was he doing?" Max asked.

"How should I know?" she said. "I took maybe three calls for him. The night shift, you know?"

Now it was Max's turn to take a sip of his drink. He was getting close. He could feel it. "What was the routine?"

She closed her eyes for a second, remembering. "Ambassador. Mr. Grayson's in a meeting now. May I have your number."

"Then what?" Max asked.

"Then the guy calls in, three or four times a day," she said. "Gets his messages. That's another thing, we never called him—nothing connects him to us, except I seen him once. Give me the money."

Max held up a hand. "Remember any of the numbers?"

"Come on, give me a fucking break, will ya?"

"How 'bout records?"

"We trash them after a week," she answered. "Besides the cops have what we had. And that ain't much. You got more now."

"What about area codes?"

"The girls said they were all over," she said. "Philly, Montana, Jersey, Detroit. All over the place. You know, national. But shit-holes, you know?"

"No," Max answered. "Tell me."

"You know, maybe there were fifty calls from Detroit, Jersey, Buffalo. There weren't none from Beverly Hills. Couple from Westchester, but Yonkers and White Plains. You know?"

Max put the money away, and started to get up. "You're bullshitting me," he said. "I saw the bill, no toll calls."

She shot him a look that could stop a taxi on the FDR. "Fuck you, asshole," she spat. "Guys like that don't leave a trail. They don't call from their office or home. Nothing that can be traced back. No message units. Nothing."

Max eased back into the seat. "Where do they call from?"

She finished her drink in a gulp, needing the liquor to cushion herself from such stupidity. "They call from offices where they pay the cleaning lady fifty bucks for an hour. They'll check into some hotel and pay cash with a bogus name. They'll get some hot credit card number from a big company. It don't matter, just as long as nothing leads back to them."

"You're kidding?"

"Right, I'm kidding," she sneered, though warming to her subject. "I knew a guy, called him Quarter Cary, know why? Cause he ran scams outta the Helmsley Palace pay phones, his private boiler room. Went in like he owned the place, with twenty, thirty bucks in quarters and a stopwatch. Three minutes tops, he'd have the Visa card number from any housewife in Iowa. Now, give me the fucking money."

"I need the mail drop," Max said, tapping the money on the table.

She eyed the clock again. "You're wasting my time," she said, then reached out, palm up for the cash. "You gonna screw me on this deal or what?"

"Can you get me the address?"

She was looking hungrily at the cash. "Yeah, I'll get it for you."

Max let the money fall flat to the table, then quickly covered it with his palm. "When?"

"Let me get back," she said. "Ten minutes give me a call on the office line."

"You know what happens if you fuck me over on this?" Max asked, not having a clue what he'd be able to do to her.

"Yeah, the same thing that happens if you don't lift your hand up," she answered casually.

Max lifted his hand, not sure if she was threatening him or making an appeal for a little mutual trust.

She grabbed the money, vanished it into the folds of her sweatsuit, and got up to leave. "Ten minutes," she said when she was halfway to the door.

Max watched her leave, then took his time finishing the beer. He had just enough cash left for a cab uptown to work. But when he was two steps from the door the bartender called out, "Hey, pal, you gonna pay for her drinks or what?"

He dialed the Seymour Answering number from a pay phone on the corner. When the woman's voice came on, Max said, "It's me."

She gave him an address in the West Twenties, just off of Fifth, then hung up.

FOURTEEN

Max hit the mail drop the next day, just before it closed. In his pocket was a cashier's check for forty-two bucks and a suitcase key filed halfway through at the center.

The place was a storefront cluttered with postage supplies, picture frames, displays for overnight film processing, photo albums, key chains, and posters advertising engraved letterhead and business cards. It was the kind of place that would open up and take on every item that every salesman and jobber through the door hauled in. If the joint made it, fine. Mostly they ran for a year or two, then closed.

There was an Indian guy behind the counter, leaning on a shelf full of jiffy bags and masking tape, looking bored.

Max brought the check out of his wallet and set it on the counter. "For Ambassador," he said, then pushed it across the counter.

"Where's the other one," the guy asked, taking the check and studying it.

Max came in toward the guy. "The other what?"

"Other fellow that come in?"

"I'm his new partner," Max said.

"New partner, check no good. Must be made out to store."

"It'll cash," Max said. "Anyone can cash it."

The guy studied the check some more, nodded. "Okay, you want receipt?"

Max moved away from the counter, toward the wall of mailboxes. "Sure, what's the number again?"

"Didn't he tell you?" the guy said, ringing up the mailbox's rent on the register and tearing the receipt from the slot.

Max, still pretending to search for the box, said, "Yeah, he told me, I forgot, okay?"

"Not allowed to give out numbers. Confidential."

"Give me a break, willya," Max shot back. "I'm not coming down here twice."

"No numbers," the guy said. "Not allowed to give out."

Max knew the guy's line was bullshit. With these joints all you needed was a fake ID—the kind you'd buy on Times Square—to sign the postal forms with. He moved up to the counter. "Okay, give me the check back."

"You paid, I put it in drawer," the guy said.

Max gave him a hard stare. "Hey, you're gonna jerk me around, I'll jerk you around. Give me the check, okay?"

"No, no, not okay," the guy said.

"What are we gonna do then, wait around 'til you close? Give me the fucking check or the number!"

The guy froze for a second, calculating the trouble caused by giving him the number, against the check. "One-forty-two," he said at last.

"Thanks pal," Max answered and walked down the rows of boxes until he saw one-forty-two at the end near the top. Through the small square of plastic he could see three letters inside, leaning against the side of the box. When he moved the key to the hole, he was praying it would go at least halfway in. It did. Then he gave it a hard turn; the key broke off inside the hole.

"What the fuck?" he shouted, loud enough to get the guy up off the stool behind the counter. "It fucking broke!"

"What did you do? What?" the guy asked, coming around the counter.

Max pocketed the top half of the key and pointed to the portion jammed inside the hole. "It broke man," he said. "Cheap fucking keys."

The Indian guy raised up on tiptoes and peered into the lock, shaking his head. "Oh no, no good," he said.

"Fucking right, no good," Max answered. "I got letters in there. See?"

"Come back tomorrow, okay."

"Come on man, don't bust my balls on this," Max said. "Go behind and get my mail."

The guy shook his head, but did it. He re-emerged on the other side of the counter holding three envelopes and threw them across to Max.

"I'll be in tomorrow for the new key," Max said and retreated out the door as fast as his Chuck Taylors could carry him.

He tore into the first letter at the corner. Inside was a two-page bank loan application. Across the top was a large red stamp, the kind you order from an office supply store. The stamp read: APPROVED in large block letters. Just under it were the slightly smaller words "Priority Customer." The form had been filled out in blue ballpoint in big block letters. It looked like a kid had done it. The applicant was a guy in South Jersey. The second letter was another application, this one from a guy in Scranton. The same red-stamped message appeared. Now, what the fuck was this, the applications originated from some Third World Spanish bank: *Banque Amerika de Pacifikca Internationale.* Attached to each with a staple, was a receipt from Ambassador for a two hundred dollar application fee.

When he opened the third letter he hit pay dirt. It was from some giveaway weekly *Pennysaver* newspaper upstate. The kind of paper that they give away at supermarkets where you advertise a used crib or '73 Plymouth Duster. There was a computerized bill attached to a length of newsprint. Max unfolded the newsprint. It was a small display ad for Ambassador Credit International.

Poor Credit? Bad Credit? No Credit?
NO PROBLEM!
Loan Consolidation. New Car. Vacation.
Home Improvements.
GET THE MONEY YOU NEED FAST!

Our international banking contacts guarantee you the personal loans you need fast! Instant approval by phone for loans from $500 to $15,000. Liberal international credit policies allow us to pre-approve loans and credit cards from some of the largest banks in Europe, Asia, the South Seas, and Middle East. As an American citizen, member of a union, veteran of the armed services, or resident of New York, you are one of the best credit risks in the world—regardless of past credit history. Take advantage now!

Just below the block of copy was the name Grayson and an 800 number he recognized as the Seymour Answering Service.

*   *   *

The big man awoke in a semiprivate room of Lenox Hill Hospital. For a long time he stayed very still, wondering if he were in prison and trying to remember what had happened.

He remembered running across the apartment for the bathroom. And he remembered not quite making it, messing the floor. Soon, he recalled, the fever was worse. He began to vomit. His stomach felt as if he were being punched again and again from the inside. When he tried to stand up, he fell, dizzy with the fever and pain.

There was a pink bathrobe hanging on the door; the angry woman had left it behind. The front pocket said Ritz-Carlton. He had pulled himself up by the bathrobe, then leaned against the door as he tried to put it on. The front of the robe didn't quite make it over his stomach. The hem came down somewhere over his thighs.

He felt himself dying. Sweat ran down his face as he staggered to the apartment door and out into the carpeted hall toward the elevator. At the elevator he messed himself again and then vomited. The wretching spasm brought him to his hands and knees as the door chimed open. Inside was a couple, a young man and a woman, both dressed in suits, carrying briefcases.

"I am dying, I think," the big man groaned, then vomited again inside the elevator. The stench was of Budweiser and bile.

The elevator doors began to close, but the big man was already halfway inside, trying to pull himself up by the rubber edge. The couple watched in horror as he lifted himself to a crouching stand, a thick strand of bile hanging from his chin.

The man, he couldn't have been more than twenty-five, tried pushing him back with a briefcase, but the big man fell forward, pinning the young man against the wall. As the elevator doors shut, the big man messed himself noisily again and collapsed to the floor.

"Push the alarm," the young man had said, stepping away. The woman began pushing buttons in a panic. The elevator jarred to a complete stop and a bell began ringing in the distance.

"Start it again, start it!" the young man cried, stepping over the big man's chest.

The woman pushed another button and the alarm stopped. The smell in the small elevator was overwhelming and the young woman began to gag.

"Help me, I am dying," the big man moaned, pulling himself up.

"How did he get in?" the young man asked, his voice panicked.

"Help me," the big man asked, then vomited against the wall in a great, gagging spasm.

The elevator doors opened, and the young man stepped out. The woman was in the corner, crying and vomiting. The young man reached back in and grabbed her by the hand, pulling her out. She half-fell, half-staggered from the elevator, still retching as the doors closed.

The doors opened twice more, revealing the shocked and disgusted faces of building residents. By the time the elevator had passed the second floor, no fewer than five people had called down to the front desk that there was a homeless man vomiting and defecating in the elevator.

When the door opened in the lobby, he crawled across the slick floor, face down, gagging. He paused for a brief moment, feeling the cool marble under his palms, seeing its rose color swirl into focus, feeling the bump of the elevator doors as they closed on his left foot and retracted again. And then the world exploded in a blinding flash. The pain surged in a jolt through his fevered head and down his spine. His arms would no longer support him, and he fell, the floor banging his stomach.

The next thing he remembered was the ambulance. The straps of the gurney tight across his chest and legs. His head immobilized.

"We got an open head wound . . . Nice QRS . . . Stabilized," a woman's voice said.

Someone patted his face and a man asked, "Buddy, what you take, huh? What were you doing? Ludes, PCP, what? What color was it, huh? Any medication?"

The big man grunted, tried to pull himself up, but couldn't.

Someone opened his left eye and shined a blinding light into it. "Start him on Narcan . . . Possible concussion."

When he gained consciousness again, they were examining him under harsh lights. Someone, a man, said, "Bleeding's stopped. We'll suture later. Who's with me to lavage? Good. Get me a sixty-cc syringe and sodium chloride solution," and measured a thick length of surgical tube against his stomach. "Start him on five-percent dextrose and half saline. Okay pal, hold tight now," the man said, and began running the tube down the big man's mouth. He began gagging again. When the tube vanished down his throat, they pumped warm water into it, then drained it out.

When the first water returned, the man said, "Okay, run a drug screen and Gram stain. Culture it. Scrape some stool off his leg and run that, too." And then he pumped more water into the big man's stomach.

FifTEEN

For a full week, Delbert Kray waded into the listings of incorporated businesses, grantee/grantor listings, property records, court liens, foreclosures, and SEC records. He'd been to small claims court, federal court, municipal court, and bankruptcy court, skimming their files. What he came up with was nothing, nada, zip, squat.

The TRW and Equifax reports had come back the day before. The guy had credit like an oil sheik, but not one credit card. The last one he carried expired three years ago. Amex. Account paid up in full. Delbert paid two hundred bucks for a cop up in Suffolk County to log on to the NCIC computer. Twenty-five million names on it and Peter Marotte wasn't one of them.

As he walked across Foley Square, Delbert ran down the list again. The Casualty File showed only a whole–life insurance policy for $200,000. It was taken out by some dead uncle, then paid up like clockwork. Neat trick, that. Usually you only saw it with the Koreans and Vietnamese. They used the policies like a bank. You could borrow against them in a pinch. A handy way to stay liquid for the long term.

The Insurance Fraud Index, the insurance industry's own secretive Big Brother database, showed only the same policy. The only paper the guy left behind was a driver's license. And he didn't have so much as a parking ticket. Didn't even own a car.

The last traces he found of the guy were eight years old. Registered as a broker with the SEC. Big deal, he passed the Series 7 exam. Place of employment: Drexel. Well, that did a whole lot of good. A dead guy traced back to a dead company.

Delbert was walking against the cold wind, heading for the parking lot behind the federal courthouse. Hands stuffed down deep in his coat pockets, he thought of what he secretly called "Sam Spade Time." These were the best times for him. This was when he could get out and act like a private eye, play the character he knew he should play in the black-and-white movie of his mind.

Sure, most of what he'd done in the past were the old-time routines, ice-picking a guy's tires so that he'd have to change a flat; sending twenty phone books wrapped up neat in a brown UPS box; or even hiring a double-jointed whore he knew, all to prove that the soft-tissue damage was a scam.

Couple of years ago he had a real good thing going, clearing three, four hundred a week in the panty business. Had guys bringing in their wives' underwear for semen tests. Checking for signs of secretions and blood type. He was popping them a hundred and a half for sixty dollars' worth of lab work. Collected so many used panties, he started packing them in Glad bags and selling them off through ads in porn magazines. But that business dried up around '88, when condoms came into fashion.

New thing now was following around husbands, wives, boyfriends, and girlfriends. AIDS made them all nervous. The wife in Rye who'd turn a blind eye to her husband's screwing around a couple years ago was digging into the grocery money now for a little peace of mind. Not just suburban wives either, now it was postal workers from Queens and sanitation workers' wives from the Bronx. Everyone was jittery. Kray knew a guy doing a good business in fiancés. Shit, few years back you got a ring and headed off to Bachrach to get a picture to send the paper. Today, they were looking for full background checks.

But here at last was a dead guy he could really sink his teeth into. You had to work at not leaving a trail. And only guys on the wrong side worked at it. And this guy, Peter Marotte, was definitely on the wrong side. He could smell it.

But it left him with two questions. Who was this guy Marotte? And why would some high-dollar lawyer be interested in him?

Instinctively, Kray knew this was his shot at the big time. Maybe even his last one. This was the one that would put his name in the papers and attract the money clients. Class divorce cases up in Westchester and Connecticut. Thieving business partners in the garment district. Industrial espionage in midtown. Discreet background checks for nervous Park Avenue co-op boards. Skimming and kickbacks in the kitchens and bars of four-star hotels. You could map the fucking city by the kind of work that needed to be done. And for a guy with the right reputation and a few newspaper clippings, the money was there.

As it stood now, he had to remember every secretary and claims adjuster's birthday just to keep his name on their Rolodexes. Personality didn't count for much anymore. And nobody respected hard work and hustle.

What those uptown stiffs wanted was flash. A good suit and pretty manners.

And everyday there were more of those slick articles opening shop. Snot-nosed punk kids just off the DEA or ATF payroll. They could waltz into those midtown offices and pick up the corporate work like they owned it. Four-hundred-dollar suits and more electronics than Radio Shack. Spectrum analysis, physical sweeps, security debriefings, neat fifty-page reports churned out by a Mac computer and bound in black folders labeled CONFIDENTIAL. All bullshit. But bullshit that paid like six bills a day.

Delbert could feel them out there sometimes. Feel them squeezing him. A few years ago they started on the big-money jobs, like corporate security. Then they began working their way down. Already, he'd heard stories about these kids—even women for chrissakes— parked in their Volvos and vans outside some Jersey motel with a pair of night-vision goggles, beside them a Nikon with a hundred-millimeter lens and high-speed film or camcorder, doing divorce work.

Sure, they looked good in court. But court wasn't where you made your bones in this business. All the court and depositions in Kings County didn't mean shit when you had a 240-pound lunatic in BVDs coming at you in the hall of a midtown hotel with a busted J&B fifth in his mitt and the receptionist from his office screaming like a banshee from the bed. That's what used to count. What still counted. Keeping cool and getting the tapes or the kind of pictures that told the story—start to finish.

Delbert crossed the street, wheezing slightly now, and headed for the parking lot and his car. Okay, balls to the wall on this one, he promised himself. And don't let any of those punks take it away. First thing tomorrow he'd check out the woman, that waitress Marotte was shacked up with.

Max rolled out of bed to the insistent ringing of the doorbell. Even as he was dragged from sleep, he knew it wasn't his doorbell, but the one for the main house. It had been maybe a year and a half since it rang, and he'd nearly forgotten it was wired to the rear quarters.

Pulling the blanket around him, he moved through the narrow hall, down the winding stairs, and into the kitchen. Suze kept on sleeping, rolling onto his spot under the blanket.

When he hit the entranceway, the marble cold on his feet, the doorbell was still ringing.

He didn't bother to check the closed-circuit monitor mounted just inside the entranceway; rather, he opened the door, pulling the blanket tighter around him with the first blast of chill air.

Two guys in winter suit coats stood on the steps, kneading their gloved hands together from the cold.

"May we come in?" the first guy asked.

Max, blinking into the cold, studied them. Both were maybe thirty, thirty-two. They had short-cropped hair and WASP features. One wore a pair of tortoise-shell glasses. A couple of years ago they could have passed for Ivy League, now they looked like lawyers. Junior partners at a second-string Wall Street firm.

"Yeah, well, not really," Max said, and freed one hand from the blanket to close the door.

"Treasury," one of the guys, the one with the glasses, said, then made his hand vanish inside a coat pocket. When he pulled it out, the hand was holding a leather case with an ID and badge.

The hand holding the ID had a college ring. It was from Cornell.

"Yeah?" Max began to mumble.

The guy not holding the ID, the one without the glasses, said, "Yeah," and walked past Max into the hall.

"Don't you guys need a warrant or something?" Max asked, closing the door and following them into the paneled hall.

"Or something," one of them said casually, looking around. "Nice digs. Where's your girlfriend?"

"Sleeping," Max answered. "You know, I really think you guys need a warrant."

"We could get a warrant," the other said, stopping to study a painting of some long-dead, gray-haired ancestor of Denny Mcbride. It was a huge gilt-framed thing, maybe four feet high. The Mcbride was wearing a tux and sitting in an easy chair with a hunting dog at his feet. He was smiling like a guy who'd won all the marbles, or at least the biggest ones.

"But it wouldn't be to search the place," the other guy said, now studying the painting too. "It would be for your arrest."

"What'd you suppose it would cost today to have something like this done?" the other one asked.

"I don't know," Max answered, determined to play it cool as he stood behind them. "Call Sears and find out."

Both of the guys shot him hard looks. The one with the glasses and the class ring said, "I'm Agent Targin, and this is Agent Reddick."

Max turned and headed for the kitchen. "That's great, you want coffee?"

They followed Max through the darkened living room and formal dining room toward the kitchen. When they passed the long table that sat twenty-six, one of the agents said, "You entertain much?"

"Not much," Max answered, rounding a corner and pushing through the double doors into the tiled kitchen.

The timer hadn't gone off on the Braun yet. Max nudged the dial down and took one of the two seats at the butcher-block table in the corner.

One of the agents, Reddick, boosted himself up on the kitchen's center island, under a collection of copper pans, while the other looked around.

"Christ, it's two in the afternoon," the sitting agent said. "What time do you get up?"

"Is that an official question?" Max answered. "Or a rhetorical?"

On the far counter, the Braun sputtered, a thin stream of coffee began to sputter into the twelve-cup pot. Max restrained an urge to replace the pot with his mug.

"You made some calls," the other agent, the one walking around said. He was at the door to the walk-in freezer, studying the thermometer at its side.

"The telephone company sent you guys out?" Max asked, his eyes glued to the coffee pot. A voice inside his head reminded him not to talk to these guys. Not without benefit of a lawyer or at least a cup of coffee.

"One call you made was to New Jersey," the sitting one said.

"Another was to Todd Manion," the walking one continued as he came around the island to face Max. There was a certain dramatic flair to it. Max had to give them that.

"You guys, you got like an act, right?"

"Listen up pal," the sitting one said, hopping down off the island. "You made three calls. The one to Jersey's to the mother of a murdered woman. The other to a murder victim."

Max got up, walked across the room, still clutching his blanket, grabbed a mug from the sink, and filled it with coffee. "So, what you want to know?"

The two treasury agents were standing side by side now. Max could see that they were nearly identical in height. Day players, he thought, Cop Number One and Cop Number Two. "You want to tell him the rest of it?" the one named Reddick asked.

"You tell him," Targin, Cornell alum, answered.

"You picked up some mail the other day," Reddick said, obliging his partner. "For Ambassador."

Max took a long gulp of the lukewarm coffee. He could feel the fear rising up in him. The kind of fear that meant get a lawyer. "Yeah?"

"We left those letters there," Reddick said. "Just to see who'd pick them up."

Targin added, "Now imagine our surprise when you showed."

"Know what we said to each other?" Reddick asked.

Max finished the coffee and shook his head.

"We're looking at our surveillance tapes and you come walking in, commit a felony, and split," Targin said.

"First thing," Reddick finished. "We said, 'Now who the fuck is that guy?' Am I right, partner?"

"You're right," Targin said.

They were both coming toward Max now, closing in with cold official smiles.

Max put his cup down and tried to smile back. "So, what do you want to know?"

"Same question," Reddick said. "Who the fuck are you?"

"Just a guy," Max answered, hoping to buy time until he could think of something else. Waiting for the caffeine to take hold.

They were right in front of him now, edging him back against the counter. "Next question," Targin said, the smile melting off his face. "Are you a guy with a lawyer?"

That's when Max knew it wasn't a bust. No cop who's ever gonna bust you asks if you have a lawyer. Past the Miranda recital, the word lawyer isn't in a cop's vocabulary. Something else was at work here. "Do I need one?" Max asked, turning his back on them to refill his cup.

"You might," Reddick said, smiling again. "We know enough about you now."

"Like what?" Max asked.

"Easy stuff, like that bust you took a couple years ago," Targin finished.

"Made the papers," Max said, sipping from the mug. "Probation's over, expunged record."

"How about that the NYPD sees you as a suspect in the murder of Todd Manion?"

"That's official now?" Max asked.

Targin smiled. "Let's just say it's been bandied about in a certain squad room."

"And, they're trying to tie you to the Peter Marotte and Patricia Brimmer thing," Reddick added.

"Haven't been charged," Max answered.

"They don't have much, if that's any comfort," Targin said.

"I didn't do it," Max said, then walked to the other side of the room and sat down, trying to gather the blanket around him in the most innocent way possible.

"Frankly, I don't give a shit," Reddick said.

Max waited for Targin to finish, but the guy just stood there smiling. "How 'bout you?" Max finally asked him.

Targin frowned a little and shook his head. He didn't give a shit either.

"So, what'd you want from me?" Max asked.

"We want you to stop fucking up our investigation," Targin said.

"Let me rephrase that," Reddick put in. "You will stop fucking up our investigation. One way or the other. Understand?"

Max took a long drink of the coffee. The caffeine was finally kicking in. "Is that a threat?"

"See that phone over there?" Targin said, nodding to the white wall unit. "I could make a call, right now, and have you doing three months on Rikers."

"On what?"

"The mail thing for one," Reddick said. "But that's federal. How about the homicides? You might beat it. But you won't make bail. Not with about three hundred in checking and five-twenty in savings."

Targin moved ominously over to the phone and rested his hand on the receiver. "So, what's it going to be, huh?"

Max smiled, put the mug down. "You know I didn't kill those people, don't you?"

"Doesn't matter," Reddick answered.

"Can you clear me with the NYPD?"

Both shook their heads; the movement was only slightly out of unison. "Can't do it, not on a local level."

"You can make me a confidential informant, offer immunity."

"Guy's been watching too many movies," Reddick said without turning to face his partner.

"There's only one choice," Targin finished. "Step out of the way or go to jail."

"That's it, huh?" Max asked.

Both of them nodded, smiling a little. Then Targin made a slight motion with his head and they began to leave. "Enjoy your coffee, we'll show ourselves out," he said.

As they walked by the door that led up to the servants' quarters, Reddick knocked lightly on it and said, "We're leaving now, you can come out."

Max sat there for a moment, drinking the coffee, and listening for the front door to close. When the heavy door shut, Suze slid out cautiously through the servants' door. She was wearing a big black t-shirt and shivering slightly in the cool kitchen. "Max, I'm afraid," she said, sitting down at the table.

He looked across at her and said, "Me too. Maybe you should lay low for awhile, not come around."

She hugged herself against the chill, her nipples perked up in the cool air. But she was looking down, studying the wood in front of her. "That's what you want? Me not staying over anymore?"

Max went for his coffee, but it was empty. "I don't know," he said. "I don't want you in trouble, you know? I just don't know what's going to happen."

The big man awoke in the early morning. Standing over his bed was a young man with curly red hair holding a vase of flowers. "How you feeling there?" the guy asked, his face somber as his dark suit.

"Not good, want to leave," the big man said, trying to rise up. The doctors had told him the pork from the man on the street had poisoned him and the man at the door had hit him with a baseball bat.

The man in the somber suit smiled, "Not so fast, you shouldn't leave until you're fully recovered."

"You are doctor?" the big man asked.

The young man set the flowers down on the food tray, pulled a tiny eelskin wallet from his pocket, extracted a business card, and handed it to the big man.

The card said that the young man was a lawyer. His name was W. T. Zunick. It said that he was available "24 Hours-A-Day" and listed beeper and fax numbers. On the back of the card was the same information in Spanish. "It's a real tragedy. What happened to you,

I heard all about it," the young man said, then set a briefcase down on the edge of the bed.

The big man, not sure of protocol, handed the card back. "You are lawyer."

The young man waved the card away. "That's right. Me lawyer, you patient. Together we're going to make those bastards pay."

"Pay what?"

The young man opened the briefcase and pulled out a microcassette recorder. "Pay what? Pay a lot. You were assaulted in your own home. My God, in your own home by an employee of the building. Got your skull bashed in with a Louisville slugger. Just the same as if they came into your living room."

"How did you know this?"

The lawyer grinned shyly. How he found out was that he deals with ER health aides, nurses, EMS crews, and even a couple of doctors—residents anyway—in every hospital in the city. A legit call earned them fifty bucks. If the patient took him on, it went up to a hundred. "Are you kidding?" the lawyer said. "It's a tragedy, what happened to you. I mean people are talking about it. When I heard about it, I *had* to come down."

"Who is talking?" the big man asked, worry creeping into his voice.

"Who specifically doesn't matter," the lawyer said. "Now what I want to do is have this doctor I know examine you. He's the best. A specialist."

"Doctors here," the big man said. "Hospital filled with doctors."

"Yeah, but they're not *your doctors*," the lawyer said. "What you want is *your own doctor*. This is America. Everyone's entitled to the doctor of his or her own choosing."

" . . . And my own lawyer?" the big man asked.

"Right!"

The big man's head was pounding beneath the heavy bandages. He was beginning to feel sick again. He scrunched down deep in the bed, pulled the thin sheet and blanket up to his chin. "I cannot afford lawyer," he said.

A smile crossed the lawyer's face. "Now, that's the best part of it," he said. "There's no fee. None at all, unless we're successful. I'd take the case on a contingency basis. That's how sure I am we can win. As a matter of fact, this initial consultation is free."

The big man tilted his head, eyes narrowing. This was indeed a strange place. It was a city of free lawyers. "I do not need lawyer or doctor," he said, then closed his eyes, pretending to sleep.

"Yeah, sure pal," the lawyer said. "I'm leaving my card, in case you change your mind. Better yet, I'll give you a call in a couple of days. We'll talk about it, okay? And remember, that building carries a couple million dollars in insurance."

Sixteen

Julie came bouncing through the door, wearing a black cowl-neck sweater and tight jeans. "Guess who I talked to today?" she sang as she headed for the office to stash her coat.

Max, behind the bar, counting out the bar's bank, two hundred in twenties, tens, fives, and ones, said, "Don't know."

"A Hollywood producer," she called, then re-emerged from the back. "He's interested in the story. He told me we could go into development like in the summer."

Max stopped counting and fitted the drawer back into the register. "What story?"

"The murder," she said, moving cautiously now as she approached the bar.

"Yeah? Which one?"

"I can't tell you his name yet. We're still in the talk stage. He said he read the story with 'great interest,'"

Julie said, easing up on a barstool. "Said he saw me on the news and was moved and impressed. That's how he put it, 'moved *and* impressed.' He just came into town, and he wants to see me."

"I meant which murder?" Max said, coming down to the end of the bar near the waitress station. "Which murder moved and impressed him?" He could see her reflection in the mirror. She was grinning from ear to ear.

"Pat and Peter, of course. Who'd want to make a movie about Todd? Anyway, he wants me to track the case," she said. "You know, until it's solved. Then we can talk some more. He thinks maybe I could play Pat. He's thinking made-for-TV. Cable probably, but maybe network."

It didn't surprise Max. The story made the papers. Some of those guys subscribed to clipping services. Anything with a little bit of sex and violence was up for grabs. Some forgotten reflex gave the story sharp focus in Max's mind. Three or four friends, young women who come to The Big City in pursuit of fame and fortune. One's murdered after the second commercial and the three muddle along toward happiness. One married. One tragic. And the third a success.

"So, what do you think now?" Julie said, leaning victorious across the bar. "I just left his hotel."

Max arched an eyebrow dramatically.

Julie made a face and said, "It's not like that. He's got a suite at the Marriott Marquis. It's bigger than my apartment."

Before Max could answer, the door flew open and stayed open, a blast of chill air filling the bar. Lynn, the mink blowing around her, stood in the doorway like a gunfighter from some CinemaScope western, circa 1952. "You fucking scumbag," she said. She spoke very distinctly, pronouncing each word precisely. The Duke never said that.

Julie, somehow oblivious to the Wicked Witch of the West entrance, cried, "Lynn! Terrific news!" in her best ladies-who-lunch voice.

Lynn let the door close behind her and walked up to the bar, boots echoing across the floor of the empty room. She cut Julie a hard stare and said, "Take fifteen minutes down the street."

"Now?" Julie asked, stunned. "But it's cold out."

"Like right now," Lynn said, keeping her eyes on Max. "Put a coat on."

Julie bit her lip once, then retreated back to the office and grabbed her coat. Lynn didn't say anything until the door had shut behind the waitress. "What kind of complete fucking idiot are you?" she asked through clenched teeth.

"How many kinds are there?" Max asked back, then began moving for the Glenlivet. This was going to be a hard one.

Lynn dug in her bag for a cigarette, found the last one in the pack, and lit it off a red disposable. "Don't play around, not at all," she said, inhaling deeply. "And don't start drinking my liquor, you fucking mutt. I'm pissed off. I'm really fucking pissed off at you."

"What's up?" Max asked, taking a cautious step forward.

"For starters, I got treasury agents nosing around my bank accounts," she said. "You wouldn't happen to know anything about that, would you?"

Max, not wanting to lie, asked, "What'd they want?"

"What do they want, they want information, moron," she shot back through a cloud of smoke.

"I don't think it's anything to do with the bar," Max said.

"Well, tell that to Simon," Lynn answered. "He's got to find that a comfort."

Max knew Simon. He was Lynn's accountant. He came in twice a month to do the on-site books. The guy was as crooked as a corkscrew, but he'd walked Lynn through four IRS and two city audits without breaking a sweat. The guy was unshakable. Did ten years as a city auditor, then jumped to the IRS. He put in something like ten years on the fed payroll before setting up shop for himself. He ate government bean-counters for breakfast, chewed them up, and spit them out. "Simon's nervous?"

"Nervous?" Lynn asked back. "The fucking guy is popping valium like they were Tic-Tacs. He's a basket case."

"Doesn't sound like Simon," Max said. "Maybe he needs to get away for awhile."

Lynn leaned heavily on the bar, warming up to the punch line. "That's what he's afraid of, getting away for awhile."

"Does he know what they're looking for?" Max asked, leaning against the back bar.

"It doesn't matter what they're looking for," Lynn answered, moving in close, right over the bar.

And Max knew she was right. Whatever they were looking for couldn't possibly be as bad as what they might find. Lynn's books were cooked into numerical fictions that would gray the hair and freeze the blood of ten ordinary accountants. Kickbacks from liquor reps, the phony payrolls, the dummy receipts, and phantom contractors were only the scams Max knew about. "Look, let's just stick together on this thing, okay?" Max said, not sure what he meant, much less if it would calm Lynn down.

"Stick together?" Lynn asked, as if she were somehow struck partially deaf. "What are you talking about, 'stick together?' What's this 'stick together' shit? Maybe with Miles you can pull that big asshole buddy routine. But that just don't cut it, ace."

Max toughened up the pitch. Funny, he thought, how in these moments of crisis, he felt strangely detached. "Look, they're fishing, just trying to rattle your cage," he said, coming closer and making eye contact. "It's nothing to do with the bar."

"It better not, you fucking mutt," Lynn said.

A young couple drifted in, wanting to get out of the cold. Lynn turned, catching them in a glance, cigarette dangling in her set mouth, and sent them in a wide arc, nearly plastered to the wall.

"Excuse me," Max said, grateful for the interruption.

He met the couple at the end of the bar, just as they were taking off their coats, probably afraid to leave. He tried to smile when he took their order. They stared back, like they were expecting maybe Rod Serling to step out of the office and explain just what alternative universe they'd walked into.

They ordered Wild Turkey, rocks, and an Absolut, rocks with lime. Lynn kept glowering down at them. The girl, still all dressed up from the office, snuck a few quick looks back at Lynn, then finally settled her eyes down at her hands, folded neatly in her lap. The guy paid for the drinks, grabbed his off the bar, and put down half of it.

When Max walked back to Lynn, she was still staring at the couple. "You didn't proof them," she said, just loud enough for the couple to hear.

"Lynn, they must be twenty-seven," Max answered. "Just quit acting like such a fucking bitch, will you? For once?"

She brought her full attention back to Max and said, "Bitch? Pal, you haven't seen bitch. The only reason you're still behind this bar is 'cause you send the kid postcards. Now, you clear this shit up or I promise you, when I get done, you won't be able to get a job serving hotdogs in the Port Authority."

Max leaned over the bar, getting right in her face. After all, what could she do? "Lynn those guys are federal agents. How should I clear it up, write a congressman?"

Bringing the cigarette away from her mouth in a long mean stream of smoke, she began pointing it directly at Max's left eye. "I don't give a shit," she said, stabbing the Chesterfield forward in the air to drive her point home. "Make these guys go away, now. Before Simon gets an ulcer, and I rip your fucking balls off."

Then she was up and out the door. Max could practically hear the couple let out a sigh of relief. He focused at a spot on the wall across the bar. Outside he heard a blare of horns as Lynn cut the Saab into traffic.

When the door opened again, it was Julie. "Boy, was she ever pissed off," Julie said. "What'd you do now?"

                          *   *   *

They released him from the hospital after two nights.
Now, the big man stood in his sublet apartment waiting
for dark. He had a telephone call to make. Not willing
to risk a call from the apartment phone, he needed to
venture out and use a pay phone.

It was just about noon on the island. Thinking of it,
he could almost smell the sea, the plants, and the rich
volcanic earth. Thinking about home in this cold place
made him ache worse than the thirty stitches across the
back of his head where the doorman had hit with a
baseball bat.

When he grew bored with waiting, he drank a
Budweiser tallboy and watched Oprah. The apartment
was hot and the bandage on his head itched. By the third
beer, the itching became unbearable. First he tried to pull
the gauze and tape off in one piece, like a hat, but it
would not move. Then, very slowly, he picked away at
the tape and unwrapped it. When it was completely off,
he opened another beer and walked into the bathroom to
look at himself in the mirror.

One entire side of his head was shaved from the
center. His scalp looked white. Just above his ear, in
a neat crescent, ran a row of black sutures, extending
nearly the entire length of his head. Between the black
stitching, blood had dried and clotted. The skin was
stained with brownish antiseptic. The doctors told him
to keep the stitching dry until they could take it out in
a week.

Now he had to call home. He had news. That afternoon he had called his free lawyer who said that in two
days, the court would accept his plea bargain of reckless
driving. There would be a fine and "points" on his
license. A small price to pay to be away from New York.

When the sun was completely below the horizon and
the lights of the other apartments were on, the big man
slipped into the too-small shearling coat, eased the knit
cap over his head, and walked out the door.

"Hey, how's it going?" the doorman in the burgundy
uniform asked.

"Good," the big man answered and kept moving.

"Hey, real sorry 'bout the other day. You ain't gonna sue or anything, are you?"

"No."

"Cool. You wouldn't get shit anyway, you know? But don't eat no more of those bum kabobs."

"Yes," the big man answered and kept walking.

He caught a cab on the corner and told the driver to take him to the bus station. He made all of his calls from the bus station—Port Authority—hoping they might be harder to trace.

Traffic was sparse on the ride down, and the big man relaxed a little, watching the neighborhood change from white to black, from rich to poor. From stone to neon. When the driver pulled up between the two sections of the Port Authority, the big man paid him and stepped out on the sidewalk.

This, he thought, was the strangest place of all on this cold island. Fifty or sixty people had built tiny huts from cardboard, wood, and plastic sheets against the walls of the bus station. He did not understand it. With so many buildings, surely there were places for them to live. Even on the poorest islands, people lived better. But here, on the richest one, they lived worse.

Inside, on the main concourse, were kiosks of pay phones. But he avoided these. The announcements on the loudspeaker made the already faint connection even harder to understand. Upstairs, up an escalator, in a deserted section of the station, was a small wall of phones that nobody ever seemed to use. The stores, a bakery and record shop, were closed, offering him some privacy and quiet.

He had two rolls of quarters in his pocket, and when he reached the line of phones, he took both out and broke them open across the edge of the steel shelf. He dialed the operator, who put him through to the international operator, who told him to deposit thirteen dollars.

Even before he had finished feeding the quarters into the slot, he saw the boy. Not more than seventeen, *meauli*, a black guy, in a warm-looking down jacket, he was holding a black shopping bag that said "Saks Fifth Avenue" across its side in red script.

The old man came on the line, and the big man looked away from the kid. Without giving his name, he said, "In a week. I am leaving in a week. Do you understand?"

The old man paused, as if writing it down, and said, "Yes, in a week. Is that all?"

"I was sick and got hit on the head," the big man said.

"Sick and hit on head," the old man repeated. "Okay now?"

"Yes," the big man answered. "Only two days in hospital."

"Two days," the old man said without sympathy.

"Yes," the big man answered.

"Very good," the old man said, then hung up. In a few minutes the old man would relay the news to Australia.

The big man gathered up the rest of the quarters off the shelf and put them in his pocket. Once again he could smell the island. See the sky and the water in his head.

The voice at his side snapped him out of his island reverie. "Hey, hey, yo," the kid was saying.

The big man turned, saw the young man, and said, "Yes."

"Look what I got man, check it," the kid said, then opened the mouth of the shopping bag.

The big man looked down. Inside the shopping bag was a dark gray plastic box and much black wire. "A box," the big man said.

"Damn right a box," the kid said. "Fifty bucks and you be cable-ready."

The big man looked up and met the kid's eyes, which seemed a little crazy. "I do not need a box," he said. He had no way of knowing that cable boxes were hot commodities. Thieves regularly passed up CD players, amplifiers, and televisions in favor of the box. Jewelry and a cable box could be carried out under a coat or in a Saks bag, for instance.

All the rules had changed since crack. The days when cabbies would cut across two lanes of traffic to pick up a dope fiend with a sheet loaded with swag were long gone. The friendly heroin user who would sweat through a cab ride after a boost, then slip the cabbie a ten as a tip were history. A crackhead might just as easily slip a screwdriver into the back of the driver's neck.

"I do not want a box," the big man said and began walking.

But the kid kept pace, dancing along at his elbow. "Man, what are you worried 'bout, huh?"

"Nothing," the big man said.

"Look, look, check this, I got my partner here," the kid said. "Used to work for a cable company. He hook you up good."

Just ahead of them, another boy, this one white, with blond greasy hair down to his shoulders, stepped out from a bank of pay phones. The white kid was pale, with bad skin. He was wearing a ripped black leather jacket with a filthy t-shirt under it.

The big man kept walking, eyes straight ahead, as the two teenagers walked on either side. With both of them talking, he had lost his thoughts and made a left turn through a door marked EXIT. The stairway ahead was closed, barricaded with a folding metal gate.

"What, you don't need a box, man?" the white one was saying. "I'll hook it up fine. Get you HBO, Disney, Cinemax, whatever the fuck you want, man."

"Watch yourself a little MTV, man's gotta want his motherfucking MTV," the black one said.

"Guns-and-fucking-Roses, man," the white one added. "Madonna. Little Axl action."

The big man turned, saw the two boys blocking his way to the door. They had seemed small and harmless out on the lobby of the bus station. Now, they still seemed small, but not harmless. They were like wood rats. Nervous. Trapped. "No box," the big man said. "No Disney. No MTV."

"That was your last fucking chance," the black one said, then cast a look over to his partner.

"Coulda been rocking out, man," the white boy said, rolling his shoulders as he moved forward. There was a knife in his hand. The blade was at least six inches and curved.

"Now, give me the motherfucking watch," the black one ordered, moving in. There was a screwdriver in his hand. It was big, the kind that could open a locked door. Even in the dull light of the stairway, he could see that the end had been ground down, sharpened.

"And the wallet, man," the white one said.

"My watch?" the big man asked, holding his wrist out to display the gold Rolex President with thick gold links.

"He don't mean my fucking watch," the white one said.

As the big man reached over to unfasten his watch, he moved slightly to his left, so that he was standing sideways facing the white one. Then, as his fingers touched the clasp, he moved out suddenly with his right hand, and grunted, "*Aitae!*"

The white kid, startled, brought the knife up, thinking the guy was a martial arts expert, though what he said translated as "eat shit."

The big man grabbed the knife hand just beneath the frayed cuff of the jacket, his fingers easily meeting around the bony wrist, and pulled down as he brought his left hand up, hard. The heel of his hand smashed into the white kid's face, flattening his nose beneath the force of the blow. He felt the cartilage flatten and snap like a wet vine. The skin beneath his palm suddenly went limp as he gave his meaty hand a quick half-twist, grinding the ruined nose against the kid's face. The knife clattered to the floor. The big man's coat ripped, up under the arm.

As the big man released the knife hand and turned, he saw the other kid lunging with the screwdriver. He knew then that he shouldn't have turned. The sharpened blade of the screwdriver sank deep into his thigh. The pain shot through him in a hot jolt as the flattened head of the stainless shaft connected with bone.

The pain brought a bass cry from the big man's mouth and brought him all the way around. The kid withdrew the screwdriver and stabbed out again. This time he hit him square in the stomach, the bloodied shaft sinking nearly to the plastic handle and driving the big man against the folding gate.

"Motherfucker," the kid said, but before he could pull the screwdriver back, the big man struck out with both hands. Making them into cups, he clapped them together on either side of the kid's head.

For an instant, the only thing that held the kid up was the big man's hands. His grip on the screwdriver relaxed as his eyes went unfocused. The world had gone silent for him forever.

The white kid staggered to his feet, both hands up to his face to stop the blood and the pain. The black kid took an unbalanced step back, his eyes wild with panic as his partner pulled him by the coat.

The last thing the big man could remember seeing, as he slumped against the gate, was both kids moving hunched and limping through the door.

They found him twenty minutes later, in a small pool of blood. Next to him was a Saks Fifth Avenue shopping bag and sticking out of his stomach was the Stanley Tool screwdriver.

Seventeen

It was another one of those mean, gray days. An icy rain had fallen during the night and the clouds still hung threateningly in the sky as the temperature dropped.

Suze sat across the table from Max, drinking her coffee, munching wheat toast, and looking over notes for a class. He sat there studying her, thinking, is this it, sitting across a table not talking?

"Hey, Suze?"

"Yeah," she answered, distracted.

"What're you studying for?"

She didn't look up. "Psych. Got a quiz."

"Yeah, well just say it's all about sex and you'll ace it."

She lifted her head slightly, brushing a strand of hair out of her eyes. "That's Freud, nobody believes in Freud anymore."

She could have been talking about Santa or the Easter Bunny. "Yeah?" Max asked, interested. "What do they believe in?"

"Chemistry," she said. "It's all chemistry and electricity. Peptides, neural impulses, proteins. You know, we're just sacks of chemicals. Memory, personality, fear, everything."

Now, there's cheery news, Max thought, and took another sip of coffee. Why not? Everything's reduced, finally. For Miles and Todd, it was pussy. For Lynn, money. Now everything is rendered down to the essentials.

And lately, he'd only seen Suze late at night and when he got up. Somehow over the last few months they'd reduced the relationship to bed, breakfast, and a few brief appointments during the day, mostly lunch.

Just stripped the thing down to essentials. Instinct and habit. Maybe that's when it falls apart, he mused, when there's nothing left.

"Max, anything else?" she asked, only slightly annoyed.

Max brought himself back to earth, realizing she was still staring up, waiting for him to ask a question or signal that it was okay to get back to the notebook. "Just curious," he said, and took another drink of coffee. Maybe he should have taken a weekend away from the city with her.

She turned her head back down to the notes. Twenty minutes later, she was kissing him lightly on the head and hurrying out the door.

Max got up, poured himself another cup of coffee from the Braun, and went back to the table. It was still early; he had three or four hours to kill. On the floor by Suze's chair was one of those women's magazines. As far as he knew, those magazines were her sole remaining vice. She read eight or ten of the things a month. Max picked it up and started leafing through it.

Bunch of ads for makeup, more for clothing. Six pages of color photos featuring negligees that promised to "Put The Sizzle Back In The Bedroom."

All pussy wears out, Miles had said. Well, someone was making a buck off the fear.

Halfway through the magazine was a quiz, "Test Your Love Quotient: A Couple's Compatibility Guide For Today . . . And Tomorrow." Gratefully, she hadn't taken the multiple-choice test.

Keeping score in his head, Max began answering the questions. When he turned the magazine upside down for the answers, he calculated his total a half dozen points into the "Danger Zone."

Fuck it, he thought. *Lynn's going to can me. The feds are going to throw me in jail. And I'm reading compatibility tests.*

There was a number on top of the loan application, five digits and a bunch of writing in Spanish. But the more Max looked at it, the less it looked like Spanish and more like gibberish. The guy, Peter Marotte, could have just made up a language to stick at the top of the application. Something that looked foreign.

Sitting in a coffee shop at noon, he tried pronouncing it to see if he recognized the accent. When he left the coffee shop, he headed downtown to the Berlitz office in Rockefeller Center. The woman at the reception desk explained that he was in the wrong place. Their translation center was downtown. Max insisted he just wanted to know what it was, not to have it translated. She vanished into the back office with the letter-for-letter transcription that Max had made. Ten minutes later she came back. Sorry, don't know it. Try downtown.

He'd try the UN first, save the subway ride. Walking into the main lobby, he approached a guard. The guard sent him to information. Information called up to the interpreter services.

The young man in a blue blazer at the desk frowned, read the words on the paper letter for letter, nodded, then spoke a few hurried words in French.

"So, what is it?" Max asked, when the guy handed him the slip of paper back.

"It's pidgin," the guy said. "We can't be certain of the dialect."

"Pigeon?" Max asked back, not sure if the guy was putting him on out of some sadistic need or what.

But the guy was bright. "Not like the bird," he explained, more politely than he needed to. "Pidgin. P-I-D-G-I-N. Mix of English, French, Melanesian," he said.

"Who speaks it?"

"South Seas," the guy said. "Apparently there's something like three or four hundred dialects. This note pertains to a bank somewhere."

The phone rang in a bar in Queens. The bartender picked it up and said, "Yeah?"

Two men sitting at a back table watched as the bartender came around the bar. When he approached the back table, he leaned down low and whispered something into one of the men's ears.

A few minutes after the bartender spoke to him, the man lifted himself up from the chair and walked out into the cold midday air. He walked the three blocks briskly, hands jammed into the pockets of a tweed overcoat, to a pay phone at the base of an elevated subway. Then he took out two dollars in change and dialed a number in Jersey.

When the phone was picked up on the other end there was silence, except for a short raspy breath. He said, "It's me."

"There's a problem," a voice said. It was the voice of an old man.

"Yeah?"

"I'll send someone out."

"I'll be here."

"Not at the new place?" the old man asked, wanting to be certain.

"Naw, I'll be at the old place."

"Good. I never liked that new joint much."

"Okay, good."

"Tonight."

And then the man hung up. It was the longest conversation he'd ever had with the old man. He wondered if his stock was rising. After all, the way he arranged to bring in the shooter and take care of Bonanza, the little thieving prick, was pretty slick.

EiGHTEEN

The big man would be out of the hospital in a few days. The screwdriver had punctured a portion of small intestine, which the doctors at St. Clare's had expertly resectioned. The detectives had been around twice, each time asking if he had seen his assailants. The second time they came, they showed him pictures of the two boys who tried to rob him. Both were treated and released from the same hospital. Luckily, he had wiped any fingerprints from the screwdriver and knife. He did not want to go to court.

As he lay in bed, listening to the tiny television of the man next to him, he thought of the two boys. They were amateurs in his opinion. If they had wanted to kill him, it would have been easy enough. Push the screwdriver up under the ribs and into the heart. Instead, they had stabbed it straight in. Amateurs. The entire city was filled with those who did not know their own trades.

"Yo, man," the guy in the next bed said. "Should see the shit they got on 'Donahue' today." The man was Spanish and enormous. Four hundred pounds, at least. There were many things wrong with him. Before he became sick, he had a profitable business selling drugs. Now, he could no longer keep up with his business.

The big man, feeling groggy from his two o'clock medication, rolled over toward the curtained partition, dragging the IV line with him. "Don't look at 'Donahue,' " he said, getting comfortable. "Like 'Oprah' better."

"I hear you, but Oprah ain't got shit on," the voice said. "Single mothers again. Phil's talking some shit with this guy who cut off his dick 'cause he wanted to be a woman. Now wants to be a man again. Suing the doctors that did it. That's some wacky shit."

The big man closed his eyes, listening to the drone of the talk show next to him. "Doctors can't put it back?"

"Man, those things don't grow on trees. You got a cigarette?"

"Don't smoke," the big man said.

"That figures," his roommate answered.

As the big man began to drift off to sleep, he heard Donahue saying "My good man, this is America, land of the free . . ."

"And home of the motherfucking dickless," the roommate finished with a laugh.

*   *   *

Max didn't even want to think of the phone bill. It took him most of the early evening to get in touch with the bank in the South Seas. The numbers at the top of the loan application were five digits and didn't include a country code. When the language problem finally reached a dead end, he gave up and called through a phone company translator. He was leaving a paper trail a mile wide for the treasury agents.

The translator was very professional and spoke with a slight Oriental accent. He asked her to inquire about a loan he applied for. When she came back asking who exactly he was, he said that he was from New York.

"Sir, the bank representative would like your name," the translator said.

"Just tell her I'm from New York," Max answered.

"Sir, the bank representative would like to know the nature of the loan."

"It was a personal loan."

"Sir, the bank representative would like to know when and how you applied."

"I saw their ad in the newspaper a couple of weeks ago."

"Sir, the bank representative said that they do not advertise in North American papers."

"Tell her it was through their loan coordinator or whatever you call it. The ad was in the paper."

"Sir, she has stated that they do not have any personnel or authorized intermediaries in North America. She would also like your name and address to further pursue the matter."

Max hung up.

As he stood there behind the bar, he thought of what Dwayne had told him about Marotte. Specifically, he was thinking of the 'round-the-world vacation. Maybe Marotte had mixed a little business in there along the way. Picked up some loan applications from banks and used them for the scam. If anybody actually wondered if the banks existed, they could look them up in some directory. And that was the beauty of it, Max realized.

The bank was so far away, it would take months before
anything happened through the mail. All the attention
would be on the bank. In the meantime, Marotte would
have changed mail-drops and the company's name. And,
most people, he reasoned, would write off the two hundred. Chalk it up to experience and move on.

Most people. Probably somebody didn't move on and
came after Marotte. If he could hand the treasury suits
a murder and the NYPD a bank scam *and* a murder
motive, they would maybe turn the heat down a notch,
maybe even forget about him. And Lynn would get off
his back.

Delbert Kray did what he swore he wouldn't do. He
drove to Jersey to see the dead girl's parents. They were
twice removed, but maybe they'd know something. And
a chance at someone who knew something was better
than what he had, which was not a fucking thing.

What he had was a dead guy with no paper trail. Even
the Medical Information Bureau didn't have anything
on Marotte. The guy didn't even carry health insurance
for the last five years, which is where the MIB got
most of its information. But the waitress had paper;
she was covered under her father's policy. Listed her
address in Jersey, probably to stay on the policy. In
the last five years she was treated for vaginitis ten or
twelve times, though all that meant was that she had
regular checkups and the doctor wanted to get paid.
Putting that down meant insurance would pick up the
tab.

And she was spending on credit like crazy, a green
Amex with five grand a month charged to it and a
Visa from some bank in Delaware with another couple
grand a month on that one. Most of the charges were
from some uptown bar called Todd's Joint. She was banging the plastic pretty good. For a waitress who maybe,
if she was lucky, took home twelve or thirteen hundred
a month, she was spending like a surgeon's wife. And
max-paying the cards—clearing the balance out every
month.

But Kray figured that it was explainable. The last three bills showed rooms and restaurants at three A.C. casinos. Just looking at the Xeroxed copies of the bills made him start humming "Everything Old Is New Again." Wiseguys were washing their money that way twenty-five years ago in Vegas. Going into a casino and buying big-time chips, then cashing them out a few days later and calling them winnings with a check from a casino to prove it. Probably the dopers were doing it now, too.

She might have been a pro; maybe somebody turned her out, but Kray didn't think so. What he thought was that she was fronting for somebody, probably her boyfriend. The moves she was making were like inviting the IRS in. All of it amateur action. If she wasn't already dead, then she'd be hanging in the wind a year down the road.

As he eased the Fury into the flow of traffic for the Lincoln Tunnel, he reached on the seat beside him and found the Joey Bishop CD. Joey Bishop always cracked him up, and as it was, he could use a few laughs. At least.

He was sorry the moment he pulled into the driveway and blocked the handicapped van. The house wasn't much to look at. A tiny prefab on a fifty by a hundred lot. Twenty years ago you could buy it for twenty. Today maybe it would bring seventy-five; ninety, if you were lucky.

Kray opened the door and slid his thick legs out. He wouldn't bother with his coat. Something about a guy standing on your stoop shivering always made them open the door.

He rang the bell twice, and the door opened a crack. For a second, Kray didn't see anyone, then down at waist level, he saw the guy in the wheelchair.

"Yeah?" the guy asked.

"I'm investigating the death of your daughter," Kray said. That was always the best approach. Never say who exactly you were until they asked specifically. Let them think you were a cop, at least until you got inside.

"You're not a cop," the guy said. It wasn't a question.

Kray lost some of his cop posture. "No, I'm an investigator with the insurance company." No law against saying that.

"Cops don't dress that shitty," the guy said, pleased with himself. Kray could see now that the guy was around forty-five, maybe a little older. And not fat, like you'd think a guy in a wheelchair would be, but skinny. And with a face that had plenty of character on it. A guy who worked for a living before life sat him down in a chair. He was wearing khakis and a light summer shirt beneath a thick cardigan, which meant he didn't get out too much in the winter, needed to count pennies on the heating bills, and his wife knitted.

"May I come in?" Kray asked, figuring he had a shot. Maybe the guy was lonely.

The guy gave him a quick once-over and said, "Yeah, why not?" Then he opened the door and wheeled back. "Don't let all the heat out. Cost a fortune to heat this place."

Kray stepped in and shut the door. It took him about six seconds to size the place up and put a price on it. Bookcase full of *Reader's Digest* condensed. Another halfway filled with *National Geographic* and thick paperback romances. Hummel figures over the fireplace along with pictures of the girl. Furniture that was bought on time maybe fifteen, eighteen years ago. More framed pictures of the girl scattered around the end tables, and across the coffee table. It was neat and clean, but you could burn the joint to the ground and not collect more than ten grand for the furnishings without lying.

"So, what do you want?" the guy in the wheelchair said, positioning himself dead center in the room.

"May I sit down?" Kray asked.

"Why not, I'm sitting," the guy answered without much enthusiasm.

Just by the guy's timing, Kray could tell it was a line he'd used like ten or twenty thousand times before it had gone stale, if it was ever fresh. That's what the pros had, timing and the talent of keeping it fresh. Youngman could do the "Take my wife . . ." bit from now 'til they ice-skated in hell and it'd still sound fresh.

Kray gave a small appreciative smile at the joke and sat on the couch. "Like I said, I'm investigating the unfortunate murder of your daughter and Mr. Marotte. If there's anything you can tell me about him . . ."

"You mean, you're investigating that asshole Marotte, not my daughter. But then, she didn't have any life insurance, did she?"

Delbert smiled again. "Well, yes. If there's anything you can tell me about him . . ."

"He was a prick," the guy said. "I knew he was a prick the first time he showed up. The way he looked down on us."

Delbert forced the smile back down. The guy's delivery was better when he wasn't trying. "Looked down on you, how?"

The guy wheeled in closer, leaning forward slightly as his hands worked at the chrome wheels. "Sneering, like he'd just smelled shit," the guy said. "Like he was too good for us. Like that."

"Can you remember anything else?" Delbert asked. "What he was doing, for a living?"

"Nothing honest," the guy said, coasting in even closer.

Delbert felt a slight tremor of excitement. The trail was getting warm. "You suspect he was involved in something illegal?"

"Or close," the guy said, twisting his mouth around like he smelled something bad.

"How close do you think?"

"Real close. Right up to the line," the guy said. "I want to show you something. I'll show you how close."

Then the guy was gone, wheeling like a maniac into the back of the house. Delbert sat there listening to the tick of a cheap carriage clock in the dining room, smelling coffee that was brewing somewhere.

When the guy returned, he had a FedEx tyvek envelope in his lap. "This is how close," he said, wheeling up to Delbert and tossing the envelope over with one hand.

Kray caught the thing and reached a hand tentatively inside, not knowing what he'd be pulling out. When his hand came out, it was holding a fat bound folder whose covers were fancy embossed stock.

"Know what that is?" the guy asked, challenging Delbert.

Kray read the cover. It was a private placement memorandum for an oil well in Texas. A limited partnership. It was, he knew, a license to steal.

"That's a hundred thousand dollars you're holding there," the guy said.

Kray skimmed through the pages. He didn't doubt it. He'd seen these before. And this one was a classic—bar charts, column charts and columns of numerals, and geologists' reports.

The whole thing looked official as hell, right down to the name of the Dallas law firm that put it together. If Kray didn't know better, he would almost say it was legit. But he did know what it was. And he knew the way the deal worked.

The way it worked was out of a boiler room, with college kids earning minimum wage cold-calling from lists of big-money people, like purchasers of private planes, for instance. They shuffled through the wealthiest one percent of the population with one mil in assets or an annual income of two hundred grand who were willing to take a chance on a joint venture.

When the callers finally found qualified leads, they'd put them through to one of the two dozen vice presidents. And then the pitch would begin. Oil wells! Two-hundred-percent return on investment! "Was out there on site the other day and I'll tell you that soil was all but muddy with oil, sank ankle-deep in my Tony Lamas." They always talked like that, with pictures. Sometimes they even sent them pictures—Polaroids of a drilling tower against a big, blue-sky Texas landscape. And even the Polaroids were faked. Pictures of pictures. The Polaroid camera mounted to a stand above a professional eight by ten, just a little tilted to make it look hand-held. It was easier that way; you could run off forty or fifty without leaving the office.

What they got was shares in a lease for a well that had been tapped out since the fifties. Start them off small, ten or fifteen to drill and test. Then come back with good news and pop them for another twenty thousand. Thirty-two units to a well at thirty grand a pop. For the big guys—the ones with money—it's maybe make a trip down to Texas, where their new best-buddy veep meets them at the airport in a limo, gets them laid, buys them a hundred-dollar hat and a steak dinner. Worst thing that happens to them is a hundred-percent write-off. But little guys that stumble into it get burned and it's the end of the world when that last telephone call comes.

"Marotte sold this to you?" Kray asked, slipping it back into the envelope and noting the name on the return, "Flying Eagle Enterprises, Ltd."

"Sold it to me," the guy said, sadly. "Took most of what I got for the car accident that put me here."

Kray handed the envelope back, thinking that the dead guy, Marotte, was a real asshole. "He sold this to you when he was living with your daughter?"

"No, that's how they met," the guy said. "She went down to see if she could do anything. Get the money back. She came back with him. Not a real fucking bargain, huh?"

Kray could picture it. The crippled guy must have gotten on a list with the insurance money. Maybe he bought something big or maybe these guys were going after insurance awards now.

The girl goes down there to Texas, she's maybe twenty-one or twenty-two and outraged. Somebody's ripped off her crippled dad. So, she starts knocking on doors. Better Business Bureau. State Attorney General. Chamber of Commerce. Maybe she even sees a couple of lawyers. Chances are she cried more than a little when everyone told her "Sorry, kid." Finally, she goes up to the offices. And there's Peter Marotte. If he's doing well, then he's wearing Armani, drinking Dom, and leasing a nice house. Maybe even driving a leased Porsche.

"Did he ever return any of the money?" Kray asked.

"Three thousand is all," the guy said. "Then the SEC closed them down."

And Kray could picture that too, the way the feds swarm in and tape everything, even the phones. That's why Marotte left Texas and came home to New York. And that's how he got the girl. He could have said they'd pay back her father together. Maybe she saw the light—crime does pay.

"You wouldn't happen to know what he was into a little more recently, would you?" Kray asked.

"Said he'd gone into business," the crippled guy answered. "Loan brokering."

"Loan brokering?" Kray asked. "You mean like home equity deals? Second mortgages?"

"Yeah, like that, I guess."

"Wouldn't remember the company, would you?"

"Never told me," the crippled guy said. "Know who might know?"

Kray shrugged. Smiled. Just a working Joe trying to get through a day's work and grateful as hell for any help.

"This bartender my wife saw," the guy said.

"Yeah?" Come on pal, just a little help here and I can get the fuck out of Jersey.

"Helped my wife out. When she needed to get Pat's things out of the apartment," the guy said. "Has contacts with the police department or something."

"You know where he works?" Kray asked, leaning slightly forward now. "The bar?"

"Joint in Manhattan," came the answer. "Upper East Side. Wait a sec and I'll get the name."

"Sure, take your time," Kray offered, smiling.

NINETEEN

Max found Pete and the boys sitting around a pile of papers, coffee cups, and half-eaten danish at the coffee shop. Pete was reading *Variety*, the others were swapping sections of *Newsday* and the *Times*. Shit, it's like a still life, Max thought, except for positions. This time Pete was facing the door.

"How's it going?" Max asked.

Pete stared up from the paper, his eyes focusing over the top of his half-glasses, then stood up.

"What's up?" Max said.

The two others buried their heads deeper, eyes fixed on newsprint, not reading, just staring.

"Step into my office," Pete said, then led Max back out the door. "A little walk talk."

When they were outside, Pete moved in close. He wasn't wearing a coat. It was maybe twenty degrees, but he didn't look cold. He was too scared or pissed off, or both, to be cold. "It's about those kids that were killed," he said.

"Yeah, that's what I need to talk to you about."

Pete put a hand out, fingers together; he pressed it right against Max's chest. "You don't need to do any more talking," he said, his voice serious, lips barely moving. "You need to listen. No more fucking around, kid."

"I got a lead on the thing," Max said. "I need you to pass it along."

Pete moved the hand from Max's chest to his shoulder. His fingers came together hard, even through the coat Max felt the pain. "Pass it to who, huh? You know what the fuck you stepped into?"

"You know, to your pals," Max said, but with draining

enthusiasm. "The detectives on the case. It'll take some of the heat off me."

"There is no fucking case," Pete said. "Do you hear me? No fucking case."

"What about the detectives that came around?"

Pete's fingers closed tighter. "Listen to me," he said, coming in close. "There is no case because the feds came in. Shut down the whole NYPD investigation."

"Shit."

"Shit is right," Pete answered. "You want to tell someone, tell it to the feds. See how much they listen to your bullshit."

"So, what is it I do, huh?" Max asked. "Just wait around for them to come with a warrant?"

Pete gave a nervous glance over his shoulder, into the diner. "Look, if it were me, I'll tell you what I'd do," he said. "Pack up and leave for a couple of months. Go out to L.A. Get some sun, call agents. Do the thing out there. You didn't do it, so you got nothing to worry about but what number sun block to use."

"I can't," Max said. "I make a move I lose the apartment, the job. The whole thing. It doesn't matter anyway because I don't have the money."

Pete let his hand drop in an attitude of pure disgust. "Okay, just stay out of the feds' way, lay low."

Max looked up and down the avenue. Traffic was light, almost no one on the sidewalk. "They've already been around."

"FBI?" Pete asked.

"No, treasury guys, looked like lawyers or something."

"Jesus," Pete said, visibly awed.

"Is that worse?"

"I don't know," Pete answered. "What's worse than murder? That's what it's gotta be, to get a murder investigation killed. A double murder investigation."

And Max thought, a triple, if you count Todd.

"Somebody called in some favors, you know?" Pete said.

"Money?" Max tried. "That's what they handle, money, right?"

"Serious fucking money," Pete said. "That's what we're talking about, some serious fucking money. Not some waitress doubling up on credit card slips for the extra tips."

"Like a couple hundred thousand?"

Pete blew on his hands, warming them. "Like maybe a couple mil, just to think about it. Just for somebody in D.C. to *think* of making a call."

The big man was tired of bed. Tired of listening to the tiny television that the guy in his room played from morning until night. Tomorrow they were releasing him. But right now, he needed to get up.

Sliding his legs over the bed, the big man felt a sharp pain in his leg and where his abdominal muscles had been sutured. His entire midsection ached, but he fought the pain and lowered his feet gingerly to the cold floor. When he finally managed to get up, he was surprised that he walked like an old man, hunched over.

"Yo, you should check out the action on 'Magnum' today," the guy shouted from behind the curtain. "That's like your people, right? All that Hawaiian Don Ho shit."

"Going for walk," the big man said.

"Yeah, don't get lost, huh?"

"No," he answered. Then, using the IV stand for support, he began shuffling out the door.

Five minutes later, two men entered the room. Both wore driving gloves, which was not unusual given the cold weather. One of them was carrying a large potted plant in a metal vase. It was important that the vase was metal, in case they happened to pass a metal detector. Inside the vase, under the styrofoam base, was a .25-caliber Raven semiautomatic. A piece-of-shit gun that sold for maybe eighty bucks. But it was a street piece, the kind you could throw down for the cops to find and have them think dope dealers.

The first guy nodded and the second closed the door. It took the first guy about three seconds to empty the flowers and extract the styrofoam base, which had been hollowed out and the silencer inserted. The tiny gun slipped neatly out from the styrofoam.

The first guy, whose name was Anthony, had opted for a gun. Get too slick, maybe use an injection, and the police clock you for a pro. Use a piece-of-shit gun that looks like it came up from Virginia on a bus, and it's just another drug hit.

From behind the curtained bed, the two men heard the television. A syndicated rerun of "Magnum, P.I." "And how are we feeling today," the guy with the gun, Anthony, said, edging open the curtain with one hand.

Inside, on the bed, a fat man slept. The boys were right, he looked Spanish. Anthony held the gun six inches from the guy's chest and fired three times. The gun made a popping sound, not the "phppt" noise of television suppressors.

The guy shot bolt upright, eyes wide open, like he had springs on his back.

Anthony shot him twice more in the chest and that laid him out.

"Come on, hurry up, willya," the second guy at the door said.

"Just finishing now," Anthony replied, unscrewing the silencer, as he stepped back through the curtain. He'd drop the piece in the trash on the way out. The silencer, which was aluminum, he'd stomp down later and drop somewhere in Brooklyn.

Then the door opened, slowly at first, then wider. The two men froze. An IV stand came into view, creaking through the open door on wobbly wheels. Then a foot in a hospital slipper, then another foot.

Anthony moved forward, the silencer and gun already concealed in his pocket. If they moved fast enough, the guy wouldn't remember a thing.

"This is my room," the big guy with the IV stand said.

The guy was one of the biggest individuals Anthony had ever seen. And the instant he spoke, Anthony knew he'd shot the wrong man.

The big man sized up the situation immediately. Gunshots were coming from the tiny television; the air smelled unmistakably of cordite. "You leaving now?" the big man asked.

"Yeah, we was just going," the guy who wasn't Anthony said.

The big man held the door open and shuffled aside, bringing the IV stand with him.

"See youse," Anthony said, moving toward the door.

"Yes," the big man replied.

That's when the other guy, who wasn't Anthony, slammed the door shut. Anthony took a second, and managed to pull the gun from his pocket. But a second was all the big man needed. He lifted the IV stand and swung, first one way, then the other. He could feel the sutures tear and the pain shoot through him. Then the heavy base of the stand connected, hitting one of them in the jaw and shattering it, and grazing the other one's wrist, knocking the gun from his hand.

Both the big man and Anthony moved for the gun, which had skidded under the room's sole chair. With his first step, the big man knew he wouldn't make it. The guy was just too fast. Before he could reach the chair, the guy had reached it and was kneeling to retrieve the gun. The other one, with the shattered jaw, was moving now, swinging.

The first punch hit the big man solid on the back. The second one was to the kidneys and sent him doubling over in pain.

The one with the gun was turning now, coming up from the floor. He fired once, hitting the big man in the arm, the unsilenced blast loud in the small room. The big man felt the pain sear through his upper arm. The bullet scorched through the flesh before exiting and striking the man with the broken jaw in the throat, sending him to the floor.

When the guy fired again, the gun clicked on empty.

The big man fell, letting gravity carry his considerable weight downward, where he landed on the sprawled man with the gun, crushing most of his ribs.

TWENTY

The big man's arm hurt badly, though in truth the wound was not serious. Nothing more than a burn. But his leg still pained him. And everywhere were policemen. They asked him many, many questions about the man he shared the room with. It took him a long time, but he came to realize that the policemen believed the men wanted to kill the roommate and not him. The big man wanted to believe that as well, though he knew it to be untrue. What he believed was that the dark forces of this cold, crowded, stone island wanted to take him apart.

Something was terribly wrong. His luck had turned against him in some way that he could not imagine. Even if he escaped the bad luck of this island, he could not go back home. Ever.

Now, with most of his money gone, he would need to get more. He would sell the watch. Early in the morning, while the policeman slept outside his door, he dressed carefully and shuffled into the hall. The pain was everywhere. His stomach, his arm, his leg, his head, they all hurt.

Walking down a stairway, he exited by a pair of large, green dumpsters, then walked east to Fifth Avenue. The watch was worth ten thousand American dollars. That would be enough. Perhaps more than enough to fly to San Francisco, California, and purchase a green card and naturalization papers as a cousin he had never seen had done. If he was lucky, after a few months he would move on to one of the Hawaiian islands.

It seemed to him that he walked for a long time. Finally he asked a man where he could find a jewelry store. Tiffany's, the man said, was just a few blocks up the street.

When he found the store, he saw that it looked like a bank. Yes, this is what he needed. He entered through the revolving doors and asked to see the watch man. A small, bony woman with pale skin, lipstick the color of blood, and hair that looked like graying black stone, pointed to the wall on the right. He shuffled over, feeling the eyes of the men in blue blazers on him.

It took him a long time to reach the glass counter. When he finally made it, he was sweating. His arm and stomach hurt more. A young man, also skinny, approached without smiling.

The big man removed his hat, revealing the shaved portion of head and the thick black sutures. "I would like to sell watch," the big man said, leaning heavily on the counter, sweat now stinging his eyes as he unfastened the clasp of the Rolex.

"Well, sir," the young man answered, hesitantly taking the watch, though paying more attention to the hospital wristband fastened to the big man's wrist. Two men in blue blazers hovered nearby, then edged closer.

"I would like to sell," the big man said again.

The young man glanced at the guards, then at the watch, expecting yet another counterfeit. He would look at it politely and dismiss the man quickly. The guards, retired cops, would only cause a scene. Then he noticed the second hand. The way it paused and appeared to tick back with each beat told him it was genuine.

When the young man took the watch in his hand, he knew it was genuine by its weight and by the way the case was filed down at the point where the bracelet joined it and where the serial number had once been. He raised an eyebrow significantly toward the security guards, and said, "Yes sir, just a moment, please." Then he vanished into the back room.

The big man supported himself on the glass, staring down at a display of other watches. And suddenly it seemed that the young man was gone for a very long time. When the big man looked up again, a young woman was passing by, holding a dark blue velvet cushion with a diamond necklace on it. "I came to sell my watch," the big man said. "Boy has been gone long time."

The young woman did not look up; rather, she paused briefly. "He's probably checking the serial number," she said curtly. "A security procedure in estate purchases."

The explanation sent a jolt through the big man that brought him upright. The watch had no serial number. It had been removed long ago, when the watch was first stolen from a New Zealander on holiday who made the mistake of wandering drunk around Pago Pago Harbor.

He was about to leave when the young man returned. But he was not carrying the watch. "Sir, if you'll follow me," he began.

But already the big man was moving, walking backwards with upraised palms. "I do not feel good," he began to say, then turned, pulling the knit cap back on.

"Stop him!" the young man said in a voice that was oddly calm and low. "Stop him immediately."

Two hands grabbed the big man by the arms, one of them pressing painfully against the wound. He shook off the hand of one guard violently, as the other guard moved in front of him. With his good arm, he thrust out, striking the man on the chin with the heel of his hand and sending him staggering backwards against a case. A small, polite gasp from the onlookers exploded around him as the pain shot through his stomach and arm.

Two more guards were coming toward him now as the big man staggered for the door. When he saw he could not move past them, he stuck his good hand into his pocket and said, "I have gun."

The two men in blue blazers froze, then parted to let him through; another held the door to the side of the revolving doors open for him. When he reached the street, he staggered forward, turned west down Fifty-seventh, and vanished into the crowd as best he could.

Max, still shaken from his talk with Pete, was standing behind the bar at opening time and pushing down the urge for a Glenlivet by talking old times with a former model named Dawn.

She hit it big in the early eighties with the kind of sophisticated, monied look that the exclusive stores and designers were using for a few years. Her agency booked her like crazy on the New York, Paris, Milan circuit. Print ads, catalogs, runway work, and a few television spots kept her in constant motion.

When the dust settled, she had something like a half mil in the bank. She married briefly, divorced, and got the co-op on the West Side. Now she was thirty-one or two, still moisturized like it was a religion, and worked sporadically, background in commercials, voice-overs, and a few ads. Anything that took five days or less, offered residuals, and was shot on film stock, which meant national spots. Odd to think about it, she was playing mommies now. But they were using fourteen and fifteen-year-olds made up to look like twenty-five, so anything was possible.

Maybe she worked three weeks out of the year. But that was enough to pay maintenance on the co-op and for a time-share in Vail and another in Maui. She was an early-evening semiregular who came in for nostalgia like twice a month.

"The eighties were a dangerous decade," she said. "All my friends, it's like they self-destructed."

Max came forward, pulled the soda gun out, splashed some club soda on the bar, and began wiping it down with a bar rag. Got time to lean, got time to clean, as they say. "Yeah?"

She took a sip from her drink, Campari and soda, and looked up. "Nothing personal, you know," she said. "It was just all the coke. Like people went crazy or something. It was a dangerous time to have money."

"You should have tried it broke," Max said, tossing the bar rag across the cooler.

She shook her head slightly, banishing the idea. Then took another sip.

"So, what was your secret?" Max asked.

Dawn smiled and made a little motion with her head. "You know, when I first started in the business, my agent said, 'It doesn't last. Five or six years is all you have, if

you're lucky. Make the most of it. And if you're thinking
about a movie career, your chances are better trying to
be an astronaut.' "

"They tell that to everyone," Max said.

She took another sip. "But I was nineteen, you know,
new in town. I believed her. And she was right. Only I
got seven years, almost eight, out of it."

Max took her glass and refilled it. "You should send
her a card, like a thank you," he joked, returning the
glass.

"I would," Dawn answered. "Except she developed a
problem with her nose. Started basing, then went out to
L.A. to clear it up and I never heard from her again."

A little while later, Dawn was out the door on her
way to a date, when the fat guy walked in.

Max took one look at the guy and wondered what
the fuck kind of night is this gonna be? The guy was
wearing a dark-blue polyester suit, baby-blue shirt, wide
tie, and gray London Fog topcoat. And all of it about
four sizes too small. He looked like an honest Health
Department inspector, which meant a broke one.

"You Max?" the guy asked, leaning on the bar without
taking the coat off.

The guy had an official tone of voice, but there was
plenty of bluff in it too. "Yeah?" Max answered, coming
forward.

"Yeah, well, seems we got some mutual friends," the
guy said, sitting down. "Canadian Club, rocks."

"Yeah?" Max answered and found a bottle of the
stuff under the bar, left over from some distant past,
and poured the drink into a rocks glass.

"The Brimmers?" the guy answered, smiling, taking
a sip, and watching Max's reaction over the edge of
the glass.

Max felt the tips of his fingers begin to go a little
numb and hoped his face wasn't giving anything away.
He leaned against the back bar and shrugged. Maybe
it was nothing—some uncle poking around. The guy
looked like he could be from Jersey. Maybe a trucker
or dispatcher, but there was a meanness around the eyes

and mouth. The kind of expression that meant, "Maybe I'm outta shape. Maybe I'm old. But fuck you, mean can pull me through. So don't fuck with me."

"You like a friend of the family?" Max asked.

The guy took his time in answering, fishing into the pocket of the topcoat and pulling out a bent cigarette. He put it into his mouth and lit it off a crumpled book, not expecting Max to offer. "Yeah, like that," he mumbled, once he got the cigarette going.

"Yeah, like what?" Max said, coming off the back bar a little. "Like what, exactly?"

The guy set the cigarette down into the molded tin ashtray, took another drink, and put the glass down carefully. "Like I'm a friend of the family," he answered.

"Yeah?"

"Yeah," Kray answered, knowing the conversation was going nowhere, and added, "a good friend." Then he reached into his pocket, pulled out the neatly folded fifty, and slid it across the bar.

A couple of regulars came in, straight from work, and took up positions at the opposite end of the bar. Bourbon water. Vodka martini, straight up with a twist. Max loitered as long as he could, serving them. When he turned, the fat man was holding an empty glass and motioning for a refill.

"So, like I was saying," the fat man said as Max refilled the glass. "I was just wondering what the deal was with that murder and all."

Max set the fresh drink down, noticing that now there were two fifties, fanned out at his edge of the bar, so he'd be sure to see them. "It's a police thing," Max said and made no move for the fifties, not even to break them for the drinks.

The guy took a drink and stubbed the cigarette out. "I heard you did some work for the Brimmers," he said.

Max studied the guy for a second, moving in from the back bar. "Let me ask you something?"

"Shoot," the guy said quickly, taking another sip.

"Are you a cop or what?" Max asked.

"Used to be," the guy answered, casually.

"And now you're, what?"

The fat man exhaled and looked Max in the eye. What was that supposed to mean, that he wasn't bullshitting? "Now, I'm investigating the case, privately."

"For the Brimmers?" Max asked, knowing the family didn't have the kind of money to hire their own investigator.

The guy lit up another cigarette. "For a concerned party, let's say."

Max thought it over briefly. Best way to get this guy out the door was to give him a dead end. "Okay, here's the deal," he said. "The mother comes to me a couple weeks ago and asks me to help her get some shit out of the daughter's apartment. I know a guy who used to be a cop. He gives me a number and some advice. That's it."

"Okay, pal, sorry to bother you, huh?"

"Sure," Max said, walking away. But he'd gone maybe two steps when Julie came through the door. He noticed she was wearing the same outfit she had on the day before and was smiling.

"Max, Lynn's really pissed off," Julie said, heading straight to the edge of the bar, then lowering her voice. "She heard that you were still asking around about the murders."

When Max turned, he saw the fat man smiling. "I'll talk to you about it later," Max said.

"Sure, but . . ." Julie began.

When Max turned back to the fat man, he was heading out the door. So were the two fifties.

TWENTY-ONE

By four in the morning, it was winding down to another one of those two-hundred-dollar nights. Nothing to complain about. Max had maybe thirty in the tip can. Somewhere, he knew, there were bars doing decent business. The city always had five or six hot clubs that turned them away for two, sometimes three golden years before fading into obscurity. And there were sports bars, kiddy bars, rock-and-roll joints, discos, gay bars, dyke bars, and theme bars. All of them doing good business.

The thing was, a bar reaches a point where nothing helps. Barmy's was dying of old age. And the only thing that would revive it was a transfusion of some serious money.

But even now, in its enfeebled state, they were hanging on. Max figured they could hang on forever, if they didn't do anything stupid or halfway. Still, Lynn wouldn't be happy. But what did she want? The place would never be what it was. Already the vultures were circling, other bar owners and wannabes looking to buy out the lease. There was still enough money floating around for someone who thought New York needed another bar and had a good line of credit or bullshit.

It took maybe ten minutes to herd the walk-in traffic out the door and set up the half dozen regulars at a back table.

"Know what's wrong," one of the regulars asked, coming up from the back for a refill. He was one of the old advertising crew. Forty, balding, and scared. Fifteen years ago he'd been a whiz kid. A bright guy with a future. Now his future was history. He was hanging on for dear life to a third marriage and a slipping career.

Well now, there was a question, Max thought, and hit the guy with a buy-back of J&B over a lonely ice cube at the bottom of the rocks glass. He could have meant anything. Something about the Yankees lineup or the mayor or the president or the Japanese. "Lotta stuff," Max said, too tired to start thinking about lists or worry about professional bar wit.

The ad guy smiled, steadying himself on the edge of the bar with one hand. "The thing is, people are too fucking smart," he said with an air of authority. "Too smart for the old bullshit."

This brought Max up fast. "Yeah?"

"Yeah, absolutely," the guy said. "Everyone knows it's all falling apart. Everyone. Guys at the top grabbing as much as they can, fast as they can. Everyone at the bottom, just pissed off. Old bullshit just don't sell anymore."

It was about the smartest thing Max had heard at four in the morning in a long time. "Got any answers?" he asked.

The guy smiled a knowing, strangely pleasant smile. "Yeah, gotta get some new bullshit," he said.

Max laughed politely and nodded the guy away. He walked back to the table with a deliberate and nearly dignified slowness, the way all drunks walk.

When he saw the guy settle into the table, Max pulled the drawer and headed back to the office, Julie following.

"So, you going to count receipts now?" he asked, closing the door behind them. Next thing, Lynn would be hiring spotters. Guys who sit at the bar and watch the bartender, counting buy-backs and studying the register. Usually they were bartenders or managers down on their luck. Max always thought of them as hired guns. Bounty hunters. They weren't all that hard to spot and usually they were charming.

Julie locked the door. "Listen, Max, something really fucked up is going on," she said.

"You mean besides that game you're playing with Lynn?" he said and began counting twenties.

She moved from the door to the folding metal chair, sat down, and said, "Give me a break, will you? It's like real weird. People are watching me, you know?"

Max finished counting twelve twenties and added a ten to total the bank he started with. "Nobody's watching you," he said, rubber-banding the bills.

She got off the chair and picked up a newspaper from on top of the file cabinet, the *Post* with the story about Pat and the guy, Peter Marotte. Saw the story and dropped it. "Maybe it's like the FBI or something. Cops, you know?"

Max stopped counting out the night's take and watched her move from the file cabinet to the chair, then back. Her jaw muscles were working pretty good. Her eyes dilated. She fished a small pack of tissues from her pocket, pulled one, and wiped hard at her nose. Now, here's a familiar picture. "Little tense tonight, are we?" he said. Then tried to remember how many trips to the ladies' room she'd made that night, but couldn't.

"Fuck you, asshole," she muttered and threw the tissue at the garbage can under the desk, missing it.

It could have been one of the regulars who gave her a bump when Max wasn't looking, but he doubted it. What worried him was that maybe it was a gram dealer who snuck in and was looking to work a contract with her. She'd steer the clientele to him in trade for a few lines a night. It took two years to clean the dealers out; he wasn't going to lose ground now. "Who gave you the sniff?" he asked.

"I'm trying to tell you something and you're asking about that?" she said, moving in close, getting right in his face. "And maybe I bought it on my own time. Or didn't that occur to you, huh?"

Actually it hadn't occurred to him. When was the last time a waitress bought blow on the Upper East Side? Probably back in '87. Probably there was a brass plaque to commemorate it in the rest room where it happened. Max put the money back in the cash drawer and stood up. "Look, I could fire you right the fuck now," he said, surprised at how pissed off he was.

"You think all those guys, out there, are straight?" she argued. "You're living in a fairy tale. Just 'cause you don't do it anymore."

"They're not fucking staff," Max said, actually raising his voice. "Get it? They are not staff."

For a second it looked like she was going to cry. Then she moved back. "Look it was an eighth that the producer left. He was afraid to take it back on the plane. It was like a going-away gift."

"How long have you been up?" Max asked, seeing now that she looked drawn.

"Yesterday, last night, all day today," she said, sitting down. "But I gotta tell you about the guys following me. I think it's about Pat and Peter."

Max counted back. She'd been up for thirty-six hours, propped up by blow. That sounded about right for paranoid, even with the shitty blow that was going around now. He'd once tried to get a film editor who'd been up for forty hours into a taxi. When the cab pulled up at the curb, the guy's face went crazy with fear. "Don't you know, they're not real taxis anymore. None of them!" But the thing that scared him the most was coke psychosis. Guys who went crazy on it were unstoppable. "Look, how much do you have left?" Max asked and held out his hand for the blow.

"I gotta tell you what's been going on," she pleaded.

"Julie, give me the blow, and we'll talk," he answered.

She reached into her apron reluctantly and pulled out the brown vial. Max held it to the light and saw maybe three or four lines worth left. "Shit, you did all of it?"

"No, I shared some," she said. "Can we talk now?"

"Yeah, okay," he said, pocketing the vial.

"Look, I wasn't completely straight with you, you know," she started, moving around the room, turning her back on him.

"No shit," he said, sitting back down. "No fucking shit."

She turned, fast, then stopped short. "Listen, okay, it's not about the blow or Lynn or that stuff," she said, fishing another tissue from her pocket, then forgetting about it, using her sleeve. "You know, I had a thing with Todd."

Max already knew, but decided to clear up the chronology a little. "This before or after he had a thing with Pat?"

"It was like during," she said.

"During?" Some lurid instinct put the thought in his head and it must have come out in his voice. If anyone ever wrote Todd's life story it would begin, "Dear *Penthouse Forum* . . ."

"Not during-during, but like around the same time," she answered, annoyed.

"Okay, I get the idea," Max said.

"Well, Pat was like pissed off at him," she said. "So she talked me into letting her and Peter use the phone in the hotel room."

Slowly, the pieces were starting to fit into place. The Marotte guy was using the room for the loan scam. "What about the bills?"

Julie leaned back against the door and raised her eyes to the ceiling, studying the criss-cross of electrical wiring. "See, it was like perfect," she said. "He never saw the bills. Neither did his wife. They went straight to the business accountant. The accountant just paid them. And he had a platinum Amex, so he had late checkout time."

Max thought it over. Yeah, it made sense. "So you'd hang out in the room, after Todd left?"

"I'd tell him I wanted a bath or a nap," she said. "He'd split, and I'd call Pete and Pat and they'd come up."

"And use the phone," Max finished.

"Well, yeah. But it was just a couple times, like three or four," she said, voice rising in a slow panic. "But now they're all dead. Everyone in that room's dead, except me."

Max stood up and retrieved a bottle from the far corner of the desk. It was a bottle of Glenfiddich left by a salesman. "Look, have a drink," Max said, pulling a plastic go-cup from a stack of them in the desk drawer.

She watched as he poured two fingers into the cup. "What were they doing? I mean that somebody would kill them for?" she asked. Then added, "I hate scotch."

"Drink it fast then," Max said, handing her the cup. The liquor would smooth out the coke jitters, but not much. He could remember nights when he'd gone through a six of beer and a pack of cigarettes trying to get to sleep.

She gulped the scotch and made a face. "And now, they're after me," she said, holding out the cup for another hit.

Max poured another shot into the plastic cup. "Listen, this is what you do," he said. "Go home. Go to sleep. Lock all the doors and put the telephone in bed with you. When you get up tomorrow, take a long shower and come into work. Okay? We'll figure something out then."

She drank down the scotch and put the cup back on the desk. "Shit, you know, it's all turned really bad," she said. "I called the movie producer. Twice. He wouldn't return my call."

"Julie, give me the bank, okay?" Max asked.

She counted out the money from her apron and handed him a roll of fives and tens.

"Okay," he said. "Now go home. We'll talk tomorrow."

She grabbed her coat off the hook on the wall and vanished through the door. Max finished counting the take, banded the bills for night deposit, separating out credit card slips, house tabs, and entered it all in the book. When he went back out front, the regulars had vanished. Lynn was behind the bar in her mink, pouring herself a Remy, Chesterfield hanging out the side of her mouth. "Who's been giving the waitress blow?" she asked.

"A guy from L.A., but he's not around anymore," Max said, moving up behind the bar next to her.

"I don't want any more than necessary in the place," Lynn said, stepping neatly around him to the other side of the mahogany. Max noticed she was wearing heels, but didn't make a false step on the planking. "This isn't '86."

Max poured himself a scotch and added ice. "I'll man the perimeters. What's up with the treasury guys?"

"Got bored, went home," Lynn said, stubbing the cigarette out. "You staying out of that thing, right?"

Max took a drink and said, "Yeah."

"Good," came the answer, and for the first time, Max noticed an odd hint of weariness in Lynn's voice.

"What's up, bad date?"

"Movie, Chinese, honest to God I'm tired of it," she said.

"What, the dating?"

Lynn searched her purse for another pack of cigarettes, couldn't find one. "The everything," she said, cutting the search short and pulling out the ledger. "Total out, will you?"

Max totaled out the register, the blue numbers of the readout drawing a resigned sigh from Lynn as she copied them down. "So, what's the deal? Blues? PMS? What?"

"I was born with PMS," Lynn answered, closing the book and returning it to her purse. "I'm just tired of the whole fucking scene, you know? I'm tired of losing."

"This place'll be here forever," Max said.

Lynn ignored him, finding a Chesterfield wrapper with a lone cigarette in the pocket of the mink. "Two years ago, I could have sold the joint. Now, I'll take a hit on it if I try to sell."

"Sell it and buy what? Tax-free bonds? CDs?" Max asked, leaning against the back bar.

"Could have bought into a temp agency," Lynn said. "All Wall Street accounts. Place had a little deal where they charged applicants to take courses in word processing and that bullshit. Lotta companies using them, to avoid benefits."

"No good," Max answered, smiling. "There wouldn't be anyone around to abuse. Besides you'd have to wake up before noon. And what would you do, sit around giving typing tests and looking for some kid off the bus from Ohio who'd go down on the personnel manager so you keep the account?"

"They're opening another one of those topless joints," Lynn said. "Looking for investors."

Max just grinned. It wasn't even worth a reply. The new topless joints were slick items. Brass, glass, and ass. Five-dollar-a-beer places for what was left of the expense account crowd. Lynn could probably make a go of one of those on her own. But that took something like a half mil, minimum. And the millisecond they started trolling for investors in a bar, that was the time to grab your hat. Because the stealing started before the doors were opened and continued right through until the money for the lawsuits and countersuits ran out.

"Shit, Max, what the fuck's gone wrong?" Lynn said, blowing a stream of smoke across the bar and studying the sparse traffic outside.

Max knew what went wrong, just about everything, but instead said, "Look, coast for another year or two. See how this thing shakes out. You remember what Miles used to say."

" 'A saloon in New York is like a life preserver on the Titanic,' " she quoted, then allowed herself a small laugh.

Max got home around dawn, walking quickly down Third. By the time he reached the door, his toes were numb in his Chuck Taylors and he wanted to sleep for about a week.

Suze was asleep, rolled into a small ball beneath the covers. He watched her for about a minute, her face illuminated by the light from the hall. Then he closed the door and undressed.

When he crawled into the warm bed, she mumbled something and unscrunched a little, rolling comfortably toward him, and he thought, nothing wrong with that.

TWENTY-TWO

The big man used what remained of his money to buy twenty cans of salmon, fifteen cans of corned beef, twelve-liter bottles of Coke, and a case of Budweiser tallboys. He would stay in the apartment eating the salmon and corned beef and drinking the Coke and beer until everything stopped hurting and he was well enough to move about again. What he really wanted was some boiled green bananas in coconut cream, but now mistrusted all food that did not come in a can or bottle. Everything in this place he mistrusted, most of all the people. People who lived as these people did could not be trusted.

Since the Tiffany store had stolen his watch, he would need to find some money.

At the end of the first week, the phone that hung near the door and was connected to the lobby rang. The big man rose slowly from the chair, pulling himself away from the Oprah show, and answered it.

"Yeah, there's a guy down here for you," the doorman said. "You want I should send him away?"

The big man thought a moment, then said, "Who is here for me?"

"Guy says he's your lawyer," the doorman said bitterly. "What should I do, send him away?"

The big man thought some more, covering the mouthpiece with his hand. "Let him come up," he said finally.

Five minutes later W. T. Zunick was ringing the apartment bell.

"*Talofa*," the lawyer said, in the worst Samoan the big man had ever heard. "So, you're up and about, huh? And holy fucking shit, look at that head. Disgusting. Gotta get a picture of it." He was wearing a double-breasted gray suit with a gray shirt, a gray tie, and gray shoes.

"You said in hospital, you could get money?" the big man asked, moving aside to let the lawyer in.

"Bet your ass we can get you money. Big *talas*, right? That's what you call them? *Mucho talas*," the lawyer said. "Did some checking, on my own, for free, found out the building has a two-point-five-mil liability policy."

"When do I get money?" the big man asked.

The lawyer sat down in the chair and opened the eelskin briefcase on his lap. "Now, that all depends," he said. "But first we have to sign you up."

The contingency contract was four pages long. The big man did not read it. Neither did he ask why it had already been notarized.

Kray sat in his car smoking and consuming the last of five Egg McMuffins. For a bartender, this Max guy lived pretty plush. It was a good tree-lined block in a great neighborhood. Probably couldn't touch one of those brownstones for under three-five. It was the kind of place they advertise in the back of the Sunday *Times Magazine*.

He'd been sitting there for about two hours when he saw the two guys come up the street and ring the bell. They were plainclothes cops, Kray could tell by the way they walked. Maybe even bureau guys from the looks of their suits. City cops, Kray thought, didn't know how to dress. Spent a lot of money on Italian and French crap. Lotta times they looked like guys selling Toyotas out of a dealership in Queens. That was one thing Hoover did: made his men dress like bankers or lawyers. And put a spy in the classes to take notes.

Kray stubbed out his cigarette and watched as Max opened the door and let them in. From the look on his face, he was none too pleased to see them. That was good. It meant that he wasn't talking. But Kray would give odds that they were looking into the Marotte murder and that his hunch had paid off; this Max character knew more than he was letting on.

Forty minutes later, the two feds walked out the front door and back down the street. Kray waited another ten minutes before going up to the door and ringing the bell.

"Shit, now what the fuck do you want?" Max said, standing in the front door. He was wearing a sweatshirt and jeans.

"Pal, this is opportunity ringing the bell. I want to save your life," Kray said, smiling. "You got problems with the feds, I can make them go away."

"What? You're like a Jehovah's Witness Protection Program?"

Kray smiled and said, "That's pretty good for early in the morning. It's early for you, right?"

It was one in the afternoon. "Yeah, it's the middle of the night," Max said, closing the door. Upstairs Suze was showering; he wanted to spend some time with her. She had the dinner shift and they had maybe an hour and a half before her only class of the day.

"There's a coffee shop around the corner on Lex," Kray answered, blocking the door with his foot. "I'll meet you there in twenty."

Kray slid his foot back off the stoop, and Max slammed the door in the fat man's face. Then, against his better judgement, he showered, shaved, changed, and walked out the door heading for Lex. When he got there, he was a half hour late and hoping the fat guy hadn't waited.

But there he was, sitting at a booth in the back, taking up a table for four at the tail end of the lunch shot, smoking a cigarette, and reading the *Post* over a cup of coffee.

Kray smiled a small smile that still showed plenty of meanness and motioned Max over. "See, now here's what we got," he said, folding the paper as Max eased into the booth. "We got a dead guy that I want to know about and two live guys you want out of your life. Am I wrong here?"

"Keep going," Max said, trying to say as little as possible.

"Now, like I said, I'm working for some concerned parties on the murder," Kray said. "So you tell me what you know about the dead guy, Marotte, and I'll see what I can do about calling off the feds."

Max took the menu from the waitress. "Yeah, how?"

"Look, I got a contact inside," Kray said. "Flat out, I'll tell you, I can't promise nothing. But I can make the call."

Max studied the fat guy for a long time. Right now he had nothing and he was on everyone's wrong side. This guy was maybe on a side that could do him some good. "Okay," he said at last. "What'd you want to know?"

Kray smiled again, wider. "Start here," he answered. "Tell me what this Marotte guy was up to. And tell me about the chippie, the waitress."

And Max did.

From across the street, Treasury Agents Targin and Reddick sat in their car, watching. "Now what the fuck is this?" Targin asked.

"You get the fat guy's tag number?" Reddick asked.

"Yeah."

"Then let's run it and see what the bartender's up to."

The phone rang in the bar in Queens, and the bartender picked it up. From the back table, a group of four men watched as the bartender stood perfectly still, nodding slightly. Then he carefully put the phone down and walked over to the table. It was the way he walked that silenced the men.

When he leaned to one of the men on the end and whispered something in his ear, the others watched for a reaction. They were not disappointed. First the color drained from his face, then he flushed bright red.

The three others watched the slow drama as the older man smiled, nodded, finished off his anisette, then rose from the table. He moved stiffly, like a sleepwalker, or like a dead man, which is what he was, or more precisely, what he'd be in a couple of hours.

He was halfway to the el when he felt sick, right down in the pit of his stomach. Instinctively, he brought up the roll of Tums from his coat pocket, bit off three, and chewed them quickly. He'd been around enough to know that when things went as bad as they'd been going, it didn't matter if you were a good earner or not. The feds weren't playing around anymore, and neither were *the boys*.

He walked by the pay phone, heading for his car. Then he thought better of it and got on the F train into Manhattan. He hadn't been on the subway for years. And when he reached Forty-seventh Street, he got off and found a pay phone.

He chewed the last of the Tums as he punched in the number. The old man's voice sounded distant and cold. Nothing new there, but he had a bad feeling.

"We need a sit-down," the old man said.

"Yeah, like where?" he answered, his chest tightening.

"Meet a couple of the guys up at the new place," the old man said. "We have to put this situation right."

"Yeah, sure," he said, his mouth dry. "The new place, not the old one."

"A little change of ambiance, maybe a little change of luck," the old man sang, then hung up.

That's when he knew the old man was going to wax him, when he sang. The old man never sang unless he already reached some conclusion. A guy with a problem didn't sing, only guys with answers. He stood there for a long time, hand on the phone, thinking about who to call.

Finally, he dialed information and got the number for the FBI in downtown Manhattan. Again he waited, thinking that he'd probably need a lawyer to work out the deal. But the last lawyer he had was courtesy of the family. Fuck it, he decided, he'd do it himself. He could deal better for himself than any fucking shyster.

He dialed the number quickly and asked for the Organized Crime Unit Task Force. When a woman came on the phone, he gave his street name. There was a long pause, then a guy came on the line.

The guy said, "Yes?"

"You know who I am?" he asked.

"I know who you say you are," the man said.

"You got a picture of me?"

"I can arrange to get one," the man said.

"Look, I wanta deal, understand?"

"What makes you think *we* want to deal, if you're who you say you are?"

He paused, taking in a deep breath of cold air. He'd never ratted anyone out in his life and now, at fifty-two, well it was a helluva time to start. "For one thing, I know who killed Bonanza DeVecchio and why. Interested?"

"Interested in talking, anyway."

"I'll be there in half an hour," he said.

"Don't come here, we'll send someone to pick you up."

Well, fuck me, he thought, the feds offer car service for rats. And then he gave them the address.

Twenty-Three

By the time Max finished with Kray, it was nearly four and Suze would be long gone. Another missed connection, but this time it was his fault.

He headed over to the bar to do inventory and think over the options. He could feel himself sinking deeper into it. With each new person he met, the thing just got more tangled. Todd, the Marotte guy, Julie, the dead girl, her folks, and the feds. And now, there was this new guy, Delbert Kray, and whoever the fuck he was working for.

Halfway through inventory, Max realized that he was down to his last bottle and a half of Absolut. He could trot off to the liquor store and bury the expense in petty cash, but by now he probably had ABC agents watching the bar. And buying liquor retail was illegal. So was keeping the lemonex in empty gin bottles.

Fuck it, he thought, and went for his jacket. He was almost to the liquor store when he remembered Todd had borrowed those two bottles of peach schnapps. He caught a cab uptown to Todd's bar.

The place was on Ninety-second and if it wasn't a kid-dy bar, it was close enough. Popular with the suburban kids just out of school and on their first rent-paying jobs. The kind of store where the kids came in with thirty or forty bucks in their pocket and spent it all. On weekends he'd get two or three hundred people a night through the door. It added up very quickly, especially when it was mostly all cash.

Todd had the presence of mind to hire a huge black guy, a graduate student in finance or something at Columbia, to work the door. Nothing scared the white kids from the suburbs more than a ferocious-looking black guy at the door. And the guy that Todd hired was built like a linebacker, but was one of the smartest guys Max ever met in the bar business. Though he couldn't prove it, Max always suspected that the guy wasn't in it for the money. What could he be taking home, two, three hundred a week? And the guy was too smart to get off on proofing twenty-two-year-olds at the door.

Probably he was doing some independent field work in human nature. In a year or two he'd be gone, vanished into a think tank or still scaring the shit out of the same kids, only then from behind a desk at some bank or brokerage house.

Todd's Joint was an old neighborhood bar he'd taken over when he saw the tide of Yuppies advancing past East Eighty-sixth Street. The middle gate for the bar was open, which was a good sign, and when he peeked in the window, he saw the door guy sitting far in the back, reading.

Max knocked, saw the guy raise his head, ready to signal they were closed, then he recognized Max and smiled. When he got up from the stool, Max noticed that he marked his place in the thick book with a sip-stick.

"How's it going?" Max asked, trying to remember the guy's name. He was dressed in a tight-fitting short-sleeve workshirt and jeans from L.L. Bean.

"Good, good," the guy answered and opened the door wide to let him in. "Max, right?"

"Yeah," Max said, then remembered the guy's name. "Jerry, right?"

The guy closed the door and nodded, "What's up?"

Inside it was dark, except for a gooseneck lamp tilted to the book at the waitress station. Todd hadn't done much with the place since he took it over. He kept the original bar, back bar, flaking mirror, and row of shelves over the opposite wall. He filled the shelves with bottles of the forty varieties of beer he sold. The old chrome and vinyl stools were gone, sold off as kitsch art to a Soho dealer, and replaced by cheap wood. The booths and pool table were gone too, leaving the place wide open, the better to pack the kids in. There was a new CD juke with external Bose speakers and one of those PVC-tube coin-operated basketball games. The basketball game alone probably took in three hundred a night.

But the real genius of it, Max thought, was that Todd probably opened the doors for less than twelve grand in renovations. The idea was to take over a store and not spend a fortune on fixtures and all the other bullshit. Hang a new sign out front and put in a good juke and whatever game the operator suggests. The only concession to decor Max could see were oversized comic drawings mounted to the wall behind lucite. Old-time stuff from the Sunday comics, *The Yellow Kid*, *Little Nemo*, and *Dick Tracy*. And that was smart too, gave the lonely guys something to do while they drank, besides standing around looking like losers.

"Manager around?" Max asked.

"You're looking at him," the guy said, smiling slightly.

Something must have shown in Max's face. Something like surprise that he hoped wouldn't turn into a race thing, which it wasn't. It was more like, *who promotes a door guy to manager?* And it was a school thing. He'd seen maybe a dozen guys get hooked on bars, even smart ones. It didn't matter if they were working the doors, bartending, or barback. Something about the party every night hooked them. The excitement lasted maybe five years. "Yeah?" Max said.

"Just 'til we get the bullshit cleared away," the guy said. "What is it, doing the books, the inventory, ordering, watching the staff?"

"Look, here's the thing," Max said. "Todd borrowed a couple bottles of schnapps. I was wondering if I could borrow back a couple of Absolut and call it even."

The guy stood there for a second then said, "Yeah, I remember him coming back with them."

"Deal?"

Jerry walked around the bar and Max followed to the service gate. There was a half-finished soda in a pint beer glass where he'd been sitting. The book was a thick biography of Keynes. "Here's the Absolut and a couple bottles of schnapps," Jerry said, pulling bottles from under the bar. "Send someone up with the vodka next week."

"You got something I can carry them out in?"

The guy pulled an empty carton that once held wine from under the ice bin. "*Voilà*," he said.

Max began loading the bottles into the slots and folded the lid down. "So, some shit about Todd, huh?" he asked, just to be saying something.

"He was a smart guy," Jerry said, leaning comfortably across the bar. "But he went stupid hooking up with that other one. That Marotte asshole. Number-one bad move."

Max sat down, uninvited. "Yeah, how'd he hook up with him?"

"You want something to drink?" Jerry asked.

"Soda's good," Max said.

Jerry scooped some ice into a wine glass and filled it with the soda gun. "I heard you were looking around," he said, pushing the glass over to Max.

"From who?"

"Couple people talking," came the answer. "I didn't believe it. Didn't think you were dumb enough to get involved."

Now, what was the answer to that? Max settled on, "Yeah, I was dumb enough. Come on, give me the story."

Jerry grabbed his drink from the bar and smiled. "These guys, the treasury guys, aren't playing, you know?"

"They've been up here?" Max said, feeling his mouth go dry.

"Carried out the files," Jerry said. "Didn't even pack them in boxes. Sealed them and carried them out with handtrucks. Stepped all over the crime scene. Pissed off the police techs, big time."

"Todd was shot here?" This was a new one for Max. Again, he'd missed the facts. Somehow he'd assumed Todd was shot in his apartment.

"Back room," Jerry said. "Around this time. You know I got receipts up thirty-two percent the week it happened."

No surprise there. But why was the joint still open? To work that took some juice and he thought of Janey's family. "So, how was he hooked up with that guy, Marotte?"

Jerry shut his eyes and lifted his head, so that it looked like he was staring at the ceiling, thinking. When he brought his head down, he was smiling. "Would I be telling tales if I told you Marotte worked here?"

"As what, a bartender?" Max said. "Come on, I would have heard if Todd put him behind the bar."

"Consulting Assistant Manager," Jerry said, still smiling. "Brought in a lot of business."

"Yeah?" It was starting to get interesting. "What kind of business, Wall Street types?"

"His girlfriend for one," Jerry said, serious now. "That girl that got killed."

"What, like an actress/model crowd?"

"Just her," Jerry said, getting ready to deliver the payoff. "She charged maybe four grand a month between

Amex and Visa. Brought in another two or three in cash."

Jerry didn't have to draw a picture for Max. Todd took on Marotte and paid him twenty-five hundred a month for a no-show job. The dead girl's credit card charges went into the bar accounts, through bookkeeping. That would cover Marotte's salary, and then some. The cash more than likely went into Todd's pocket.

The deal left Marotte clean. He was probably using the bar as place of employment for his taxes. Listed himself as an independent contractor. If he was doing well at the phone scams and whatever other scams he was working, then the couple of grand was chump change that gave him something to put down for the IRS and the pay stubs to prove it. The money Todd pocketed probably paid the lease and parking for the Mercedes, if it wasn't listed as corporate under the bar.

"Interesting, no?" Jerry asked.

"Yeah, it's real fucking interesting," Max said, thinking of the girl, Pat Brimmer. The whole deal left her out in the cold. It would have been hard to explain if anyone started asking questions. She'd be left twisting unless she had some real good reason why she was charging more on the plastic than she took home from the waitress job. Sure, she could talk about Marotte, but guys like him could vanish. And the girl would take the fall. Marotte didn't have to set her up, but he did. She's the one the feds would pin everything on.

"Got it figured?" Jerry asked, arching an eyebrow and offering a smile.

"Yeah, real class guys, huh?" Max said. "Know anything else?"

"Two things," Jerry answered. "Marotte, he used the place to apply for a carry permit, and I know we never had this conversation." Then he came back from around the bar to open the door for Max.

Ten minutes later there was another knock at the door of Todd's Joint. Jerry looked out at the darkening street and saw a fat man blowing into his cupped hands to keep them warm.

Jerry waved his hand in the international bar language for "We're closed," but the fat man kept knocking.

Outside, standing in the cold, Kray mumbled under his breath, "Come on you big fucking spook, open the fucking door."

Jerry rose from the seat, thinking the fat man was maybe a liquor salesman and let him in.

TWENTY-FOUR

For three days the lawyer, W. T. Zunick, came and took the big man to doctors in Queens, Brooklyn, and Long Island. They visited five doctors. The first was a general practitioner; the second, a chiropractor; the third, a psychiatrist; the fourth, a neurologist; and the fifth, an orthopedic surgeon.

It was not a problem hiding the bullet wound and the other wounds from the doctors. They only looked at his head. A nurse weighed him, measured him, and took down a medical history. The neurologist had written a prescription for pain. The psychiatrist, a nervous lady who chain-smoked, handed him a prescription for anxiety she said he had. The lawyer paid for the prescriptions—Talwin, Prozac, Halcion, Tylenol 3—and pocketed the bottles. Later, he'd sell the medication for more than double the over-the-counter legal price to a guy he knew—a disbarred lawyer who owned an executive search firm downtown. The guy used the shit to dope his clients up before interviews, relax them or hype them. Used to be, the guy did a good business selling piss-filled catheters for drug testing. Tape the catheter under a guy's arm and run the tube to his zipper. Got fifty bucks a pop for a three-dollar item, less what he spent on piss. Now, that was one crooked sonofabitch, the lawyer thought.

After each visit, the lawyer would reach into his pocket, give the big man twenty dollars, and say, "We got 'em by the fuckin' balls."

They rode in the lawyer's car, which was tiny. A pocket Bearcat scanner, wedged between the bucket seats, monitored police calls. The big man had no way of knowing that the lawyer owned another car—an '88 Jag—because he would never drive it to work. After years he'd found the small car was easier to pull off onto the shoulder of the BQE and Cross Bronx Expressway at accident scenes and less conspicuous when he drove it uptown.

Often, the lawyer's beeper would make noise and then he'd grab frantically at the car phone, sometimes steering the tiny car across two lanes of traffic. The big man had never been so afraid in an automobile. Whenever the beeper would go off, even when they were stopped at a traffic light, he would reach up with both hands and hold tightly on the dashboard and shut his eyes.

At the end of the third day, the lawyer said, "Now we *really* got 'em by the balls. I'm gonna fax the insurance carrier, developer, and bank the letter of representation tomorrow. Next day they get the reports FedEx. I'm gonna make it real easy for them."

"When do I get money?" the big man asked.

"Hey, I'm working as fast as I can, you know?" the lawyer said, bringing both hands up off the wheel. "See, usually we'd file a criminal case against the doorman. But I figure fuck it, we'll use the criminal charges to lean on him with. Let 'em know that if he plays ball with us, the worst that happens is, he's outta a job. Besides, we already got the cops' incident report and EMS paperwork. Let the claims adjuster chew on those for awhile. Won't even have to take it to trial."

"How long?" the big man asked, realizing he should have asked that question before. But it was the lawyer that tricked him; he thought the money would come soon. Any day.

"Couple months," the lawyer said. "They're not going to buy this one cheap. Not with that mil-plus coverage. It's a fucking lock! I'll come by tomorrow, and we'll go over your papers. Passport and all that bullshit."

"You need passport?" the big man asked, remembering his visa and passport were still downtown, unclaimed since the accident. The free lawyer downtown did not know where he lived.

"Yeah, for the CIB, Central Index Bureau," the lawyer answered. "It ain't that I don't believe you, but if they find out you sued before, it's gonna be tougher by much. Why, you need some money now?"

"Yes," the big man said, then watched as the lawyer pulled a fat roll of bills—a thousand dollars at least— from his pocket and peeled off fifty. "Remember, don't do anything. They could already be watching you."

"Who watching me?" the big man asked, taking the money.

"Those fucking insurance scumbags is who," the lawyer said. "Don't go out and lift anything. Don't party. You can party after you get the money."

Then the big man lifted himself from the tiny car and walked back into the lobby of the building.

The doorman didn't move from his seat to open the door. As the big man walked to the elevator, the doorman shouted out, "Hey, I thought you weren't gonna sue?"

"I am not going to sue," the big man answered, approaching the mailbox and looking for the key. "My lawyer is one is going to sue." Inside the mailbox was another letter from the bank. The third in the last week. He would mail them to the angry woman in Armonk tomorrow.

The big man put the letter in his pocket, turned to the elevator, and pushed the button. The door opened immediately and he stepped inside.

"Well, good luck with the insurance company, pal," Derek called. "They're killers."

The big man stuck a meaty hand on the elevator's door, opening it again. "What you mean, 'killers'?" he said, uneasily.

Derek got up from his seat and faced the elevator. "They'll be so far up your ass, they'll know every parking ticket you ever got. I hear they're cracking down on awards. Not so free with the money no more. They'll have investigators crawling all over you."

The big man didn't answer; rather, he let his hand fall from the elevator door and watched it close.

"Big fucking asshole," Derek mumbled. "In the fucking country eight minutes and he's gonna score like six figures."

It was past two in the morning when Derek walked into the bar and sat opposite the register in the center so Max would be sure to see him.

The place was starting to thin out, maybe eight or nine people at the bar, walk-in traffic, and four regulars at a back table. Derek was already half-drunk, but propped up with enough blow to keep him going through a partial tour of the after-hours joints.

"Max, Max, so what's happening with that job?" he asked.

Max poured a Jim Beam over ice for a guy in a suit at the end of the bar and said, "What job?"

"You know, that thing we talked about," Derek said, smiling and grinding his teeth at the same time.

Max grabbed the drink and took it to the guy at the end of the bar, rang up the register, and turned toward Derek. "What's that now?"

"That job thing," Derek said. "Remember when you came in and used the phone? Said you might have some shifts opening."

"Man, this is the shift," Max answered, motioning up and down the sparse line of people.

"I could talk to Lynn," Derek said. "You guys could start opening days. Open early, you know? Happy hour, huh?"

"What about your thing at the apartment?" Max tried. And wasn't it a school night tonight? he thought to himself.

"It's gonna disappear, I can feel it," Derek said.

No shit, Max thought and went to make a couple of Finlandia martinis for a couple signaling at the other end.

When he was ringing up the martinis, Derek said, "Some asshole takes a spill in the lobby and now they're gonna can me."

Max threw up his hands, "Sorry man, can't do it."

"Look, what I need is like two shifts a week," Derek said.

Julie was at the end of the bar with her tray, and Max went to mix drinks for her. When he walked back, he turned to Derek and leaned down across the bar. "Where's your brains, man? You come into a store and ask for a job in the middle of a fucking shift. You know better than that."

Derek's face kind of dropped for a second, before he answered, "I thought, you know, it'd be okay, since you guys weren't doing any business anymore—you know?"

The guy was so terminally fucking dumb, Max had to take some pity on him. He served up a beer from a keg he knew was going bad and slid it over to him. "On the house, okay."

Derek smiled wanly and nodded, lifting the beer.

When Max turned around again, the fat man, Delbert Kray, was walking through the door. It took Max a second to recognize him; somebody had seriously beaten the shit out of him. The left side of his face was covered in a bandage from beneath his jaw to just under the eye, which was blackened and nearly swollen completely shut. When he sat down at the bar, next to Derek, Max noticed that two fingers on his left hand were in a splint. Both the splint and bandages looked new.

Max walked up in front of him, thinking that he'd picked the wrong side again and said, "What happened?"

"Fell down," Delbert answered. "Give me a Canadian Club, willya. I just left Lenox Hill emergency."

Max poured the liquor, then made a motion that it was on the house when Kray made a pathetic show of reaching for his money with the splinted fingers.

"Let me ask you something?" Derek said, turning to Kray. "As a guy who fell down."

Shit, Max thought, these two deserved each other.

When Kray didn't answer, Derek asked, "You ain't gonna sue, are you?"

"Naw, only scumbags sue," Kray said and drained the glass, hoping the liquor would work on the three codeine pills he'd taken.

Derek looked toward Max. "See that, only scumbags sue," he said. "This fucking South Seas asshole takes a dive, and now he's gonna collect, big time. Motherfucker can't even speak English right."

"Yeah, what is it them people speak?" Kray asked.

The words were out of Max's mouth before he thought of them. "They speak pidgin," he said, and something clicked in his head.

"Well coo-coo," Derek mumbled.

TWENTY-FIVE

The attorney sat stiffly at the table in the basement Chinese restaurant, eyeing his water glass as if it were filled from the Hudson. He sat completely motionless, trying not to touch anything. And not moving to unbutton his topcoat. Clearly, he did not intend on eating.

Kray sat opposite him, staring across the formica square of the table, an entire steamed dumpling impaled on the tines of a filthy fork, which he waved in the air as he spoke. His left hand, the splint now stained, rested on the table.

"Eat, eat something," Kray said, again waving the dumpling toward the menu that lay untouched in front of the lawyer.

Kray had chosen the place with great care. Downtown

just off of Mott, only a few blocks from where they'd first met. Let the scumbag meet him on some unfamiliar ground, is the way Kray saw it. And to show him that just a couple steps in any direction and he's down where things aren't all that nice.

"Should I say I was quite taken back by your call last night?" the lawyer began. "It was past four in the morning. Though you sounded in good spirits."

"You can say whatever the fuck you want, huh," Kray answered, closing his lips around the pale dumpling. And sure, he was shit-faced, but so what? He pretty much had the whole deal figured out. All the pieces were in place: Todd Manion, Janey Manion, Peter Marotte, and that girl, the dead waitress from Jersey with the crippled father. It just took a few drinks and a codeine to bring the picture into focus.

The lawyer brushed off the answer; his eyes fastened on Kray's eye, which was swollen into a slitted wink above the bandage. "Your present appearance, should I assume it occurred in relation to the case?"

"Yeah, I tangled with a big nigger up in Harlem, if you want to know," Kray said, enjoying the way the lawyer recoiled slightly at the word. Go 'head and show your fucking disapproval, asshole, Kray thought, I'm sure there's just a whole bunch of black folks running in your social circles.

"And that somehow bears on the case?" the lawyer said.

"I think you know it does, asshole," Kray said. To his own surprise, Kray discovered he was pissed off. The job wasn't what he thought it was gonna be. Not at all. With these people, there wouldn't be any publicity. But with a little luck he'd be scoring some serious money.

The lawyer again recoiled, though the movement was no more than a twitch. "Should I?"

"Yeah and here's a flash," Kray said, chewing around another dumpling. "I know who your client is."

The lawyer smiled at this. It was a small, self-satisfied smile.

"Thing is, I forgot the name of the trust," Kray said, swallowing. "But it's controlled by an old biddy up on the East Side."

The lawyer remained perfectly still for a two-beat, then reached out and took a drink of the water. Kray noticed that his hand was shaking slightly. And he wasn't smiling anymore.

"See, took me awhile to figure it out," Kray said. "You wanted information on this Marotte guy."

"Go on, please."

Kray put his fork down, warming to the story. "See, Marotte was just dirty," he began. "Not dope like you'd think, but scams. Real estate scams, stocks, you name it. The guy was a real fucking piece of work. Pathological. And he was bringing in serious money the last couple of months. Fifteen or eighteen grand a month. I figure he was looking to make some kind of move where he needed clean money. My guess is, he wanted to buy something. But he needed paperwork for his taxes. Now that's all speculation, you know?"

"Indeed it is," the attorney said.

"But I'll tell you what isn't," Kray continued. "He was dirty and he was moving cash through Todd Manion's bar. The kind of money that could maybe bring heat down on your client. I'll put it in a report if you want."

"Please," the lawyer said with a twitching nod.

"Okay, the thing was, he was washing some of his money through the bar," Kray said. "Through the dead girl's Amex and Visa at Todd's Joint, uptown. He had some other things going, like moving some of it through A.C. casinos, then to the girl."

"Go on, please," the lawyer said, not committing. "We've already established that."

"Anyway, took me about ten minutes and two hundred of your out-of-pocket to get the girl's Amex receipts off a guy in their EDS department," Kray said. "Took another couple of minutes to dig up Todd's will. Turns out his share of the bar is left to some trust down in Delaware. So, I get curious. After all, the guy was married. What about the widow? Turns out, she gets a quarterly whack-up of the trust's dividends. And the dividends are sent to a Connecticut address in Wilton, leased from that same trust by Todd and Mrs. Todd Manion. The whole deal's a tax thing, right? They spend a couple weekends a month up in the country, look at the trees, listen to the birds, and all that shit, stepping around the city and state taxes. It's their official residence, right? I'd guess both have Connecticut driver's licenses and they vote there."

"It's a perfectly legal arrangement," the lawyer said.

"And the trust, what's that, a way to keep Mr. Manion's hands off the family money?"

The lawyer squirmed uncomfortably at the question.

Kray allowed himself an appreciative smile. "So anyway, turns out the trust, which is named after the biddy's father, is controlled by the biddy, your client."

"The trust itself is our client, if you must know."

"Yeah, whatever," Kray said, motioning with a newly impaled dumpling and leaning over the table as he spoke in tones of hurried, or at least condensed, conspiracy. "Anyway, I figure the bar's worth two hundred and ninety, two-seventy-five K. Probably more with those comic-book drawings on the wall. Did some checking. One they got hanging there, *Little Nemo*, is worth twenty-five K. So maybe this Marotte guy was using the place like a bank, too. Hanging his deposits on the walls. Either him or that Todd guy. Todd probably got off on that, hiding money from the feds and his wife on the walls. By the way, treasury missed them. Anyway, maybe the bar nets another sixty or seventy a year for the owner if he plays it straight with the taxes."

"Approximately," the lawyer said with a tone of reluctance bred of discretion. "Continue, please."

Then, just to torture the fucking shyster, Kray took the dumpling into his mouth and chewed slowly. When he was finished with the dumpling, Kray said, "Seventy grand isn't much of a lifestyle for a guy like that Todd. Here he is, married to this rich girl and all and he's pulling in seventy K. Shit, she was getting more than that, almost double, just breathing. Plus, he had expensive tastes."

"We've established Mr. Manion's profligate ways," the lawyer said.

"Here's the deal. Maybe your firm sent down an audit team, with the widow's approval of course. Found the Amex charges for a couple of grand a month billed to a dead woman and hired me to find out if there was anything that tied the bar into something illegal. Then there was maybe two or three thousand billed to hotel rooms in midtown on Todd's card. The biddy musta loved that, huh?"

"We only sought to avoid embarrassment," the lawyer said. "Even the hint of it."

"Yeah, the old broad probably still worries about that," Kray said. "Fuck, sixty or seventy grand a year, she'd sacrifice that to avoid the fuss. And it was pretty smart having me move on it from the other direction."

"The other area of concern is the possibility of Mr. Manion and Mr. Marotte's involvement with organized crime, the Mafia."

The question took Kray by surprise, but not much. He shook his head. "Both of them, they were loners. But tell me something, counselor, have the feds moved on the bar yet?"

The lawyer twitched and shifted in his seat. He couldn't have been more clear if he'd nodded. "Is that pertinent to this conversation?" In fact it was, and they both knew it. With the information Kray dug up, damage control would be easier.

"Probably," Kray answered. "But I'd say the trail ends with the will. What were you going to do, renounce it? Fuck, you guys probably drew it up, didn't you? Bet you gave the guy a bargain rate along with the pre-nup. Maybe it wouldn't be that hard to void. Have one of your boys whisper the right word to the judge at the club. The widow Manion hires a broker and lays the bar off quietly for next to nothing. Take about three seconds. Everything in the Manion name. Afterwards, she changes her name back. No muss, fuss, or scandal."

The lawyer let out a deep breath. "Very thorough, really, more than I expected."

"I'm glad you liked it," Kray said.

"And now, I suppose I should ask the final fee," came the reply. "The total."

"Fifty grand," Kray said.

The lawyer didn't bat an eye, he only nodded slightly.

Kray actually seemed to deflate a little. He'd spent all morning deciding on the number and now it turned out he was low. "Aren't you curious about the other thing?" he asked.

"What *thing* would that be?" the lawyer asked.

"Like who killed Todd," Kray said. "And who killed Marotte, and the girl. I got some ideas. Some things I could follow up, like that. You interested, counselor?"

"Not in the least," the lawyer said. "We'd prefer to let the police handle the investigation. As I said, we only sought to distance ourselves from possible scandal. I'll arrange for your payment to be sent over by hand, say tomorrow?"

"I got a better idea," Kray countered, pushing his small advantage. "How 'bout you send the cash over with four of those Dick Tracys hanging in the bar."

A thin smile spread across the lawyer's face. It was the first time he smiled since arriving at the restaurant. Four of the comic art originals would be worth approximately sixty thousand dollars, untaxed. In another year or two, they might be worth seventy thousand dollars. "A newfound appreciation in popular art, Mr. Kray?"

"Yeah, like that."

"I'm certain the trust would be grateful enough for your services to indulge it with, let us say, three. A bonus, so to speak."

Kray thought it over carefully, calculating the drawings as a bonus. Even three that came out on the low end, at forty K, would be like money in the bank. "Yeah, sure," he said at last. "Three's good."

"Good, good," the lawyer answered briskly, rising from the table and pushing away from it with gloved hands.

"Let me ask you something?" Kray called. "What about the other girl? Mrs. Todd."

"I'm afraid she's unavailable," the lawyer said, turning. "She's been through quite a lot."

"Yeah, she's in fucking Minnesota!" Kray yelled to the lawyer's back. "Drying out her sinuses at Hazeldon!"

The big man sat in his apartment, now growing dark, drinking Budweiser and watching the closing credits of the Oprah show scroll up the screen.

The free lawyer would return the following morning and ask for a passport and visa that he did not have. Very soon, the marshall, sent by the bank, would come for him. A notice on his door said so. Images of the old American movies he'd seen as a boy ran through his mind. Clint Eastwood. John Wayne. And that other one, Lee Van Cleef. He had no way of knowing that New York's marshall dealt almost solely in parking scofflaws, repossessions, and foreclosures. He did not know that the angry woman from Armonk's mail contained foreclosure letters until he saw the notice on the door.

He thought hard on how it had all gone so badly. He could not prove it, but he felt that somewhere in this cold city of free lawyers and big buildings, where people breathed metal air, ate poisoned food, lived in tiny rooms, and were angry, that forces he could not understand—like spirits—had conspired against him.

A commercial came on the television for more free lawyers, and the big man leaned forward and switched off the small set. For a long time he listened to the warm metal air blowing up through the floor and the cold air blowing in through a space where the sliding window did not fit quite right.

He finished the last of the beer slowly, then walked to the kitchen and opened a can of salmon. When he returned to the chair, he began to eat the salmon in the dark, but soon grew lonely and turned the television back on.

The man on the news was saying that two more children had killed themselves with guns. Then another commercial for a free lawyer came on.

There were so many lawyers in this cold city, he thought. So many lawyers that surely one less would make little difference.

Twenty-Six

Max didn't believe in coincidence, unless he had to or wanted to. On the other hand, the fed twins, as he'd taken to thinking of Reddick and Targin, hadn't been around again. So maybe that Kray guy had put a word in for him.

Or maybe he was just screwed again.

In any event, Lynn had mellowed, temporarily adrift in her own anxiety, and Julie had taken to playing up to him. But that didn't count for much. Lynn was a survivor. Two weeks, maximum, and she'd pull herself together. As for Julie, she was wounded and down. The Hollywood producer had left town and wouldn't return her calls. *Ah, Beware the Producer Who Stays at the Marriott Marquis.* And the media wasn't interested in the murders, much less hearing from the official spokesperson. Even the tabloids had moved on to the newest crime.

It was two o'clock when he crawled from bed, missing Suze and thinking of calling her. Instead of heading directly down to the kitchen, he took the other door that wound down a narrow servants' stairway and came out next to a linen closet. From there, he wandered around the house. The place was like a museum of old money. Everything was perfect, but grown just a little shabby by a generation of neglect.

Twenty-five years ago, Denny Mcbride was known for his parties. Huge, sprawling things that probably appeared near sinfully revolutionary with the rock and roll, acid-eyed beautiful people, and mini skirts thrown against the dark Victoriana of the furnishings. Today, it seemed quaint and a little puzzling to consider. The day the furnace went out, Max found a six-foot length of fluorescent black light, a stack of day-glow posters, and a broken strobe light in an unused coal bin. That's the way the wealthy organized their lives, he supposed, antiques and heirlooms in the attic, *objets d'mode* in the basement.

How many basements of his neighbors, he wondered, were filled with Nehru jackets, Peter Max art, or for that matter, Todd Manions.

Max walked into the library and switched on the light. A hundred or more of Denny's unframed canvases leaned against shelves packed with calfskin volumes and framed portraits and photos of dead Mcbrides on the walls. A thin layer of dust had collected over the writing desk crammed with knick-knacks and the mantel crowded with more knick-knacks and dead Mcbrides. The Aubusson rug was starting to look a little darker. In another week or two, he'd go crosstown, to the Museum of Natural History, and hook up with a Jamaican nanny he knew. The museum was a big nanny hangout in winter. They'd bring the kids in and let them run around the exhibits while they gossiped. Forever, he'd remember hearing one scold her young charge, "Zachry! Don't be tinking 'bout bottering tat dinosaur!"

The particular nanny he knew was in charge of an eight-month-old girl. Twice a month, she'd bring the little girl crosstown and clean the house, polish the wood, vacuum the carpets. She'd spent four years working down the street and knew how to treat the precious and invaluable. What polishes to buy, cloths to use, and cleansers to avoid were a careful art in these places.

It was a scam that more than a few of the nannies ran. Sometimes they'd leave the kids with other nannies for a few hours while they moonlighted as housekeepers. When the kids got old enough to talk, the deal was over. Still, the other ones were worse. One agency that advertised college girls from Sweden, Denmark, and

France—which decoded meant white and often from places like Nebraska—had a bad run of luck one year when a half dozen of their *au pairs* got busted for running a phone-sex scam out of a corporate raider's apartment on Fifth Avenue.

Max moved through the library on the second floor, peeked out through the thick curtains, and saw it was starting to snow. A solid quarter inch was on the ground, and traffic was backed up on the street. Maybe he'd see some business that night.

By the time he reached the kitchen, the coffee was perked. He was going for his cup in the sink when the phone rang. He picked it up and the operator came on. "Collect call to anyone from Miles," she said. "Will you accept charges?"

It took Max a second for the call to sink in. Miles never called. There were phones all over the prison where inmates could call anywhere collect, yet he never called.

"Will you accept charges?" the operator repeated.

"Yeah, I'll accept," Max mumbled, thinking that this wasn't good.

"It's me," Miles said, his voice nearly drowned out by cellblock noise.

"Yeah?"

"Listen, whatever you're doing, stop it," Miles said.

Max wedged the phone between his ear and shoulder and filled his cup. "I'm having a cup of coffee."

"Listen to me, Max," Miles said, his voice flat and deliberate. "I asked some questions about what we were talking about last time, and they reached out for me. It's not good."

"It's stopped," Max said. "All over."

There was a long pause on the other end filled up with clatter. "That's good," Miles said at last. Then his tone lightened up a little, "When you coming up?"

"What you say, in two weeks?"

"I'll pencil you in," Miles said, his voice returning to near normal. "You know, I'll be around."

Max tried to respond to the joke, but couldn't. "I'll bring some postcards."

"Great, see you then," Miles answered and hung up.

Two minutes later, the phone rang again. Max picked it up on the second ring. "Max?" Babs Binindi's voice said, then didn't wait for an answer. "Hold for Gil."

A second later, Gil Pontero came on the line. "Kid, N-G on that made-for-TV."

Max put his cup down. "What, they canceled production?"

"They canceled you, kid," Gil said, his voice cracking and echoing over the speaker phone.

"I thought we have a contract with these people?"

"Had is the operative word. *Had a contract*," Gil corrected. "They went with someone else."

Max felt something was up. It wasn't a big part, not a lot of lines, but plenty of walk-ons. In elevators, on the street, in a crowd. The way the part was written, he was a suspect through half the show. Two weeks work, at least, and above scale. That was something like ten grand, not counting residuals if they used his appearance for any promo spots. Gil wouldn't be glib over losing his ten percent. "So, who'd they go with?" Max asked.

"Some kid," Gil answered cautiously. "Another look, you know?"

Max was starting to catch on. "Off your roster, though, right?"

"As a matter of fact . . ."

"As a matter of fact, yeah," Max said. "Don't bullshit me Gil. What happened to my contract?"

"Look, they're paying the kid scale," Gil answered defensively. "Scale. And they're paying you five grand to forget it."

So that was the deal. Gil negotiated him out of the contract for the same fee. Did the favor and didn't lose a dime. "What happened to the contract?"

"Look, don't make a thing out of this, understand?" Gil said, almost pleading. "Wait, I'm taking you off speaker."

"Gil?" Max said.

A second later the agent's voice was back, close now, talking directly into the phone. "You get five grand for nothing. What kind of problem could you have with that?"

"What happened to my contract?" Max insisted.

Gil inhaled deeply. When he spoke again, his voice had changed from pleading to pissed off. "Max, your fucking contract died with that scumbag Todd Manion. Now be a good guy. Take the fucking money. Trust me, I'll take care of you in a couple of months. Send you up for some parts. Commercials, national spots, okay?"

"Yeah, sure Gil," Max said and hung up without waiting for an answer.

Max finished his coffee thinking the whole world was looking for closure. That had been the hot word going around. Closure on relationships, marriages, drug habits, careers, the eighties, maybe even their lives. They just wanted somebody to tell them it was over. A last call and the lights go on revealing the shabbiness and debris. And that's exactly what Max figured he had.

Ten minutes later Max was still mulling it over, finishing his third cup of coffee, when the door bell rang. Checking the monitor in the vestibule, he saw Targin and Reddick. The one named Targin was waving up at the camera. Real cute.

Max opened the door to them, asking, "What's up?"

"We were good guys last time, right?" Targin said, walking past Max. "Didn't lean too hard. Just checking up. Had some coffee, shot the shit a little. It was pleasant, almost."

"He's pissed," Reddick said, following his partner through the door. "You've got him mad now. Really mad."

"What? I didn't do shit," Max said, ignoring Reddick's running commentary.

"Did you hear that?" Targin said. " 'Didn't do shit.' What about a fat fuck named Delbert Kray?"

Max backed up a step. "He was supposed to square it with you guys."

A brief flash of disbelief settled across both Targin and Reddick's face. "He couldn't square shit," Targin snapped back.

"He told me he had an inside with you guys."

Targin stepped forward. "Your buddy Kray's got nothing. No juice at all," he said. "He's an old FBI guy who got canned because he sold some files to a data banker. There's a civil case pending against him because he traded blow-jobs from a car dealer's wife he was supposed to be following in exchange for letting her keep banging a tennis pro up in Putnam County. That's what kind of scumbag you're talking to."

Max felt his knees go a little weak. He moved back toward the stairs and sat down.

"Now, you're gonna start answering some questions," Targin said.

Max pressed hard with both hands on either side of his head and looked down. Reddick pulled his head back up by the hair. "What do you know about the pigs?" he asked.

"Pigs?"

"Yeah, what about the fucking pigs?" Reddick said.

"Nothing, I don't know anything about pigs," Max answered. Confusion must have been plastered across his face.

"What about the money?" Targin said. "When does it start moving?"

Max shook his head, looking from one to the other. Both their faces were stony.

"What fucking bank is the money moving from?"

"Really, I don't know what you guys are talking about," Max said.

"Then how about this," Reddick said, leaning down close, getting right in Max's face. "How are they taking the money out? What is it, cash, stamps, diamonds, what? Who's supplying the mule—the Smurfs?"

"Moving out where?" Max answered. "I don't know about any of this shit."

"Then try this one," Reddick said. "Where's the motherfucking Samoan, huh?"

Max was about to say something, but before he could, Targin broke in. "Okay, be a scumbag," he said. "But when we find that fucking Samoan, we'll tie you to him so tight you won't know what hit you. And that's a murder rap, just for starters."

Max felt the cold wet blast from the door. When he looked up again, they were gone.

An hour later, Max walked to the Lexington Avenue subway and took it down to Astor Place, came up from the renovated subway station, and walked east, looking at college kids and would-be artists having fun in the snow. Thinking that a couple of treasury agents would be easy enough to spot. When he reached Second Avenue, he turned right and headed downtown, walked a couple of blocks and had kielbasa and eggs at the Kiev Diner.

When he finished his eggs, he caught a cab and headed back uptown, telling the cabbie to get off the FDR Drive on Forty-second.

TWENTY-SEVEN

It was all going pretty good for W. T. Zunick. Already he'd run up something like three grand in out-of-pocket. Doctor bills, prescriptions, credit card receipts for gas, twelve cents a mile on travel, and even a hundred or so in bogus parking lot receipts from a place downtown near the civil court.

He figured that maybe he put in eight hours on the case, which totaled out to a billing rate around five bills an hour, less his initial investment, which was something like a hundred and fifty bucks. A hundred for the intern at the hospital, twenty for the typing service that did up the letter of representation, gas, stamps, and a couple of calls off the cellular.

The doctors' bills were all contingency, which meant they knew the risks and trusted him enough to invest

the eight or ten minutes it took to see the big guy and
work up the reports. They also knew they'd have to kick
back a hundred and a half each if they wanted to stay in
business together.

He was solid with the doctors. Not like some of those
other lawyers who had to drag in the EMS and police
incident reports to negotiate a contingency deal.

Sometimes, in quieter moments, he began to believe
that it was just getting out of control. It was only a
matter of time before the public was beginning to catch
on. Soon they'd be shopping for the best contingency
fees. Walking off the street with strong cases and full
paperwork, looking to shave five or ten points off the
lawyer's split. The whole thing was heading in a bad
direction, he could feel it.

Then, there were those lawyers out West, truly desperate characters. It wasn't enough to just catch the crashes
on a scanner, these maniacs were staging them. It started
a couple of years ago out in L.A., but was already beginning to go strong in New York. They used three or four
cars, forcing some poor schmuck, always a truck or van
with commercial tags, to rear end their guy—usually
some asshole who just got canned and was willing to
take a chance in a wreck. And they were pulling that shit
on freeways; people were dying behind those scams.

Zunick parked in a garage up on Eighty-sixth and
walked down Second to the apartment, all the time letting his brain drift back over the math, which is what law
was about anyway. He was particularly interested in *The
Specials*—the Special Damages he'd claim.

Zunick was thinking that by the time he finally sat
down with the claims adjuster, he could have the bills
for treatment and therapy up to around four grand with
a projection of a twenty grand total. The medical reports
he had were masterpieces of litigious art. Real tragic
stuff. But lately they'd all been like that. Lord help
him, he even had to tone a few of them down. Four or
five years ago, you'd start to see them around August
or September, when the doctors starting thinking about
winter, Bermuda vacations, and the new car models.

Now they all pushed the limits, all the time, like they just didn't care anymore.

Usually he was a conservative player, looking to make the sale to the insurance company for triple the total. But this time he was going for the gold, looking for four times the medical billing for pain, suffering, anxiety, and the other bullshit. He figured he could sit down with the adjuster a couple days after the insurance company's internal report hit the desk. And then he'd let them buy it for seventy-five or eighty. No fuss, a neat twenty-six-two for himself off the top. Then he'd start adding the extras like the kickbacks from the therapists and doctors, plus the cash he advanced the big man, plus the advance on medications, and his operating expenses. By the time he finished, the original seventy-thirty split would come out more like fifty-fifty without ever seeing the inside of a courtroom.

And that was the whole point of the thing, never to see the inside of a courtroom. The thing was, you had to play it smart and know just how high the insurance company would go without taking it to court. Edge up the compensation near six figures and the adjuster is gonna start talking about depositions and trial dates. And those fucks could eat up a year just on depositions and postponements. Never mind about the experts they call in, the hard thing was to keep your client in line for a year. Forget about how much you told them they stood to make or how much you babysat them, clients just couldn't resist stupidity. It was in their blood.

Leave a soft-tissue victim alone for an afternoon and he'd rip off the neck brace and start throwing his toddler around on the front lawn or play shortstop for the company softball team with fifty home video cameras pointed on him.

But the worst thing about them was their fucking greed. Tell a client what the liability coverage was and the next thing you knew, he was dragging the family down to the Javits Center Boat Show to pick out their yacht, or more often, charging the limit on the family Visa card. What did they think, that insurance companies hand over seven-figure compensation checks like the lottery? Anyway, whatever they got, seven or seventy grand, they always blew it. *Always*. It was in their blood. They were victims.

Sure, there was some bullshit on his part, he knew that. Like talking up the award and the coverage. Always open with the coverage. And say it like it's change you'd pick up on the street. Then pull out the cases, news clippings were best, trial summaries almost as good, just as long as it looked official and mentioned some outrageous numbers in compensation. But that was the fucking hook. You promise the world, and settle for a living wage. Scare them into the settlement with a line about how the insurance company hasn't lost a case and how the doctors' reports won't stand up against the specialists they'll have to see. Lay it out for them somber as hell, like a relative's died. And soon the client's begging for the seven or eight grand.

There was always disability, which was another game altogether. Kickbacks from doctors like crazy. And if the client actually had to work again, well that was just too fucking bad. *This was still America; go out and find a job*. He didn't have the time or the kind of money it took to mount an all-out case against some insurance monster.

Besides, he fucking hated court. Juries, judges, and the rest of that bullshit. What was the point when you could sit down with some adjuster and knock out a deal? Court was a dice game, but a deal was always a deal.

The lawyer approached the building's lobby and stamped the snow off his feet. The doorman was there, looking grim. For a couple of seconds, the lawyer thought about offering the guy a grand to play along, then thought better of it. The doorman looked like the kind of punk who'd go running to building management with the bribe just to save his seven bucks an hour.

"Ring up my client, will you?" the lawyer said.

"He expecting you?" Derek asked, not moving from the seat.

Attitude, the lawyer thought. This punk in a polyester

uniform with gold braid on the shoulders is giving me attitude. "Let's buzz up and find out, huh?"

Derek got up off his seat reluctantly and punched in the number. A moment later he said, "Your lawyer's here. Yeah, sure."

"He's expecting me, right?" the lawyer said.

Derek motioned toward the elevator wordlessly, and the lawyer walked through the lobby. As soon as the elevator door closed behind Zunick, Derek pulled a bent business card from his pants pocket and dialed the beeper number.

Three minutes later the phone rang.

"This is Del Kray," the voice on the other end said.

"Yeah, the lawyer just went up," Derek answered in a whisper, though nobody was in the lobby.

"I'll be there in ten minutes," Kray said, and hung up.

Kray showed up ten minutes later dressed in overalls and carrying a toolbox.

"Jesus, what happened to your face?" Derek asked, opening the door. "It didn't look that bad last night at the bar."

"You should see the other guy," Kray said, smiling. He needed this doorman. He hadn't worked with the insurance company before, but if he could get something on the deadbeat, it was a foot in the door.

"Looks like it was a bunch of guys," Derek said, coming out from behind the desk. "You sure this is cool?"

"Like I told you, it's done," Kray said with a shrug. "I'll go up, get some shit on the guy, and take it to the insurance company. If I can show the guy's ripping them off, then I got a chance at the job and you're off the fucking hook."

Derek thought it over for a second. "Man, it just seems like really fucked up, big time, you know?"

"Wake up," Kray said, snapping the fingers of his good hand in Derek's face. "This is New York, if everyone played by the rules it'd be anarchy."

Derek did a slow shuffle, hesitating. "I don't know, man."

"You better get your thinking straight," Kray ordered.

"You think that guy upstairs is confused. He ain't confused and soon he's gonna be cashing a check. It's fucked up, but it's done."

"I don't know, it's really fucked up."

"Like I said, it's fucked up, but it's done. It's math. What would you rather do, write a check for forty grand to a fucking deadbeat or hire me for maybe four or five to shred the guy's case?"

"I don't know, it's fucked up," Derek said, still wary.

Kray put the case down. "Look kid, what's the worst they can do to you, huh? Fire you? They file that claim, you're shit-canned anyway, history. Also, and I don't want to scare you here, but nine times out of ten, they file criminal charges," Kray said. "We're talking what, here? Some fucking assault charge. You want to spend your life dragging ass around criminal court fighting to stay out of the slam, while this fuck's living high on insurance money?"

"I don't know," Derek answered, shaking his head.

"Look, you called me, remember?" Kray said, moving in a little. "Don't fucking waste my time."

Derek backed down. "Go on up," he said. "What's in there anyway?"

Kray picked up the case. "What's in here is a tray of tools on top. Underneath is some more tools, power drill and shit, and a recorder. See that little hole?"

Derek nodded to the chipped side that looked partly rusted through. "Yeah?"

"There's a two-hundred-dollar mike and a voice-activated recorder attached to it," Kray said.

"Yeah, like James Bond, huh?"

"Yeah, like James-fucking-Bond," Kray said, walking toward the elevator. "Now give me five minutes to get up, then buzz him and tell him I'm coming. I want to be at the door when I hear the phone inside ring, understand?"

"Like to distract him, right?" Derek said, getting into the conspiracy.

"Yeah, like that," Kray answered, and pushed the button to the side of the elevator's door.

Kray moved as quietly as he could from the elevator to the apartment. It wasn't quite five yet, so there wouldn't be a bunch of people moving around in the halls, coming home from work, and taking their dogs out for a walk.

When he reached the door, he stood to one side, listening. When he didn't hear anything, he opened the toolbox and switched on the Olympus microcassette recorder that was taped to the underside of the tray. As he was shutting the case he heard the phone. On the first ring, he rang the bell and kept ringing it like there was an emergency. The idea was to get into the apartment. Once you got in, nobody threw you out, as long as you looked official.

The phone inside stopped ringing and Kray heard someone talking. Then the talking stopped and the peephole opened.

"We got water flooding in from your bathroom down on the floor below," he yelled, panic coming into his voice. "It's flooding those people out!"

"Wait," the voice said through the door.

Kray waited. A few seconds later, the peephole opened again. "No water," the voice said.

"It's in the walls, pal!"

"Come back later," the voice answered.

This was gonna be tough, Kray could see that. "What?" he called, making out like he couldn't hear.

"Come back later," the voice ordered.

"I can't hear you, pal," Kray said. "But I gotta get in there. Either you open up or I'm going back down to building management and have them take the door off the hinges. Bust it down. Hear me? This is an emergency."

Something inside moved, and Kray got ready. The door opened an inch, and Kray saw the big man. "Go to apartment next door," he said. "No water in walls."

Kray pushed and the door gave way as he squeezed himself inside. "I can't pal," he began. "I gotta look at your john. It's a mess . . ."

Behind him, Kray vaguely heard the door slam. But

what he saw inside just shocked the shit out of him. There was a guy lying sprawled on the floor, his throat cut and a pool of blood the size of a manhole spreading out over the parquet floor.

"Told you, come back," the voice behind him said.

"Okay, sure," Kray said, then turned fast and jammed the toolbox into the guy's gut. It hit solidly, and Kray went for the doorknob, but the big guy was blocking the door. Suddenly a huge hand came down and bounced Kray's head off the drywall.

For a second he saw stars, then managed to stagger further into the room. He moved quickly, ears still ringing, and began looking for a weapon. There was an empty wine bottle on the television, where Oprah was passing a mike to a smiling college girl with something to say. Kray went for it, but slipped on the blood as the big man moved for him.

Downstairs, Max was talking Derek up, trying to avoid the promise of a job, if at all possible.

"Look, just let me up to see the Samoan, will ya?" Max said.

"And I'm asking you again, why?" Derek said, holding his ground.

"Like I said, I think he's tied into the thing I'm working on for someone," Max said. "If he's a bad guy, that gets you off the hook, right?"

Derek thought it over, walking away. "Okay, not now, he's got company. Okay?"

Max worked his way into the lobby. "Yeah, who?"

"Like it's any of your business, right?"

"Come on man, you don't have anything to lose," Max tried. "Why protect the guy, huh?"

"Well, his lawyer for one thing," Derek said.

"Yeah?"

"And a friend of yours."

Max shook his head, "Friend of mine, who?" Then he saw them coming up to the entrance. Reddick and Targin.

"That guy Kray, you know, I met him at the bar last night," Derek answered. "He's a good guy. Gonna help me out here."

But Max wasn't listening. Targin was reaching into his coat pocket; a second later, a pair of handcuffs flashed. Cheap theatrics, but enough to get Max's attention. With those handcuffs and arrest looming large, Targin was DeNiro.

"You know, he's gonna help me out on the lawsuit bullshit," Derek said.

Max stood frozen; the two treasury guys were maybe fifty feet from the door. Briefly, Max thought of flight, skip through the back door. But then what?

"Who're these guys?" Derek asked, following Max's gaze.

Targin was swinging the cuffs on one finger as they approached. He was smiling.

Max didn't answer; rather, he began walking, numbed, out the door to meet the two men. As he moved through the revolving door, something dark flashed, there was a rush of air, a bass thump, and an explosion of snow erupted up in front of him, startling him back against the glass and sending the adrenaline pumping. When he opened his eyes again, a body lay on the new snow between him and the fed twins.

The guy landed on his back, ass first, and bounced. The impact had shattered the skull at the top, above the hairline, and scattered brains out in a thick trail that began above Kray's distorted face and ended on the second leather button of Targin's navy coat.

Oddly, Max noticed that one of Kray's shoes had fallen off. He was wearing white socks.

Reddick said something that began with "Fuck" and looked up. Instinct brought Targin's hand up to his soiled coat, but he quickly wiped his hand clean down the front when he realized what had soiled it. Then they both charged forward, hustling Max back through the revolving door into the lobby.

"What apartment?" Targin said, cornering Derek. "What floor?"

"Ah man, man," Derek moaned. "Look at that guy, look!"

"What floor?" Reddick demanded. Then added, "Treasury."

"Ah man, fuck," Derek answered, his mind grinding down in confusion and shock. "Fuck, you got brains on your coat."

Targin moved in, took Derek by the lapels, and began shaking him. "What apartment!"

Reddick moved around, picked up the house phone, and began dialing.

"You gotta dial nine first," Derek said, gathering himself together a little.

Targin released his grip on Derek and asked again, voice calmer, "What apartment he come out of?"

"Twenty-three B," Derek answered as Reddick called in 911, then hung up and dialed another number.

Targin pulled cuffs from his pocket and locked Max to the chrome stanchion with the sign on top that said, ALL VISITORS MUST BE ANNOUNCED.

"Who lives there?" Targin asked, pulling a gun.

"Samoan," Derek answered. "Big fucker."

The two feds looked at each other and smiled.

Max tested the cuffs. They weren't toys. "How'd you find me?" he asked, not sure he'd get an answer.

Targin gave him a look, and said, "Kray, we had a line on his beeper. We weren't even looking for you, asshole. There any back stairs?"

"Through the door, past the elevator," Derek said.

"You got a control key for the elevators?" Reddick asked, already moving.

"Porter got it," Derek said, eyes glued to the corpse outside.

Reddick, now breathing hard, shouted, "Where's the porter?"

Derek shrugged, knowing the porter was either in the model apartment getting laid, working his moonlight job as an usher at an Eighty-sixth Street movie theater, or clocked out legitimately on his lunch break.

"Shit!" Reddick said, then he and Targin were

gone. Targin up the stairs, Reddick at the elevator. "Tell the police we're here! Don't let anyone leave. Don't let anyone touch the body," he called back to Derek as the doors chimed open. Then to Max, "And you, don't fucking move!"

It took about six seconds for a crowd to start to gather outside and the police sirens to start working their way through traffic.

"What'd I do, man?" Derek asked plaintively, watching the crowd edge in around the body. A young guy in a suit and topcoat kicked at Kray's white-socked foot, then picked up the shoe laying nearby and tossed it onto the dead man's chest.

"Go cover him up with something," Max said, feeling a dull panic rising up in him. The fed twins said they'd tie him to the Samoan, and if the Samoan did this, then he'd be an accessory to murder. Fuck it, he thought, he'd run.

Derek was rummaging around in the doorman's desk and found an oversized umbrella for escorting residents to cabs on rainy days. It was the best he could do and took the umbrella out the door. When he opened it, the name of the building was silk-screened in eighteen-inch-high gold letters. He covered the stiff, at least the head, with it, then tried to shoo away the crowd. Oddly, it made Kray look like he was on a beach. All he needed was a piña colada in his hand.

As Derek began working on the crowd, Max tried to twist the top half of the sign off, but it was welded on to the stanchion and the post was sunk into a chrome joint in the marble floor.

Max gave the post a hard twist and the thing turned. Pulling, it came up from the joint, nearly breaking his wrist with the release of weight. The thing must have been thirty pounds.

Outside, blue police cars were pulling up to the curb. Max headed for the back door. When he reached it, the thing was locked from the inside. Targin probably locked it when he took the stairs.

Max, dragging the post, pushed the elevator button.

He'd take it down to the health spa level and get out through the service entrance.

The elevator door opened as the cops came into the lobby. Max hit the basement button and felt the elevator rise as he saw the hand-lettered sign to the side of the control panel, "Health Spa Hours 5:30 p.m.—10:30 p.m." No service to the basement.

The big man knew he didn't have much time. He did not want to throw the fat plumber over the railing of the tiny balcony, but the plumber had come after him with a broken wine bottle. He had cut him with the bottle, once across the cheek, then again over his eyes, before running out on the balcony to scream for help. At first he wanted to drag the plumber back inside and kill him there. But they fought again, and he had to throw the plumber over the railing.

The big man was bleeding badly now, his blood stinging his eyes and running down into the shearling jacket. He could feel the blood soaking into the knit cap. The towel he held to his cheek did little to stem the tide of blood.

He knew that his only chance for escape was to leave through the back quickly. As he waited for the elevator, he saw the indicator open at the lobby, then move up. As each number flashed higher, he knew with greater certainty that someone was coming for him. It was rare that the elevator traveled up so far without stopping at a lower floor.

When the elevator was two floors below him, he hid in the room where tenants left their garbage in plastic bags for the janitor to take down. Peeking through the door, the big man watched as a man with a gun ran toward his apartment.

As quietly as he could, the big man left the room with the bags of garbage and headed toward the elevator. When he pushed the button, the door opened immediately.

He would take it down to the second floor then use the stairs.

*   *   *

Max got off on two and turned the wrong way down
the hall, still dragging the sign. When he turned back, he
heard the elevator door open as he passed. Instinctively
he paused and looked in.

Coming at him was the biggest guy he'd ever seen.
And the guy was covered in blood.

It was the guy! The Samoan!

The guy pushed past Max and headed toward the
stairs.

And Max realized, if this asshole gets away, it's just
me and the cops.

Max followed, lifting the sign as he went. When he
reached the guy, he brought the sign up and swung awkwardly, landing it across the guy's back. The shearling
absorbed most of the shock, and the big man turned
quickly, glaring murderously, but not talking.

Max backpedaled, and the big man turned back to
the door, opened it, and vanished into the stairway.
Before the door shut, Max was through it, following
the footsteps down, the sign clanking alongside.

As he rounded the first corner on the stairs, he saw
the big man again, waiting for him. Huge hands were
out like a wrestler's, poised there with closed fists.

Max brought the chrome sign up in front of him in
a fighting stance, then thought, fuck it, and jumped the
three steps.

The big man turned, pivoting on his left foot, to let
Max sail by, but suddenly lost his footing. As he fell
backwards, the edge of the square sign caught him in
the eye and he brought his hands up off the rail.

Max felt himself hit the guy, and it was like hitting
a wall. Then the wall gave way and he rode the big man
down the twenty or so stairs, hearing the clank of the
metal stand as it tore at his wrist and the dull thud
the big man's head made as it bounced down each of the
concrete steps.

Twenty-Eight

Targin and Reddick sat at the bar smiling. They were dressed casual, crewnecks, slacks, and no ties. Max figured it must have been their day off or something.

Max looked across and poured a couple of drafts from the good spigot. He figured he owed them that, at least. They'd helped clear him. And he told almost everything he knew, even turned over the cheap plastic briefcase that Delbert Kray left at the bar the night he got shit-faced with Derek.

"You're a lucky guy," Targin said, taking the glass.

Reddick took a sip of his beer and nodded in agreement.

The whole thing was just civilized as hell.

Outside, the last of the gray winter snow was melting. It had taken that long to clear the mess up.

"So, what about the pigs?" Max asked. It was a question he wanted to ask for a long time.

"Yeah, what about those fucking pigs?" Targin said, still smiling.

Reddick lifted his beer and said, "To the pigs."

"Come on, give me a clue here, will you?" Max asked. He just opened and he wanted to get the truth out of these guys, before the first flurry of customers.

Both of them shook their heads.

"Okay, then," Max said, "give me a hypothetical. How's that? Change the names to protect the guilty."

"Hypothetically speaking?" Reddick asked, sipping away.

Targin nodded slightly.

"Okay, then, suppose there was an island," Reddick started.

"Samoa?" Max asked.

"Guess again," Targin answered. "Your friend was just hired help. By the way, Samoans don't speak pidgin, they speak Samoan."

Reddick began again. "Now, this island's doing pretty good for itself," he said. "Getting aid from the Russians, from the Americans. Soft loans from the IMF. Pocket change, you know, but enough. Suddenly the Soviets are gone and we cut aid. They have a couple of revolutions, but the *ratus*, the tribal chiefs, are still pretty much in charge."

A couple came in and took a seat at a back table.

"Hold on," Max said, then eased down the bar to serve them. Julie had quit more than a month before. Two weeks ago he'd gotten a call from some caterer in L.A. The guy sounded like a prick and wanted to check out her references. Max told him yeah, she'd been tending bar at Barmy's for a couple of years. A great bartender in fact. "Our clients," the prick from L.A. whined with a significant pause, "are exclusive A-list, you understand." And Max told him Julie wouldn't be a problem.

Max made the drinks and returned to Targin and Reddick. "Go on, I want to hear the rest of it."

"Well, these guys, they're not dumb," Reddick said. "They look around and see what other islands are doing. The Caymans, the Isle of Man, Anguilla, Andorra, Vanuatu, like that."

"Money laundering," Max said. "And tax havens."

"Bingo," Reddick answered, a little worried about Max's knowledge. "So they pass a bunch of laws. Banking secrecy laws and nationalize the banks, looking to sell them off piecemeal, privatize as it were. Maybe they even loosen up the tax laws a little. Thing got about three lines in the *Wall Street Journal* and two graphs in the *Economist*."

Max leaned against the bar. "Who shows up, Wall Street?"

"More like Mulberry Street," Targin said. "See the bent-nose crew's been shoveling money into Wall Street for years. Been putting their kids in as brokers and lawyers, just to keep an eye on the money and maybe do a little fancy accounting. Now this is serious money, washed through a bunch of front companies. But lately the SEC's been snooping around. There's some unofficial leaks to other agencies, local DA, justice, and like that. The Swiss are starting to relax some of their secrecy laws. And nobody knows how the EC is going to shake down. Maybe a bunch of their guys turn rats. Just say, hypothetically."

Max, seeing conspiracy everywhere, thought yeah, and maybe a couple of federal agencies aren't as close to the families as they used to be, huh?

"Maybe even they're getting a little scared, you know," Targin continued. "The market's acting kinda jittery. And maybe it's a good time to stay liquid. Or, they want to branch out. Invest overseas. Maybe buy a bank for themselves. A fallback position, maybe."

"But the banks were nationalized, right?"

Reddick smiled again and took a sip of beer. "Right. You can buy one, but only with approval of the banking honcho, who happens to be one of the bigwigs' sons. What the islanders expected were Wall Street types, insurance companies, factors, finance companies, actors, athletes, rock and rollers, mid-sized manufacturers with offshore concerns, you know, businessmen," he said. "So the bent noses find a front man. An Aussie with a good name."

"But the island guys find out, huh?"

"Maybe what they find is this," Targin said. "Now listen carefully. They find the Aussie's last asset is his good name. He went heavy into real estate, and he's coming up short. Overextended and needs a little cash infusion, as they say. He starts buying up the bank stock with a loan from a Singapore bank. Then, he borrows money from a half dozen or so Mob front companies to pay off his legit loan, using the bank stock as collateral."

"Let me guess," Max said. "He defaults on the loans. The ones from the Mob. They get the bank stock."

"Close," Targin said. "Maybe he's about to default when the islanders find out what the scam is and get nervous. If he can't buy the rest of the stock—get control of the bank—the deal doesn't go through. He's stuck with a bank in the middle of the ocean with about eight cents in assets and loans from the Mob and Singapore. Now, these guys aren't going to take thirty cents on the dollar in some bankruptcy court."

Max leaned back against the back bar, listening, his gaze going from one to the other.

Reddick, now warming to the story, continued. "So, the more the island guys back off, the more the family wants the bank," he said. "They start wining and dining the tribal hotshots, through the Aussie. You know their style. Anyway, they bought up almost every fucking pig on the place and then flew in more. That's what tipped us off, the pigs. Peace Corps worker, of all people, got suspicious."

"What about the Samoan?" Max asked.

"So, everything cools down. They're about to do the deal," Reddick said. "Then, out of nowhere, somebody, some woman out in Jersey, starts making noise about the bank stiffing her for a loan."

"That would be that Peter Marotte guy's scam, right?" Max said.

"Bingo again," Reddick answered, draining his beer and handing the glass to Max. "Now the Mob gets scared and maybe leans on the Aussie to clean up the problem. The guy's into them for a bunch of money and the notes are coming due. If the bank's got a light on it, they don't want to play."

Max took the glass and filled it. "What about the somebody in Jersey?"

"Dead," Targin said.

"And Marotte's dead," Max offered.

"Now, here's the thing," Reddick said. "We can't do shit because somebody bought a bunch of pigs. We can't do shit if some country wants to sell a bank. What're we gonna do, ask the State Department to pull their Peace Corps volunteers? But now we got a complaint from a U.S. citizen."

"So, the Aussie sends someone out to fix it?" Max asked.

"*Voilà*, that's it. The family gives him a little help, maybe, and tells him to take care of the problem," Targin said, putting his beer down. "Now you know it all. Maybe."

"What about the Aussie?" Max asked.

"Maybe the best part," Reddick said. "You gotta remember, this has been going on for months. The guy's a nervous wreck. Smoking three packs a day, drinking like a fish. Around the same time as you were wrestling the Samoan, he drops hypothetically dead of a hypothetical heart attack. Any other hypothetical questions?"

Max came up off the back bar and flipped the switch that turned on the outside lights. "Who killed Todd Manion?"

Reddick and Targin looked at each other. Finally Reddick said, "Who gives a fuck? The guy was a hound. Probably some girl. He was shot with a lady's gun. A twenty-five."

"But not his gun," Max said, knowing his fingerprints had been on the wrong gun. The cardboard-wrapped .380 automatic, Todd's gun, was still with the doorman at Todd's apartment when the NYPD stepped in.

The NYPD had cleared Max quickly. Probably he'd never been a suspect. The detectives were just pressuring him for information. The piece was reduced to paperwork. The contents of Kray's briefcase included the complete NYPD file, including the detectives' notes.

Janey's family would have leaned on someone to bury the case. The detectives had been reassigned after two weeks. Among all the official police paperwork in the briefcase, pages and pages of it, her maiden name was only mentioned once—but it was circled. So was the name of some law firm downtown.

Max wondered how much money it took to kill a murder investigation. And the answer came back, if you have to ask how much, then you can't afford it. But the one thing he knew, whoever killed Todd would never hear from the police.

"No, he was killed with another gun," Reddick said, sliding off the stool.

Targin followed his partner's lead, finishing off the beer as he stood up. "It's been real pleasant," he said. "This is a nice place."

"Tell your friends," Max said, as he watched them leave.

Max was driving a rented car and it took him a long time to find the house. He would have missed it completely, except for the handicapped van in the driveway.

As he went up the walk, he wondered if it was too early, then decided that ten on a Sunday morning was early, but not outrageous for people in the suburbs. If he left in an hour, he'd still be able to make his date with Miles upstate.

When he rang the bell, Mrs. Brimmer answered immediately. She was dressed in a pair of blue slacks and a red sweater. Dressed between winter and spring. She said, "Yes?"

"Remember me, Mrs. Brimmer?" Max asked.

She stared for a second through her oversized glasses, her memory working. "You're the bartender, right?"

Inside, a man's voice yelled from a back room and she called back, "It's okay."

"Look, I have to run, I just wanted to bring something by, okay?" Max said, then dug into his pocket and pulled out the charm bracelet. There were a bunch of little charms on it, gold cups, a tiny bike, and two new ones, a tragedy and comedy mask joined at the ears.

One of the woman's hands went up to her mouth in recognition and Max dropped the bracelet into the other. "I didn't want to just put it in the mail," he said, then turned to leave.

The woman made a noise and stepped off the porch. She studied it carefully and saw the traces of white plaster dust in the links. "Where'd you find this, may I ask?" she said, coming down the stairs.

Max was going to lie to her, then decided against it. Like dropping it in the mail with no return address, it would have left her wondering. "It was behind a tile in Pat's apartment," he said. "Up under the bathroom sink."

Her hand came up again, and she bit down on the bracelet. A guy in a wheelchair appeared in the door behind her. "Everything okay?" he called.

When the woman didn't say anything, Max raised his hands up and said, "Yeah, no problem."

"How did you know?" she asked. "Know where they kept things?"

Max did a slow shuffle, not wanting to get into it. Kray's briefcase had the uniformed officer's report from her visit to retrieve her daughter's things. The guy was thorough, probably a rookie. "The cop who let you in. I saw his log. It said that you took out a dress, shoes, and some makeup. That night you came into the bar, you said you wanted the bracelet. It wasn't listed, I just figured you forgot it."

"Pat showed me the hole when they first moved in. Peter did it. She thought he was so clever. I guess I forgot it, I just got so nervous when I found that other thing."

Max shrugged. He could picture her finding the gun. She probably put it in her purse. And when she came out with an armload of stuff, the cop wasn't about to search her.

"Was there anything else in there?" the woman asked in a small voice. "In the hole?"

"There was, but I threw it away," Max said. "I dropped it off the ferry." The gun's extra clip hadn't even made a splash when he leaned against the side railing and dropped it.

The woman let out a small unexpected laugh, then said, "You know, that's what I did with the other thing."

They stood there for a second, Max feeling like he should say something. Probably, she didn't know she shot the wrong guy. But the Samoan was dead too, stabbed in a prison hospital ward, before he could even be charged.

When Max finally did say something, he wasn't sure

it was the right thing. "If you ever wonder about that Todd guy, don't," he said. "Really, he's not worth the trouble."

"You know, I never do," she answered. "Isn't that odd?"

"No, it's just about right," Max answered, then walked away.

As he started the car he noticed that the woman had vanished into the house and shut the door.

It would be a couple of hours before he reached the prison, and that would give him enough time to think about what to say to Suze. To sort through it in his mind. She'd be home when he finished work that night. He'd make breakfast. Eggs, sausage, French toast, fresh squeezed OJ, and one of those imported coffees she liked. They'd eat breakfast and he'd lay it all out for her, what he'd been thinking.

They were heading into truly desperate times, for him, certainly, and maybe even for everyone. He didn't want to face them alone and couldn't imagine even a bad future without her. Max didn't let himself think of the word until he was nearly out of New Jersey. He'd only say it once, and if she believed him, then everything after that would be okay. No, it would be really fucking great.

CAJUN CRIME
FEATURING DAVE ROBICHEAUX
BY EDGAR AWARD-WINNING AUTHOR

JAMES LEE BURKE

A STAINED WHITE RADIANCE
72047-7/ $5.50 US/ $6.50 Can
"No one captures Louisiana culture
as well as James Lee Burke. . . it is also possible
that no one writes better detective novels."
Washington Post Book World

BLACK CHERRY BLUES
71204-0/ $5.50 US/ $6.50 Can
"Remarkable. . .A terrific story. . .
Not to be missed!"
Los Angeles Times Book Review

A MORNING FOR FLAMINGOS
71360-8/ $5.50 US/ $6.50 Can
"Truly astonishing"
Washington Post Book World

And Coming Soon

IN THE ELECTRIC MIST
WITH CONFEDERATE DEAD

JAMES ELLROY

"Echoes the Best of Wambaugh"
New York Sunday News

BROWN'S REQUIEM   78741-5/$4.50 US $5.50 Can
Join ex-cop and sometimes P.I. Fritz Brown beneath the golden glitter of Tinsel Town...where arson, pay-offs, and porn are all part of the game.

CLANDESTINE   81141-3/$4.99 US/$5.99 Can
Nominated for an Edgar Award for Best Original Paperback Mystery Novel. A compelling thriller about an ambitious L.A. patrolman caught up in the sex and sleaze of smog city where murder is the dark side of love.

KILLER ON THE ROAD   89934-5/$4.99 US/$5.99 Can
Enter the horrifying world of a killer whose bloody trail of carnage baffles police from coast to coast and whose only pleasure is to kill...and kill again.

Featuring Lloyd Hopkins

BLOOD ON THE MOON   69851-X/$4.50 US/$5.50 Can
Lloyd Hopkins is an L.A. cop. Hard, driven, brilliant, he's the man they call in when a murder case looks bad.

BECAUSE THE NIGHT   70063-8/$4.99 US/$5.99 Can
Detective Sergeant Lloyd Hopkins had a hunch that there was a connection between three bloody bodies and one missing cop...a hunch that would take him to the dark heart of madness...and beyond.